Praise
All the Olc

'With an original narrative style, a setting as enchanting as an Irish *Three Pines*, and story that unfolds as cleverly as a puzzle box . . . Absolutely charming.'

—Connie Berry, *USA Today* bestselling author of the Kate Hamilton Mysteries

'The village and its inhabitants are completely alive in this novel . . . O'Donnell handles the sentimental and the sombre just perfectly, balancing it with the wit and charm of the characters . . . A thoroughly entertaining, witty, clever read.'

—Hannah King, author of *She and I*

'Cosy crime with a sharp bite . . . has all the charm of an Irish thriller, wrapped in a soft cardigan and wearing wellies.'

—Kitty Murphy, author of the Dublin Drag Series

'O'Donnell's debut is so atmospheric in its background and poetic in its language.'

—*Kirkus Reviews*

'O'Donnell debuts with a complex and accomplished whodunit . . . Brings to mind the regional mysteries of Charles Todd, and he matches his gift for atmosphere with intricate plotting and nuanced characterizations.'

—*Publishers Weekly*

About the Author

R. P. O'Donnell was born in Boston, Massachusetts, and lives in West Cork with his two children. His essays have been published in *The Irish Times* and the *Irish Examiner*. In 2020, he won the J. G. Farrell Award at the West Cork Literary Festival. He has had two poems published in *Songs of the Susquehanna* (Bucknell University Press). *All the Old Clocks* is his debut novel.

ALL THE OLD CLOCKS

ALL THE OLD CLOCKS
First published in 2026 by
New Island Books
Glenshesk House
10 Richview Office Park
Clonskeagh
Dublin D14 V8C4
Republic of Ireland
newisland.ie

First published as *No Comfort for the Dead* in the United States of America in 2025 by Crooked Lane Books, an imprint of The Quick Brown Fox & Company LLC.

Print ISBN: 978-1-83594-011-2
eBook ISBN: 978-1-83594-010-5

British Library Cataloguing in Publication Data. A CIP catalogue record for this book is available from the British Library.

Product safety queries can be addressed to New Island Books at the above postal address or at info@newisland.ie.

Set in Espinosa Nova Pro in 13 on 17.25pt
Typeset by JVR Creative India
Cover design by Sarah McCoy, @sarahmccoy_design
Printed by L&C Printing Group, Poland, lcprinting.eu

New Island Books received financial assistance from The Arts Council (An Chomhairle Ealaíon), Dublin, Ireland.

New Island Books is a member of Publishing Ireland and the Independent Publishers Guild.

10 9 8 7 6 5 4 3 2 1

ALL THE OLD CLOCKS

A KILCRAVEN MYSTERY

R. P. O'DONNELL

NEW ISLAND

For Josh and Lauren

Prologue

When Cordelia arrived in Kilcraven, she ripped the front shutters off the parish hall. A few shingles from the old creamery came loose, and she threw them, shrieking, into Myross Wood and the Blackfield pitch. Wind and rain and the high crack of thunder – Cordelia made herself known.

Kilcraven was a quiet village, the quiet only broken by the constant refrain: God, it's awful quiet here, isn't it? Or, from the younger crowd, by the constant complaint: nothing ever happens here.

In 1988, in Kilcraven, there were rumours and a rumbling of trouble up North – but that was Northern business. Belfast could've been on the other side of the world for all the village knew. When the village talked about crime, they meant masturbation or the price of milk. There had never been a murder in Kilcraven, as far as anyone knew or could remember.

No, while Ireland itself was at a crossroads, in Kilcraven, life was the same as it always was. Round and round went the villagers, minding their own business and the business of their neighbours – the kind of village where nothing ever happened.

The villagers left Cordelia to herself and closed their windows and doors against her; outside, she threw their coal bins and drying racks and football nets into the road.

But in the front room of the Big House on the top of the hill, an old man paced nervously. It wasn't the storm that scared him. It was the noise at the door – loud enough to cut through the rattling of the windows and the pounding of the rain. A knock on the door, steady and insistent.

Could it be? the old man wondered. No, no, it's not possible—

Unless ...

And then, the door slammed open.

By the time Cordelia left the next morning, two fishing boats had capsized and half the village was flooded, from the old pier all the way down to the front door of Nolan's pub. There were trees down everywhere. Anything that hadn't been tied down was floating or flown apart. And the old man lay dead on the floor of the drawing room of the Big House on the top of the hill – a single gunshot through his heart.

Trouble, it seemed, had finally come to Kilcraven.

Chapter 1

The Kilcraven Library was usually a quiet place after closing. Especially after dark, when the aisles filled with shadows and the bookshelves muffled the dusty clock ticking and the creak of the warm walls settling against the cold night. The library fell asleep. Usually.

Tonight, however, there was another sound: the sound of steady but undignified snoring. Not the gentle snoring you might expect – like the heavy breathing of a middle-aged woman in church, for example, or a small pug – but rather, these were the full-mouthed eruptions of a woman who has clearly worked too hard.

The head librarian, Emma Daly, was twenty-six years old and on the slight side – her habit of wearing her dad's old cardigans added to the impression of smallness. Her copper hair was cropped short, framing a pale face and dark green eyes, freckles spreading high under her cheekbones. But at the moment, judging purely from the sound coming out of her – a passer-by would be excused for thinking there was a rabid dog loose in the library.

Emma's head was on the front desk, her left cheek smudging the paperwork she had been working on. Her tape recorder hissed as it continued turning, the last of her dictation trailing off into heavy breathing. Her cup of tea had turned cold and grey, and her cigarette had burned itself out in another mug long ago.

Dear Board of Trustees, the paper beneath her head started, *The papers have been printing the obituary for rural Ireland for twenty years now. Always the same reasons, always the same excuses. But why hasn't it died? It's because of places like the Kilcraven Library. For only 100 pounds per month, you can help ...*

Emma often fell asleep at her desk – she stayed hours past closing most nights. Her colleague, Maeve, often protested, insisting that the work could wait until the morning. But Emma always insisted right back. The library balanced on a razor's edge; it had only survived due to an endless stream of grants, extensions, charters, blessings – all applied to and fought for by Emma. In triplicate. She'd only been manager for three years, but now, she was the little boy with her finger in the dam. Without her, it was lost.

It wasn't just the library. The whole village was in trouble. Most of the shops had closed, and the rest were on borrowed time. Even the parish hall was shuttered for half the year now. It was only the library that held the village together, that brought some life back into the deadened streets. A rock in the stream. Some hope of weathering the tide. All built by Emma. In three years, she'd transformed the library from a glorified storage cupboard into the backbone of the community. And Maeve and Emma's dad had to agree – as much as they wished she would just get some sleep.

But they also knew that pride wasn't the real reason she worked late. And so, every night, Emma stayed past closing – filling out forms and fundraising and writing essays on footfall and lending rates. It was like bureaucratic meditation; she worked until she fell asleep at her desk. And if that didn't work, she took long walks around the village and countryside at night, staring up at the stars until her legs couldn't walk any further.

In between snores that sounded like a half-hearted stroke, there was a knock. Outside, on the library door. Once ... twice ... then a bit louder. Finally, Emma woke up, the sheet of paper sticking to her cheek for a moment.

And before she came to her senses fully, before she completely stepped back out of the dream – she heard it. Hot, panicky breath nestling in close to her ear. A small voice breaking apart. And then the room came into focus, and the door in her heart fell open.

*

The last of Cordelia had raged and pounded on the windows all morning, but it was quiet as Emma stepped outside. The air was still and calm – and all the more so for having been so wild before, like a child sleeping after a tantrum.

Emma's dad waited as she locked the door behind her. Unlike his daughter, Sam was tall and ran burly. He had a full, dark beard and most of his hair. He was a carpenter by trade but a collector by nature. His pockets were always full of odds and ends he'd found on walks – delicately coloured eggshells, for example, or old coins. Tonight, Emma saw his pockets were slightly damp, suggesting whatever he'd found had been wet.

'Sorry to wake you,' he said brightly, 'I thought you might need a torch.' He waited as she lit a cigarette. 'Jesus, you should see the lane. Two trees down across the way, and half the road underwater.'

'What about the bridge?'

'Fecked,' he said cheerfully. 'The council are going to have their work cut out for them.' He seemed almost delighted at the prospect. 'Flooded on both sides, with a couple of big branches in the middle. Nobody's getting across that bridge for a few days.'

There was only one main road in and out of Kilcraven – the bridge. The bridge was so narrow that only one car could fit on it at once, but it was better than the alternative: the winding labyrinth of unmarked country roads, split by grass and covered in cow shite. And those were the good roads – others were closer to a rumour than a road.

Sam was about to say something, but he saw Emma's face and a blotchiness that wasn't just from exhaustion.

'Bad night, love?' he asked gently.

She nodded. Her eyes were jittery and bright and didn't land on anything, like an anchor trying to catch on stone.

She stood there for a while without saying anything. He waited.

After a minute, Emma took a deep breath. She pulled her jacket around her and smiled at him. It had passed.

'God, I could murder a cup of tea,' she said as she linked arms with Sam and they made their way through the village, towards the hill and home.

In the village centre, small and brightly painted houses lined the street, close together, like a family on a couch. There was a full moon overhead; the country lanes wandered off, like dark and lovely visitors to townlands like Ballincolla and the surrounding fields. The hedgerows divided the land into small fields and the fishing boats swung slowly out of the harbour. Everywhere you looked, the world was full of Cordelia's rain.

Sam cursed as he stepped into a puddle.

'Where's that torch you brought me?' Emma laughed, knowing full well that he'd only come to wake her up.

'I said I thought you might *need* a torch, not that I brought you one.' He looked pointedly at her bag. 'And what did you bring for me?'

Emma often took books home from the library – it was how she and Sam spent most evenings, quietly reading in front of the stove.

'Is *King Lear* a bit too on the nose?'

He groaned and she laughed, and soon they were home.

*

Emma and her father lived in a house on top of the hill. The front looked out over the village and across the harbour; the rest was surrounded by hills and fields and an incompetent farmer who refused to cut a drain.

After they stamped their feet on the mat and threw their coats on the table (revealing the small bits of quartz Sam had found on his walk), Sam stuck their dinner in the oven. While they waited, they settled into their usual places in front of the stove.

'Why'd the storm have a name?' Emma asked. 'And why Cordelia? If you're going to name a storm, that one seems a bit …'

'Insensitive?' Sam asked, finishing her thought. 'Heavy-handed? Why would you name a storm after one of the saddest victims in one of the saddest plays of all time, you ask? Answer: because Americans are idiots.'

Emma laughed.

'Da … you can't say that.'

Sam shrugged.

'I don't think they'd mind. Hell, they'd probably agree.' He marked his page and closed his book. 'The storm was supposed to hit America. By the time they realised it wasn't going to hit them, or come anywhere close, they'd already named it.'

Emma frowned. Last time she checked, America was over 3,000 kilometres away.

'That's a pretty big miss, no?'

Sam shook his head. 'Happens all the time and not just to the Americans. In fairness, look what happened in England last year with your man Michael Fish and the hurricane he insisted wasn't coming. The English fecked it up too.' He picked up the jug of milk; finding it empty (and shooting a reproachful look at Emma's tea, where the last few drops had disappeared) he got up to refill it. As he walked over to the kitchen, he stopped and patted her shoulder. 'Nobody can predict the future, Emma. Not even the people getting paid to.'

She waited, knowing exactly what he was going to say next and willing him not to. It was a conversation – a monologue, really – they'd already had a million times. He opened the cupboards and started rummaging through them. But she knew he was just winding up for the usual sales pitch. And sure enough, a few seconds later, it came.

'And, you know,' he said casually, 'speaking of the future ... I was talking to Miss McGready at the shop earlier, and she said she was going to be renting a few flats in the city this spring ...'

'Actually, I'm going to go for a walk,' she said, cutting him off abruptly. Without waiting for a response, she got up and grabbed her coat off the table, moving quickly towards the door. But Sam was too quick for her.

'I know you don't want to talk about it,' he said, stepping in front of her and putting his hands up. 'And God knows I love having you here, but you must've walked a million miles to run away from this conversation. It's been four years since you moved back from the city. You're too young to be stuck here.'

Emma squared up, ready to tell him off, to tell him that she wasn't stuck, she was fighting ... but all at once, a weariness set in. Like a plug pulled on a bath. She let her shoulders hang.

'I'm trying, Dad.' Her voice cracked slightly. 'I'm trying my best.'

Sam pulled her into a hug.

'I know it's been hard,' he said, squeezing her tight, 'I know. But you can't freeze yourself in time.' Then he took a deep breath and held her at arm's length. 'I know you don't want to hear it. But it's time to move on—'

All at once, Emma was out of his arms and out the door. The night's cool air crept into the warm house; the distant sound of fog bells rolled across the harbour.

Sam hung his head. He knew better than to follow her. She was just past the gate already. He let her go.

'Will I have your dinner in the oven?' he called to her.

At a distance, he couldn't tell if she was debating whether or not to ignore him or to come back in altogether – the chill in the air would've stopped most people. Finally, she called over her shoulder.

'Yes, please!'

*

Emma didn't head off in any particular direction other than not towards the village. Her hands were shaking, but she could see well enough in the moonlight to find her usual path up past the corner of Christy's field and up again towards the Blackfield.

Myross Wood ran down from the left to the water's edge and collapsed, as if exhausted, into the sea. The bridge stepped lightly from around the corner, across the harbour to Glandore. The twin islands, Adam and Eve, looked joined, like Emma could walk across them as one hill until she finally came back to Kilcraven, tangled up among the nets and bells and bilge pumps of the old pier where the fishing boats waited patiently: red, yellow and blue. She could still see the destruction of Cordelia – two of the smaller boats were underwater – but the rest of the pier was busy under the sodium lights. The fishermen drifted from the stove and their cups of tea – half-warm and half-drunk – to the ships that would carry them to Georges Bank and the Flemish Cap.

Emma knew her dad, Sam, loved her and meant well. She knew Sam wasn't pushing her to leave – he loved their routine as much as she did. But he didn't understand. And if he didn't understand, then she wasn't sure anybody could.

The path came out from the trees on a slight rise. She was way out in the country now, in the big fields and dark woods where houses were rare. She could only see one now, in a field down below her through the trees. It was the Big House.

Emma always felt safe in Kilcraven, even on a dark lane like this one. But every so often, a line from Sherlock Holmes popped up out of nowhere. (Not exactly nowhere, of course – her anthology of *The Adventures* was falling apart, and it was her third one.) It was a throwaway line – how the lonely houses of the country, each in its own field, were filled with more horrors than any of the darkest alleyways in London. Because in the country, Sherlock argued, nobody could hear you scream. Emma shuddered: it was as jarring now as it was when she was twelve years old and living in one of those lonely houses in the country. A loving, peaceful house, of course, but lonely in its field. They lived on the edge of the village now, but every so often, on a night like this, as she stared out the window, down the hill and across the field to the village stirring restlessly in the rain, she sometimes wondered. Was Sherlock right? Was there something terrible happening? Somewhere behind those curtains, somewhere in the darkness of the house, was there a fire burning—?

A noise broke her reverie. It was coming from the house just beyond the trees – the sound of shouting. The house was dark, and at this distance the words were muffled, but it was definitely shouting. Angry, too.

Emma frowned. Mr Hollis lived alone in the Big House – he was an old man and not the type to be entertaining late at night. People said he hadn't even left the house in over ten years. As Emma considered whether or not to go down and knock on the door, a sudden *CRACK* split the air. And then a cry of pain.

A gunshot. Rifle, .38 calibre? It came from inside the house.

Emma flattened herself on the ground and crawled forwards to the tree line. Her heart was pounding, her mind racing, but her body was on autopilot, tensed and ready for action.

A second *CRACK*.

Emma had made the tree line now; this time she saw the orange flash behind the window, against the darkness.

Different this time. Not a rifle. Pistol – maybe a .45 calibre? Different gun.

She stayed as still as she could, keeping her eyes trained on the house. *Data, data, give me data!* Sherlock Holmes shouted in her mind. *An engine needs coal, damn it!*

She took a deep breath and blocked out the shouting fictional coke-head. She thought about the real world and what she had learned in another life, in Templemore Garda College.

Deep breaths. Quiet your mind. Take stock of the situation.

Two guns – that means at least two people. There could be more. Exits? From this vantage point, she could only count one door and three windows, but she had a clear line of view to the surrounding tree line. She'd see if anyone left.

If you can't help – collect evidence.

Well, she couldn't help. She didn't have a gun, for starters. She could call the guards, but the closest phone was back in the village at Nolan's pub. The council had been promising to repair the two public phone boxes for three years, and most of the village hadn't paid their phone bills so the phone at Nolan's had become a major part of the village infrastructure. But it was a long run from here.

The front door of the house slammed open. A man stood in the dark doorway, looking all around him. For a moment, Emma thought he might see her, or worse, start to head in her direction. It was too dark; she couldn't make out any features, just a silhouette. He was tall, nearly two metres – he seemed well built, but a long coat mixed unevenly with the shadows and made it impossible to tell for sure. He stood there for a second, as if he were listening for something, and then ran off towards the woods in the opposite direction and was gone.

Every muscle in Emma's body screamed against the silence; her whole body ached from tension and the cold wet ground. But she waited. Her heart pounded, but her breath, visible now in the night air, was steady. She couldn't hear anything in the woods or see any movement from the house – all she could hear was the roar of what sounded like the ocean in her ears. But she waited.

After what she guessed was five minutes, Emma stood up and slowly made her way to the house, padding softly across the dark loam, ready to hit the ground again if she needed to. There was nothing but silence. She made it to the side of the house and looked through the window. And then she gasped.

There in the middle of the dark room was an old man. He was sprawled out on the floor, eyes open, frozen, staring at the ceiling. Blood was blooming from a hole in his chest and from under his back; it pooled on the floor beneath him and there was more splattered on the wall behind him. He wasn't moving.

She had never met the man, but she knew – it was Mr Hollis.

Mr Hollis was dead.

Emma heard a low moan coming from the back of the room. It was too dark to see clearly, but she could make out the silhouette of a body slumped against the wall. She could see movement.

The man was clearly alive, but badly hurt. He needed a doctor. And the guards.

Right as she was about to leave, she did a double take. Above her, the moon shifted, and grey light spread across the man's face. And for a second, as she took in his figure, she thought – she nearly *swore* – that it was Charley Thornton. But it couldn't be. Charley was younger, and he was gone, long gone. No, no—

The man groaned again and raised his arm. He was still slumped against the wall, and he wasn't trying to get up. But that didn't matter. Because Emma saw what he held in his hand – a gun. And it was pointed right at her.

Chapter 2

Emma knew the country lanes like the back of her hand. She could have run down from the Big House to the village blindfolded. Which was good because that was essentially what she was doing now.

Night in the countryside, far away from any city or light bulb brighter than a sixty-watt, the dark is like a heavy blanket. It has a weight and a texture; you have to push your way through it.

The moon had disappeared behind a dark bank of clouds. There were no stars to speak of. Emma ran through the darkness, all the way down to the village, until she saw the light.

*

Adam Thornton, the village doctor, had a difficult job. It wasn't just the house calls or the long hours or even the hard decisions – and occasional mistakes – that made it hard. It was his proximity to the community he served.

He was their doctor, but he was also their neighbour. This came with complications.

Some complications, of course, involved payment. Adam kept his rates affordable, and he was unusually tolerant and kind – he understood that his patients struggled. But still, since most of his patients were fishermen, they couldn't afford even his cheapest rates.

So, Adam was mainly paid in fish.

His family ate fish every night of the week – and sometimes for lunch too. (After his son, Charley, moved out, he never ate fish again – he figured he'd eaten enough cod to last him three lifetimes.)

The other complication – the major complication, if you asked Adam – was his neighbours' concern for privacy around a fellow neighbour. Even if that fellow neighbour was their doctor. It came in two extremes.

In his office, they'd act withholding. Patients stood in his office, spouting or spewing from one orifice or another, pretending there was nothing wrong. They came in – of their own volition, mind you – and then stood there and acted like Doc had cornered them on the street. A man would've cut his arm to ribbons in a thresher, and he'd be standing there, acting coy.

In Nolan's pub, however, it was the opposite. There – in public – his patients sought him out; they pushed their way next to him at the bar and gave lengthy descriptions of any and all afflictions, with reckless abandon and startling candour.

It was often too much for Adam, as professional as he was.

'Please, Billy,' he'd beg. 'We can't talk about this here. Just book an appointment. First thing tomorrow – I won't even charge you.'

And Billy would take this like a bull takes a red flag.

'Doc, I can't for the life of me understand it. I have to stand sideways. Fully sideways – nearly backwards, really – to take a piss.'

Adam would whimper, 'Please, Billy. Tomorrow. First thing, in the office.'

But Billy would continue, louder now.

'And that's all well and good – but it's the same thing in bed. My poor wife – well, let's just say she has to take three steps backwards and wear me as a belt to get anywhere ...'

Sometimes, Adam had to break a glass just to get out of the conversation. And then another patient would sidle up.

'Hey, Doc! Guess what? I'm leaking again!'

And the odd thing was, it wasn't that they were drunk. They weren't. They might've had a few pints to the good, but they were never that drunk.

It came in handy, though. Adam stored the information away for the next time they were in the office and acting coy.

'Ah, Billy, c'mere to me.' Adam would squint at him dubiously. 'There's nothing wrong at all?'

'Not at all,' Billy would say, tight-lipped and blushing. 'Just looking for a physical.'

And Adam would nod politely and give him the physical. But he'd make sure to leave out a pamphlet, discreetly, where he knew Billy would see it.

And Billy, for his part, would make sure to leave a recipe with his payment.

'The key is – half a wedge of lemon and a full stick of butter. No salt, no pepper, just butter and lemon, Doc.'

So, if Adam ever wanted to have a pint or two in peace – and that's all he ever wanted – he had to go down to Nolan's at unusual hours. It could be the morning or the middle of the night, as long as he had no patients.

Which is why, when Emma came running down into the village and saw the light in Nolan's, she knew she'd find Adam there.

Nolan's was an old pub, full of dark wood and smoke. It always smelled the same – like fried onions and sawdust. This was strange because it didn't serve food and the floor was clean slate. On a normal night, Emma would've opened the door and heard laughing and shouting, the sharp knock of billiard cues from the back corner and the rhythmic thud of darts (with the occasional shriek when there should've been a thud). The bar would've been ringed by Billy and two or three fishermen at least – men that went to the pub 'for the chat' and then spoke in monosyllabic grunts, if at all. But tonight, there was only Adam and Fintan, the barman. Until Emma burst through the door.

'Jesus Christ, Emma,' Adam cried, as she fell to the ground, gasping for air. 'What's wrong – is it Sam?'

If it was anybody else, Billy for example, Adam would have thought they were drunk, or being dramatic. But Adam knew Emma well. She had gone out with his son, Charley, all throughout school. She'd always had a good head on her shoulders.

And she'd clearly been running for her life.

'Right so,' he said, quickly downing the last of his pint and putting his coat on. 'If you can't tell me, Emma, you'll just have to bring me.'

But to his surprise, she stopped him.

'Phone,' she gasped. 'Guards.'

It was then that Adam realised that she was more than just out of breath; she was trembling all over. He turned to Fintan.

'Get me a double brandy.'

Unfortunately, Fintan was a good barman, which meant that he reacted slowly to alarming changes in situations. He stared blankly at Adam.

'For God's sake, Fintan,' Adam snapped, taking off his coat and wrapping it around Emma, still hunched up on the ground. 'She's in shock, she needs something stiff, quickly.'

Fintan obliged, hastily grabbing the bottle behind him.

But Emma had already collected herself. She shook her head and managed a weak smile.

'I'm alright now, thanks, Dr Thornton. I don't think it's shock – just adrenaline and a long run.'

He frowned.

'First things first – are you hurt?'

Her smile quickly faded. 'No, but you need to ring the guards. *Now.*'

*

Emma told Adam what had happened – the gunshots, the man running into the woods and the two bodies in the house. Adam used the pub phone to call the guards, who told him they would be out as soon as they could – but half the roads were flooded, including the bridge, so it might take a while.

'Do *not* try and go there yourselves, do you understand?' the guard repeated for the third time. 'You'll just have to wait – from the sound of it, I'd say it's just dead bodies up there. So, stay where you are.'

'One of them was alive,' Emma said after the guard hung up. 'But Mr Hollis is dead. Definitely.' Her voice was flat; the brandy had disappeared and been refilled. She hadn't known Mr Hollis, which was unusual for a village like Kilcraven, but he was the first murder victim she'd ever seen in person. The adrenaline lingered in her fingertips.

Adam nodded.

'I'll do what I can for him anyway. Maybe there'll be a miracle.'

Fintan muttered something darkly to himself.

Emma frowned.

'You didn't like him?'

Fintan raised his hands, as if to say: *you didn't hear it from me.* Adam looked sharply at him, then back at Emma. Then he sighed.

'He wasn't exactly a popular man, Mr Hollis.' He thought for a moment, picking his words carefully. 'It's a tragedy, of course. And it feels strange to be sitting here waiting while there's a man bleeding out up there. But as for that fella, well, as far as I'm concerned – you try to rob an old man, them's the breaks. And as for Mr Hollis, well ...' He scratched his head delicately. 'From the sounds of it, there's nothing I can do anyway. But, even if there was, I wouldn't feel too bad waiting here, if you understand me. And I don't think anyone who was around back then would disagree.'

'Was he really that bad?' Emma asked incredulously, looking between the two of them.

Fintan made another noise, this one to say: *you're bloody right, he was.*

Adam sighed again.

'Look, he was mean. He made a lot of trouble for a lot of people who deserved much better—'

Fintan snorted.

'Trouble, is that what you call it?'

Adam held up his hands, as if to say: *no argument here.* But neither of them ventured any further than that.

The pub was quiet. It was nearly midnight now. It was just the three of them, and the darkness in the corners of the room seemed to creep into their bones, like a chill. There was something niggling at Emma's brain – a doubt, or a half-formed question.

'He must have had enemies, so,' Emma said slowly, 'people who would want him dead?'

Adam looked at her curiously.

'I'd say it was a robbery, plain and simple.' He lit a cigarette and slid the pack to Emma. 'Somebody knew he was rich, knew he was old and alone, and broke in. Hollis got the jump on him, but then the robber shot him back.'

Emma lit a match, then paused.

'But what about the other guy – the one who ran away?' She looked back and forth between the two of them, but they both looked blankly back at her. She continued, 'If the two were robbing the place together, why would he run away with nothing? Hollis was dead. His friend was hurt. Why run away? And why didn't he take anything?'

Adam thought this over. 'What'd he look like?'

Emma inhaled and waved the match out. She thought back but could only remember the vague outline.

'He was in the shadows – I couldn't get a good look at him.'

'Was he tall?' Adam asked. 'Heavy or well built?'

Emma shook her head.

'I don't know – he was hunched over and had a big coat on.'

Fintan raised his eyebrows at Adam.

'And you're sure you actually saw someone?' Fintan asked. When Emma's eyes narrowed, he raised his hands.

'Moonlight isn't like sunlight,' he said matter-of-factly. 'It can play tricks on you. Happens every time I walk up the back lane after a late night. I hear a noise, a branch breaks and suddenly every shadow turns into a fox.' He shrugged. 'I don't know what I'd start seeing if I heard gunshots.'

Emma nodded.

'And was it the moonlight or the dead man that got up and opened the door?' she asked drily. 'Or maybe the man slumped over in the corner?'

Adam frowned at Fintan. He leaned over to Emma.

'Nobody's doubting you,' he said kindly. 'The guards will take a look around and whatever they find, they'll follow. But I'd say this was just a case of a robbery gone wrong. Hollis dinged one, and the other ran away. Any bad blood, that was almost ten years ago – Hollis barely left the house anymore.'

Emma nodded. Her mind had started to race, but she tried to catch up to it now. She wasn't Sherlock Holmes. She wasn't even a guard anymore. It was up to them now. Out of her hands.

Fintan put a pint glass under the tap, but only a trickle of foam came out.

'Kicked,' he said. 'Back in a minute.'

After he disappeared into the back, Adam leaned over to Emma. 'Are you alright?' He hesitated. 'I know, look – I'm probably not ...' He cleared his throat awkwardly. 'Look, you don't have to go into specifics or anything. But as your doctor,' he looked at her kindly over his glasses, 'I have to say, I had a case of walking pneumonia the other day that looked more well-rested than you.'

Emma turned red again.

'How is Charley doing these days?' she asked, changing the subject. 'Is he still in London?'

Adam was quiet for a moment. It was clearly a well-worn subject, and not an entirely happy one.

'I'm not sure what he's doing, to be honest. It's hard to keep track of him these days ...'

She was about to ask a follow-up when a thought struck, just as Fintan came back into the room.

'I forgot to tell you,' she said to Adam, 'The man – he looked *exactly* like Charley.' She saw the look on his face and quickly added, 'I mean, it definitely *wasn't* Charley. This guy was older, much older. Middle-aged, like.'

Adam smiled. 'That's alright so—'

'And besides, I think he was a priest.'

Adam startled. 'A priest?' he asked.

Emma nodded. She had been focused on the gun in the man's hand at the time, but now that the adrenaline had worn off, the outer edges of her tunnel vision suddenly widened.

'He was wearing black – at first, I thought it was just the standard outfit for a robbery, you know, but then I saw the dog collar. And what looked like a cross around his neck.'

'Hey, are you okay?' Fintan asked. But he wasn't looking at Emma, he was looking at Adam.

Adam, in turn, was staring at Emma, his face pale. 'Say that again?' he asked, his voice shaking.

Emma glanced at Fintan. He shook his head: *I don't know.*

'Erm – he was a priest, I think.'

'And he definitely, *definitely*, looked like Charley?' Adam demanded. 'What age? About my age?'

'A bit younger, I'd say.'

Adam jumped up, knocking his stool backwards. He grabbed his coat.

'I'm going up there.' Emma stared at him.

'What?' she asked, nearly shouting in surprise. 'Now? Jesus Christ, Dr Thor— Adam! He has a gun! And what about the other guy? He's still out there too!'

But Adam had already thrown on his coat and hat.

'I'm sorry – I have to.' He looked at Fintan. 'Tell the guards where I've gone.'

Emma turned to Fintan for support, but he was still looking at Adam. The penny had dropped.

'It's not him,' he said, coming around the bar. 'Adam, listen to me. Jesus Christ, it's not him – it's been thirty years, for God's sake! What are the chances?'

Adam paused, as if wondering what they were himself. 'Smaller and smaller every day,' he said finally. 'But still not zero.' And then he threw the door open and was gone.

Emma stared at the door for a moment, wondering what the hell had just happened – trying to work her way backwards through the conversation. She looked at Fintan, who looked just as upset as she felt.

'What the fuck, Fintan?'

Fintan looked at her, blank with shock.

'He thinks it's Colm.' He looked out the window, out into the dark night Adam had disappeared into. 'Colm Thornton.'

And suddenly, Emma remembered. The name. And a story from long ago.

'Colm Thornton,' she said slowly. 'The boy who disappeared thirty years ago.'

'Thirty-two, to be precise.'

Emma hesitated; she weighed up the chances – slim to none – that it actually was Colm Thornton against the very real fact of the gun. But her hesitation only lasted a second. She grabbed her coat and ran out after Adam.

She followed him all the way back up to the house, where he found Colm Thornton, his little brother, lying slumped in the corner of the room. And she watched Adam try to stop the bleeding.

But thirty-two years was a long time, and it was a lot of blood.

Chapter 3

There was no garda station in Kilcraven. When necessary – when a villager took the night a pint too far, for example, or a TV set grew wings – the guilty party was taken to the nearest town, Skibbereen, fifteen minutes away. But even Skibbereen wasn't exactly a city. Which is why when the call went out that night, only the sergeant was available.

Sergeant Noonan had not been having a good night. He'd directed traffic on the edge of town for nearly ten hours – getting soaked to the bone from both the rain and the abuse. Sergeants weren't supposed to do this sort of grunt work, but it was only him, Liam and another guard who had called in sick, so he didn't have a choice.

'I've been waiting here twenty minutes, mate, cop on!'

These were his neighbours, like. Hurling abuse at him from their cars while he held up their day by a few minutes for vital road work that he hadn't exactly planned himself.

'You ... fecking ... you absolute ... LANGER!'

Surely, they could understand that he wasn't the one who had set up the digger in the middle of the road, right? Wrong.

'C'mere ye dozy fuck!'

Noonan waved and nodded at them all – and added an additional five minutes to their delay each time.

By the end of his shift, he was exhausted. He wanted to crawl back home to his microwave and his television and his cans of cold lager. But as soon as he sat down in his car, the radio squawked to life.

'Sergeant ... come in, Sergeant ...'

Noonan reluctantly picked up the radio and clicked.

'What is it, Liam?'

Cordelia had made ribbons of the airwaves; instead of an answer, all that Noonan heard was a burst of static. He swore up and down – Liam always called on the wrong channel. Noonan made a series of indignant noises about Liam's incompetence, his weight, his lack of even the most basic radio-handling and his propensity for wearing odd-coloured socks. But on his end, Liam only heard a rush of garbled static.

'What was that?' There was a pause. 'Sir?'

Noonan took a deep breath and tried again. 'For feck's sake, Liam, what is it?'

Liam's response faded in and out of the airwaves, but Noonan heard enough to make him instantly forget all about the patchy reception and his wet clothes.

'I said ... (static burst) ... there's been a shooting ... (static burst) ... two victims, up at the Hollis house ... (static burst) is dead ... I repeat ... Hollis is dead.'

Noonan turned the ignition and slammed his car into gear, the tyres spinning uselessly for a second on the asphalt before grabbing hold. He flicked his overhead lights on and swore at the feeble beams. The bridge was closed, covered in branches and mangled buoy lines; Noonan would have to go the long way around, cutting through a field or two. And pray that the report was wrong.

The back roads of West Cork are a peculiar labyrinth – the country lanes twist and turn, run around and then double back until you wish you'd brought a map. Or breadcrumbs. Or a passport and a change of clothes. And then, whenever you reach your soul's last fingertip and you think yourself totally, hopelessly lost – the road runs up along a ridge and falls away, and there you are. Noonan knew he'd get there, alright, but it would take some time. Too much time. And at least two or three wrong turns. He tried to focus on the road, but his mind kept coming back to the same thought.

Hollis was dead. Murdered. It had started.

He had to get to the Big House before anyone else did.

Chapter 4

Frances Thornton was doing her usual inspection in the bathroom mirror. Tonight, she found a lump on the underside of her jaw.

Frances had diagnosed every bump on her body over the years, with a whole list of possible ailments that would make even Munchausen grow faint. But she'd only just noticed this one. It was very exciting.

'Cancer of the lymph nodes,' she said, running her fingers over the bump in the manner of a professional. 'Possibly just the start, but give it time.' She nodded darkly into the mirror. 'It'll get there.'

Jimmy was at her feet, rooting around in the cupboard under the bathroom sink. He'd been under there for nearly five minutes (looking for his denture glue, apparently) but she couldn't get more than a grunt out of him. She tried again: 'Maybe it's my tonsils. Could be my tonsils.'

Another grunt from under the sink. 'Of course, I read something about—'

'Why do we still have so many sanitary pads?'

She frowned, her fingers still feeling her neck for bumps. 'What?'

'Sanitary pads,' Jimmy repeated. 'We've still got hundreds of sanitary pads down here; they take up half the bloody cupboard. Are we expecting company or something?'

'Jimmy, are you listening to anything I'm saying?' asked Frances, looking down at him sternly – or at least, as sternly as she could look down at a seventy-year-old's bottom waving in the air. 'I just told you I might have a lymphoma, and you're banging on about ... Jesus, I don't even know what.' She poked his bottom. 'What are you even looking for?'

But Jimmy was distracted again.

'There's something wrong with the pipe here, love. The U-pipe, I think it is.'

Frances rolled her eyes. Something about piping and plumbing appealed to Jimmy in a way that would've made Freud quite happy. He'd never done any actual plumbing, of course, and he wasn't about to start now. She went back to diagnosing herself in the mirror. *Cherry angioma ... that was something, wasn't it?*

Jimmy let out a series of grunts and twisted around on the floor. 'Frances, love, I really think we've got a problem here.'

'What do you mean?'

He tried to put it in terms she'd understand. 'It's a contusion, like.'

'A contusion? What are you on about?'

'There's a leakage here.'

'Ah. That's not a contusion, so, that's a haemorrhage.'

'Haemorrhage, fine. It needs sorting all the same.'

'Then call the plumber.'

Frances heard a loud sigh, followed by a series of exploratory knocks, an object coming loose and a pained squeal. She addressed his waggling posterior.

'Will you call the plumber so?' There was a long pause.

'Okay, love.'

'Now, back to my lymph nodes ...'

*

Jimmy had a lot of time to stick his head in the cupboard these days. After he retired, the only place he had to be was in the post-office queue every Friday morning to pick up his pension. The rest of the week, he was as free as a bird. A free, tired bird who suffered from vertigo and a prostate the size of a watermelon.

It took a while for Frances to get used to having him around the house so much. Every day. Even for two people who loved each other as much as they did, they suddenly had a lot of extra time together. And a lot fewer things to talk about.

When she'd imagined his retirement, she imagined days of cleaning and cooking and shopping while he sat on the couch reading about ships. But it turned out even Jimmy had a limit to how many ships he could take. And in an even bigger surprise, it turned out that Frances had actually quite enjoyed her old routine, as dull as it might sound, and her time alone. When Jimmy got bored, he started following her around the house.

Which was fine. Until he started making suggestions as well.

'Why don't you brush the counters, wipe them down and *then* sweep the floor,' he'd say, as he watched her clean the kitchen. 'The way you're doing it, you're spending twice the time making it half as clean.' Frances would stop and glare at him until he got the message and toddled off back to his chair. But then twenty minutes later, he'd hop back up and start again. 'And what about if you moved the bin over here instead? That way, it's right next to the chopping board and you can sweep the scraps right in ...' And so on.

But she loved him. And the last thing she wanted to do was to make him feel unwelcome. It's just that after a while, she found herself dangerously close to pulling an Agatha Christie, and even *she* wasn't sure if she meant disappearing for two weeks or poisoning his food.

Eventually, Frances came up with a strategy. She began narrating, out loud and with startling detail, all of her medical complaints. As a hypochondriac, she was a natural. There was always plenty of material to work with – various organs wobbling or going haywire altogether, vast entrails of potential danger, not to mention a whole litany of mysterious burps and whistles that surely invited discussion, if not conversation. Poor Jimmy never stood a chance; he had a weak stomach. And even if he didn't, Frances's descriptions bordered on the obscene.

'Love?' Jimmy would ask innocently, peering into the cupboard. 'Why are you spending so much on the name-brand cleaners? Own-brand is half the price, and you'd never notice the difference. Or better yet, just mix a bit of bleach into some water and presto, you've got some cleaner.'

She would sigh – deeply – and then turn to him with the same innocent tone.

'Have you ever heard the term *marinating bladder*, Jimmy? No? Well, let me tell you what's happening to mine ...'

Jimmy would try to explain the profit margins of own-brand packaging, but by the time she had got to the description of what she called 'post-urethral discomfort' he would run up a white flag and find his interest in ships renewed.

*

After Storm Cordelia blew herself out and the night came up to the window, tired and worn-down, Jimmy sat in his favourite armchair. There was a fire in the stove next to him and a new book on his lap. He was happy as a man could be – if it weren't for the door. The damn thing wouldn't knock.

'Has he not called yet?' he asked for the third time that night. And for the third time that night, Frances said, 'No, no – not yet,' her hands worrying over her knitting. 'But you know how forgetful he is. Besides, half the village is flooded.'

Jimmy grumbled to himself.

He put down his book and went out to the kitchen. He made a cup of tea for Frances and took a small cake out of the fridge: he'd bought it that morning and hidden it behind the three tubs of Dairygold in the fridge.

Where had they gone wrong? Adam called over a good bit, but he barely had time to finish a cup of tea before he was running out the door again. And here, on his mother's birthday, he had yet to call in at all. Jimmy understood he was busy, of course – Adam was the village doctor, and this was the beginning of flu season – but surely he could've dropped in a card or something. It was half nine, for God's sake. The more Frances pretended it didn't bother her, the more Jimmy knew it did. Her eyes kept darting to the window at every small sound outside.

And Colm ... well ... that was a wound that had never healed. A wound that they had never understood enough to heal. Across all these years, it still hurt. Especially on nights like this.

One son forgot, and the other was in the wind. Where had they gone wrong?

Jimmy brought the cup and saucer out to the sitting room and set them down in front of Frances; then he produced the cake from behind his back. She gave a big watery smile.

'Ah, Jimmy,' she said quietly, touching his cheek. 'There was no need.'

He waved her off. 'Will I bother with the candles?' He knew the answer.

'God no. It's perfect.'

'Happy birthday, love.' He gave her a long kiss. 'Will we do the birthday kisses?'

She laughed and shoved him gently.

'I don't think anyone can do seventy kisses. Even you, Jimmy Thornton.' She kissed him back, then nodded in the direction of the kitchen. 'C'mon, off you go.'

'What do you mean, love?'

'Get yourself a drop – oh, don't act all coy. I saw you got a new bottle and everything.'

He laughed with her, then did as he was told.

But as he settled into his chair, he found himself frowning at the empty spot where the telly used to be.

'It's okay, love,' Frances said quietly, without looking up from her knitting. 'Sure, I don't miss it at all.'

Jimmy sighed.

'I just feel wrong.' He gestured at the glass of whiskey. 'Getting this while—'

Frances cut him off.

'Jimmy – how often do you get a new bottle?' she asked firmly. 'Today's my birthday, and I won't have any whingeing on my birthday.' She worked out a particularly stubborn purl with her finger. 'Things will change, and we'll be able to afford it again. Or they won't – in which case, we may as well enjoy ourselves while we can.'

Jimmy sighed again. But she was right. He picked up his book, and soon they were back in their happy little orbits.

*

An hour later, the warmth of the stove and the blanket and the whiskey had sent Jimmy to sleep. Frances was in the kitchen, rinsing out her mug. She stared out the window, into the black.

She remembered a birthday long, long ago. Before Colm disappeared. He was only eight years old. Adam, a few years older, gave her his present first – a bunch of loose teabags and a bottle of hand soap. Adam was a very literal child, and, as he said, 'Well, Mum, you're always drinking tea, you're always washing your hands and you're always complaining about how much things cost.' He shrugged. 'And I couldn't afford the mug.'

Adam's was a practical love; he was Jimmy all over. She'd kissed and hugged him until he begged her to stop, but he was secretly pleased. And then it was Colm's turn.

Colm, who couldn't look anyone in the eye and, even at eight years old, still hid behind her if he had to speak. He stood up on the footstool and sang her a song he'd written, especially for her.

She'd never cried so much in her life.

Seven years later, Colm was gone. And every day of the thirty-two years since, she saw him standing there in the sitting room, in his bare feet and too-small pyjama top, his eyes shining and proud. And every day, she prayed that the world had been kind to him. That it was still kind to him. That he was ...

She shook her head. *Positive thoughts. Positive energy.*

They'd got a letter, five or six years ago, saying that he was in the North and had joined the priesthood. But it was anonymous, and when they went looking they couldn't find anything. It was hard to know what to think. Some days she didn't know which was harder, the grief or the hope.

A commotion outside the front door interrupted her reverie. She stood for a second, still staring out the window, lost in her thoughts. The commotion came nearer. It was a man's voice. Adam.

She wiped her hands and took off her apron, hanging it neatly on the hook next to the hob.

She'd prefer that he didn't show up drunk, but he *had* shown up. That was something. And who knew, maybe he had some more teabags and hand soap. That boy was still in there somewhere. She might just need to get some coffee into him before he woke the whole village.

She went downstairs and opened the door. When she saw him, she nearly fell backwards in fright.

'I'm so sorry, Ma ...' he was saying, his face full of shock and hurt. 'I'm so, so, sorry ...' He was closer to babbling than to talking.

He was covered in blood.

As Frances listened to him, her face began to mirror his. Someone was dead, that part she understood – Mr Hollis. He was dead; but it wasn't his blood on Adam's shirt.

It was that part that she couldn't follow.

'Adam, slow down – what do you mean?' she asked. 'What do you mean, Colm's back?'

'Colm's back,' he repeated. 'He's still alive. They don't know if he's going to make it. But ... oh God ... he's under arrest. For murder.'

Frances didn't remember hitting the floor.

Chapter 5

'Can you walk me through it again?' Garda Liam asked. 'Just take it from the top.'

Emma sighed wearily.

She'd been through her story twice already, and Liam still had the same earnest but uncomprehending look on his face as he did when they'd started.

Liam sat in front of her, across a table; his boss, Sergeant Noonan, leaned against a wall in the far corner, watching impatiently. They were in one of the Skibbereen Garda Station's interrogation rooms – the only interrogation room, in fact. The table was wooden, the chairs were made of metal. It didn't exactly have a single lightbulb swinging on a chain, but it was close. The only thing that made it less like the movies was the small slice of cake in the corner. It was left over from a birthday party two days before.

Sergeant Noonan had asked Emma to come to the station to make a statement, but she was having trouble getting through to Garda Liam. She'd repeated the story twice now.

Liam flipped through his notebook again, clearly trying to find the place where he had lost the thread.

'I think ...' he said, sweat glistening on his forehead, 'I think, you had said ...' He flipped a page again and was confronted with the back cover. 'Hang on a second here.'

From behind him in the corner, Sergeant Noonan pulled a sympathetic face at Emma. Or at least, what he thought was a sympathetic face – in reality, it made him look incontinent. He was in his fifties and suffering from a bad dye job. From what Emma knew of his reputation, he deserved both the incontinence and the bad dye job.

'Not exactly our finest operative, Liam here,' he said. 'But Garda Eamon is out sick this week, so we'll take what we can get.'

Liam blushed, and Emma felt a wave of pity for him. Where Liam had an open, nervous face, Noonan's was thin and reedy – his eyes darted around the room and, again, down her shirt. If anyone in the room had her sympathy, it was Liam.

'What about the third man?' she asked. 'The one who ran away? Are you out looking for him?'

Noonan rolled his eyes.

'Let's see here,' he said, coming over to the table and taking Liam's notebook from him before he could start flipping through it again. 'Ah, yes, here. You said you saw a man. Who you can't describe.' He glanced at Liam meaningfully. 'A person of no known features, who was wearing a coat. Which was ... dark.' He leaned in mockingly. 'Think closely now, are you sure it was dark?'

Emma started to answer, but Noonan ignored her. He sat down next to Liam.

'Well, that about solves it, so,' he said. 'We just need to find a man. A man of average build, who was last seen possibly wearing a coat, and who quite possibly isn't even of average build.' He looked up at Emma and leaned back in his chair, smirking. 'Now, does that sound about right? Shall I call it in?'

Emma was a patient person. And even if she wasn't, she had spent a year at Templemore, the lone woman in a class of one hundred – she knew how to fake it. But that little performance had burned a lot of fuse.

'I told you,' she said calmly. 'He had his face turned away, and he was in the shadow of the house. I couldn't get a good look at him, but surely you can get footprints. Or maybe he left something in the house—'

Noonan held up his hand.

'Thank you for the advice on how to do my job,' he said coldly. 'But we have no reason to believe that this was anything more than a burglary that went tragically wrong, both for the victim and for the burglar.' He looked at her. 'Singular.'

Emma changed tactics.

'Okay, you think it was a burglary.' She nodded. 'I get it. But there were two of them. That other man is still out there, possibly armed. *Definitely* dangerous.' She paused. 'You have to warn people.'

Noonan scoffed.

'We're not going to start a panic just because you're scared of the dark.'

Emma's jaw clenched. Somewhere deep in her brain, a web of fingers frantically tried to catch the burning spark racing along the fuse but missed. And suddenly, the spark vanished into the powder.

Liam seemed to sense the impending explosion and quickly changed the subject, pulling out a spare notebook from his back pocket for good measure.

'Maybe if you could just take us through Dr Thornton's reaction one more time—'

'His reaction,' Emma interrupted, her voice incredulous, 'to finding his long-lost brother on the floor of a dead man's house and close to dying himself?' Liam started frantically flipping through his notebook, even though it was empty. 'Right, well, as you can imagine, he was very upset.'

She'd caught up to Adam halfway up the village, but she couldn't get a word out of him. She couldn't even get him to slow down to check if the coast was clear before he went into the house – he just burst through the open front door.

He barely stopped to look at Mr Hollis – but Emma could see the old man was dead. The blood was dried and clotted – flies flitted across his pale blue lips. It was horrible, but the sort of horrible that demands to be looked at, to be made small. Only a guttural, primal noise coming from the corner of the room made her look away. The noise was coming from Adam, as he knelt over the priest.

'He recognised him, of course,' Emma said quietly. 'Colm wasn't conscious, but after Adam got the bleeding to stop, he found a pulse.'

That was all she needed to tell them, as far as she was concerned. They didn't need to hear about the screaming. They didn't need to know that she saw Adam raise his fist to his unconscious brother twice, and then twice restrain himself. They didn't need to know that she had to pull him off Colm in the end.

Liam stopped flipping through his notebook. 'Are you okay?'

Emma almost smiled; it was the first time either one of the guards had acknowledged that she might be upset.

'I suppose. Just a bit shook up.' She shifted on her seat; the cold metal was making her legs go numb. 'Where's he been this whole time? Colm, I mean. Where's he been the last thirty years?'

Noonan and Liam both answered at the same time. 'We don't know.'

'Belfast.'

Noonan glared at Liam, who turned red and went back to his notebook.

She started to say something to Liam, to comfort him, but Noonan was impatient.

'And then what?' he snapped. 'After Dr Thornton found a pulse.'

Emma lit a cigarette, waving the match out after.

'And then you came through the door. You can tell him what happened from there.'

'Right, so.' Noonan looked at Liam. 'Let's pick that up later, shall we?'

'I'd rather go through it now, actually,' Liam said. 'If you don't mind. *Sir*,' he added quickly.

Noonan sighed in frustration.

'Once I had the scene in hand,' he began, 'I made the decision to transport the assailant—'

'The gunshot victim,' Emma corrected. Noonan ignored her.

'To transport the *assailant*,' he repeated, 'as well as his attending doctor and the witness to Bandon General as quickly as possible, and then brought Miss Daly back here to take a statement.'

Liam frowned at Emma. 'We haven't got much of a statement yet.'

Emma had no idea how to respond to that.

'And what about the crime scene?' Liam said, as if to himself. 'What did it look like?'

Emma stared blankly at him.

'What did it ... I'm sorry, what sort of question is that?'

As Liam flushed and immediately started sweating again, Noonan took over.

'Yes, Liam, that's enough of that.' Noonan said, through gritted teeth. 'I can answer that. The inside of the house was in poor condition, very poor – I needed to sweep through the scene and secure any evidence before we left. There were rats, you see, and even twenty minutes with a dead body can be disastrous ...'

Liam shuddered, and another bead of sweat dripped down his pale face. Noonan nodded grimly.

'Yes, I know. But unfortunately, there was nothing more to learn.' He glared at Emma now. 'The scene had already been spoiled.' It was clear he believed Adam's medical attention was either unnecessary or, at least, partly her fault.

He was right, though. Mr Hollis was a hoarder. She'd only caught a glimpse of the other rooms in the house, but it was enough; there were boxes scattered all over, newspapers and ripped-up cushions. The kitchen was overflowing with dirty dishes and sour laundry. She might not have seen any rats, but they certainly fit with the decor.

But Noonan was hiding something, she was sure of it. He'd rushed them out of the house and had seemed more upset that they were there than about the dead and dying men in the front room. And why did he keep insisting there was no third man?

Emma wished she could read Noonan from his clothes or track his movements from a stray detail on his shirt, like Sherlock would. Unfortunately, she didn't have the ability to identify, at a glance, 140 different types of tobacco ash. She couldn't place him just by noticing that there was a cat hair on the left shoulder of his coat; she wasn't even sure it was a cat hair at all. And in fairness, Sherlock himself solved most of his cases through elaborate disguises or his network of homeless children. He really only ever used his deduction to impress Watson.

So, other than the fact that Noonan may or may not have come in contact with a cat recently, she couldn't deduce anything. But the whole village knew that Noonan was sleazy. Maybe not fully sinister, but he was definitely not fully on the same side of the law as his badge either.

'Anything else in that notepad of yours, Liam?' Noonan asked, in a tone that made it clear he had answered his own question. Liam shook his head vigorously, scattering a few drops of sweat loose.

'Now then, Miss Daly,' the sergeant said, putting both his hands on the table, 'you have been most helpful, and you are now free to go.' He regarded her coldly. 'With our thanks.'

But Emma didn't move.

'But what about the third man?' she asked again. 'For God's sake, he's still out there—'

Noonan held up his hand.

'Will you shut up about the third man,' he said, an edge creeping into his voice. 'As I've said, we have heard enough, and we thank you for your time.'

'I trained at Templemore,' Emma argued. 'Inspector class. I think I—'

'*You* trained at Templemore?' Liam asked incredulously. He looked down at his notebook again. 'I thought you were a librarian.' Noonan's eyes narrowed, and he pounced on this new direction.

'Yes, Miss Daly here was one of the top recruits up in the city,' he said, with a smile that didn't extend any further than his mouth. 'But it didn't work out.' He leant forward, his eyes hardening. 'Which is why she had to move back down here, to live among us simple country folk again.'

Emma flushed but ignored him. She turned to Liam.

'You said he didn't find any footprints. But there should have at least been mine and Adam's. So, if there were none, then that doesn't rule out—'

'Enough!' Noonan shouted suddenly. Emma flinched. Liam dropped his notebook and practically dived under the table. 'Now, that's quite enough. I won't stand here and listen to a lecture from a bloody librarian, and I sure as hell won't have you starting a panic in the village for no damn reason. There were no footprints, and that's the end of this.' When Emma didn't answer, he slammed his hand on the table.

'Do you understand me?'

Emma looked at Noonan in disbelief. She didn't buy the robbery. Not that she wanted Adam's brother – Charley's uncle – to be guilty of simple murder either. But any idiot could see it wasn't a robbery. For one thing, who goes to a robbery dressed up as a priest? And what kind of burglar breaks into a house, murders someone and then runs away without at least taking something for their trouble? At least for the additional twenty years of jail time?

Besides, one peek through the window would've told any burglar that the old man had nothing valuable – at least, not unless they wanted to dig through mouldy boxes to get it. And Colm was seemingly living in Belfast; why would he come all the way to Kilcraven to rob someone? It didn't make sense. None of it made any sense. So why was Noonan pretending it did?

She tried one more time, her fists clenching and unclenching under the table.

'I can take you to where I was,' she said, in an even tone. 'To exactly where I was standing, and where he ran – maybe you looked in the wrong direction.'

Noonan rolled his eyes at Liam. Liam returned the look with a confused one of his own.

'Look for ... for footprints, was it?' Noonan said, picking up a pen and pretending to write in Liam's notebook. 'Does the librarian have any other tips?'

Emma stood, knocking the chair over behind her, but before she could say anything, Noonan held up his hand.

'That's enough of that now,' he said sternly. He gestured for Emma to sit down again. 'Please.'

Emma stayed where she was. Noonan exhaled in frustration.

'I'll remind you, Miss Daly, that you trained in the city. They have problems that we don't have down here.' His voice hardened. 'And I'll *also* remind you that you were kicked out of the force. Now, you can either be a disgraced ex-inspector or a librarian. You decide.'

Emma turned sharply on her heel and made for the door. 'Oh, and Miss Daly?'

She paused, but she didn't turn around. 'Yes?'

'I may not be from the big city, but I knew Garda John Byrne. I knew him pretty well, in fact. And, well ... people don't forget something like that. Do they?'

She could hear the smirk in his voice. Was it a warning to back off? Or a reminder that nobody would listen to her if she didn't? Or did he just want to hurt her, to see her squirm? Either way, he got what he wanted.

She slammed the door behind her. But not hard enough. As she walked down the hallway, the muffled sound of laughter echoed in her ears.

Chapter 6

The air in the garda station office had a funny charge to it – a rattle, like a wasp trapped behind a fluorescent light. It was the sort of charge created by tension, exhaustion and an overcompensation of bad coffee.

Emma shook her head. There was clearly something else going on here that Noonan was hiding – whether it was about Mr Hollis, or the third man, or even Colm Thornton, she didn't know. But there was nothing she could do. As much as she wanted to march back in there and beat their fecking heads against the desk until some sense fell out – there was no point. That comment about John Byrne made it clear. She'd done her part. It was over.

Noonan was right – she was a librarian now. And it was time to get back to the business of the library. She checked her watch as she headed for the exit; it was nearly half one in the morning. She'd be wrecked for work tomorrow, if she made it in at all.

'Hi ... Emma!' a voice called from across the room. 'Emma, over here!'

Jimmy Thornton hurried across the room to her. Behind him, Frances and Adam sat on the waiting room benches, looking miserable. Adam hadn't changed out of his shirt; it was still covered in blood.

'You okay?' Jimmy asked, putting his hand on her shoulder. 'They didn't keep you this whole time, did they?'

Emma waved it away.

'Never mind me, how about you? Any news from the hospital?' Jimmy steered her out of earshot of Frances and Adam.

'It's not looking good,' he said quietly. 'He's alive, but they don't know much more than that. Adam patched him up pretty good, but the bullet hit his lung. They say they're hopeful, but …' He trailed off.

Emma nodded. Then she thought of something.

'Look, just a heads up – the guards are particularly thick tonight. They think they're playing Columbo. And you've never met two people less suited to the role of Columbo in your life, like.' She rolled her eyes. 'But they kept asking why Adam thought it was Colm. I think they're wondering if he was involved somehow.'

'I asked him that myself.' Jimmy looked across the room at Adam, who sat slumped in his chair, his head in his hands. 'He said his first thought, anytime there's been a stranger in the village, is that it's Colm. Come back, like.' Jimmy explained about the anonymous letter, about Belfast and how they'd been told he was a priest. 'And of course, even as a kid, everybody always said how much Charley looked like Colm. In all that time, he never gave up hope that his brother was alive and might come back one day. And then tonight, of all nights, he was right.'

He sat down heavily. Emma quietly sat down next to him. She waited. The hum of the overhead lights and distant murmured conversations all blended together with the occasional clatter of a typewriter. *Tick tick tick* went the keys. *Chime. Slide. Bang. Tick tick tick.* Emma waited.

'We called every parish in the North,' he said quietly – like he was reminding himself. 'Every church, every parish hall. Every year, we'd travel up there and spend a week just knocking on doors, showing his picture around. But all the parishes said no. They'd never heard of him.' His voice hardened sharply. 'He told them to.'

Emma had sat at Jimmy's kitchen table with Charley a hundred times as an awkward teenager, desperately trying to impress her boyfriend's family. But she'd never seen Jimmy cry; never heard him talk like this before.

'Thirty years,' he said, shaking his head. 'I thought he was dead. God, I wished he was dead. We could make our peace with that.' He looked over his shoulder at Frances and Adam. 'I don't know what this is going to do to them. To her. I honestly don't.' All around them, the typewriters clattered on. A phone rang, then another. Jimmy patted Emma's knee and stood up.

'Anyway, love,' he said with a forced cheeriness. 'Sorry to keep you. Just been a long night.' He lit a cigarette. 'Now. I need to go find these guards and tell them to feck off out of it.'

But as he walked away with Adam, Emma could see the frightened, wounded look still lingering on his face. The tears still in his eyes.

Just give it time, she thought. *Just give it time.*

*

Frances sat on the hard-backed bench – her knees and back erupted in creaks and cracks and small moans as she stood up to greet Emma. Frances pulled her into a hug, her body shaking with sobs.

'I'm so sorry, Frances,' Emma said, her words muffled by a tangle of hair and shoulder pads. 'I'm so sorry ...'

'I know, love,' Frances said, 'I know ...'

*

Sam was waiting outside for her with the car. As soon as she left the building, all of the adrenaline and tension and fear fell away – a trap door snapped shut, leaving nothing but exhaustion in its wake. Sam nearly had to carry her the two metres to the car. She dozed on the ride home and then collapsed into bed. She didn't even have the energy to set her alarm for work tomorrow.

But just before Emma fell asleep, a last thought kept swooping and swirling. Something Frances had told her just before she left the station.

Charley Thornton was coming home.

Chapter 7

The Protestant church in Kilcraven was well regarded, if not well attended. It was at the top of the hill; the parson was a firm believer in preserving wildlife habitats, particularly for bees, and he let the grass around the church grow tall – wildflowers and chestnut trees burst up all around the headstones of the small cemetery beside it. Little by little, year after year, the church crouched lower and lower behind the young forest.

It became a popular place to visit in the last warm days of autumn – for all ages, at different times. The elderly came in the early morning: for them it was a nature reserve, with a clean stone path and plenty of benches. For the rest of the day it was given over to small children and their parents, hunting for the conkers that lined the path. And then, as the day turned into evening, the teenagers came.

You could quietly disappear just off the path into the tall sweetgrass, surrounded by bluebells and snapdragons and small blackberry bushes. Two people could lie down and hide from the world as long as they wanted or needed.

And on the off chance they were discovered, far better to be found by a parson than a priest.

*

At dusk, when the blue-dark sky mixed with the first drop of moonlight, the bats that lived in the church's old bell tower started to stir and rustle and stretch. Eight years ago, on such an evening and in such a light, Charley and Emma walked slowly up the church path. The parson saw them out his sitting-room window and briefly thought they were coming up to the church. But then the girl broke into laughter and pulled the boy down the path, and they disappeared from view. With a sigh, the parson pulled the blind down and went back into the kitchen. Outside, Emma had dragged Charley far enough, and she spun around as he lifted her up, tucked her legs to the side and gently laid her down on the grass. It felt wet; her cotton blouse clung to her back. She was still in her uniform. She smiled as he ran one hand through her short hair, the other disappearing beneath her skirt. They'd forgotten to talk.

'Hey,' she said breathlessly, after a minute.

He stopped and smiled back at her. 'Hey,' he said.

Charley was the same age as Emma, but he was wearing work pants and a white undershirt, with sawdust clinging to the folds. His eyes were flecked with yellow and flashed blue and green all at once.

She smiled and pulled him slowly against her. But then, she waited.

He frowned.

'Hey – are you okay?'

She nodded, but her eyes were bright and wet.

'I just realised – this is the last time I'm going to have this uniform on.'

'Take it off, more like,' he said and grinned.

Emma pushed him, but it was playful again. She was old enough to start feeling nostalgia for things that hadn't ended yet, but young enough that the moment passed quickly.

'Three more months,' Charley said.

'Three *beautiful* months,' she answered.

'And, after, when you've settled into your fancy new college digs, I'll come visit—'

Emma put her finger across his lips.

'No promises,' she said. 'We promised. No promises we can't keep.'

Charley nodded, his face serious for a moment. Then she moved one hand up under his shirt and the other beneath his belt buckle, and he abandoned the thought, and all thoughts in general.

They pulled at each other, digging their bodies out of cloth and buckles and buttons, firm lips on soft, pale skin.

His tongue was on her chest, her stomach, between her legs. She twisted, she grabbed his hair, she pulled him up, up into her; she arched further down into his mouth. A shudder, a gasp, and then she collapsed, holding clumps of grass that she'd pulled out of the ground.

He crawled back up to her. She ran her thumb along his jaw – his chin was still wet – and they both laughed. He rolled onto his back beside her.

She looked down between his legs. 'Can't lie on your stomach, eh?'

He laughed again.

Then she was on top of him, pushing him deep inside her.

*

They'd been lying quietly for a while, tangled up in each other – sweaty and warm – when the night suddenly erupted above them. Black, shuddering wings flew out in a great sigh across the violet sky.

'Bats,' Charley murmured.

Emma ran her hands absentmindedly across his chest. 'What?'

'Bats – they live up in the bell tower.'

Emma frowned. 'What's so interesting about bats?'

Charley stared at the sky.

'There was one in the boathouse a couple years back. Luke was running around trying to kill it with an oar – but it was just hurt and trapped and scared out of its mind. I tried to do something, bring it to a vet, like, but ...' He shrugged. 'No vet would take it; they bother the livestock, apparently. So, I took care of it for a while.' He looked over at her; she had her eyes closed. 'But anyway ... I have something for you.'

He reached into his bag, and he handed her a book – an anthology of Sherlock Holmes.

'I saw your old one was falling apart,' he said, his face turning red even in the cool air. 'It's not to replace that one, I know your mam gave it to you – just if you want to give it a little rest now and then – save some wear and tear, like.'

Emma flipped through the pages greedily – the names of the adventures she knew by heart but couldn't stop reading. 'It's beautiful,' she murmured. 'I'll think of you when I read it.'

'And I'll think of you when I'm reading the stories of your own adventures,' he said quietly, watching her. 'The first female inspector, the first female commissioner ...'

It was Emma's turn to blush now.

'Come here,' she said, and threw her arm across his chest, her lips trembling along his neck. 'Let's not think about that yet.'

But they did. The air was heavy with bluebells and cherry blossoms; the wind and stars moved gently through the trees up above them. They wondered quietly about the future; the girl who wanted to change the world, to give it justice, and the boy who believed she would. The night was soft and sweet and, there in the tall grass, it was all for them.

Emma fell asleep. Charley didn't notice.

'Bats are delicate, you know,' he said quietly, his fingers running gently along her arm. 'They're sensitive to changes that we can't see.

Even other animals can't see them.' He shook his head in wonder. 'Little, tiny changes. But they notice. And when they notice, they start to disappear.' And then he fell asleep too.

Dusk fell gently away, dropped slowly like a stone through dark water. The boy and the girl lay in each other's arms, asleep, but up above them, the stars kept spinning.

An hour later, when the parson looked out the window again, they were gone.

*

We all have one night, one moment in this life that was created just for us. That was theirs – Emma and Charley, eight years ago.

Afterwards, after she left for college and he left for a job in London, they fell out of each other's lives. They didn't speak; they wouldn't have known what to say if they had – they'd both grown up and lived and changed so much. But they never forgot the feeling of that night, among the wildflowers and tall grass, the sky held up by the dark chestnut trees.

And now, eight years later, life had decided that that was long enough. Something was pulling them back together. And they could both feel it, and they both wondered if maybe the universe believed, occasionally, in second chances.

Chapter 8

The morning broke slowly over Kilcraven. The sun dragged itself up over the horizon, at first only managing a pale blue light. Little by little, though, it started to nudge its way through, and the clouds reluctantly shuffled out of its way. By the time Emma was outside and on the footpath to work, the day had arrived.

The village was quiet. It was quiet every morning, in fairness. The little shops that used to line the street had closed down over the past decade, shuttered one by one, until only one remained: Deasy's, or 'the shop' as it was known locally.

The shop had been standing in the middle of Kilcraven since 1842. It was a small shop, but it prided itself on supplying a little bit of almost everything: a range of groceries, baby products, toiletries, the odd bit of clothing and hardware, as well as seasonal furniture. There were baby dolls and propane tanks, baked goods and, occasionally, a bike or two. It could be expensive, but it saved you both the time and the petrol of going into town. For over a hundred years, that was the business model (give or take the invention of the automobile).

The N71 road, on the other hand, which ran through West Cork from the city down to Skibbereen, was built by an army of architects, engineers and traffic consultants who envisioned it less as a road for people and more as a brutal arm of commerce. It was a road built for lorries on a schedule, for commuters and for tourists. The N71 was a shipping lane – it didn't so much cross West Cork as barrel through it, the low green hills turning into the wake of a great ocean liner. It was an ugly road, built for ugly reasons, but it connected West Cork to the world – and West Cork loved it.

Unfortunately, though, the N71 didn't go through Kilcraven. The villagers put up a sign on the turn-off from Leap, but it was no use. Now, the world passed by Kilcraven without even slowing down. And it was easier than ever to leave the village and go somewhere they didn't just have a little bit of almost everything – they had a *lot* of *absolutely* everything. They had whatever you wanted and whenever you wanted it.

The exodus was swift and entirely in one direction. Kilcraven struggled to keep up. Its main road used to have five pubs, two grocers, a post office and a chip shop. Now, it was down to just the one pub, the library and the shop – and the library was a miracle while the shop was on its last legs.

In 1988 *The Economist* declared that Ireland was doomed. They made the case the country should be taken behind the woodshed and shot, for the sake of all involved. Kilcraven didn't need *The Economist* to read the writing on the wall – it was all around them in the empty storefronts of the village.

It was a short walk from Emma and her father's house on the hill down to the library, but Emma always took the long way around, across the causeway. She liked to let her mind stretch out a bit before she got behind her desk. A hazy mist lay across the harbour and the surrounding fields. The footpath echoed as she walked; her footsteps running down along the causeway to the old mill, then running back around her up the hill. It was the only sound for miles.

At breakfast, Sam had waited until she had her mug of tea in hand to ask about the night before. She gave him the short version, but still he saw right through her.

'Don't get involved,' he warned. 'Burglary or not, something like this is going to upset a lot of people. I don't want you getting caught in the middle.'

She busied herself spreading butter on toast. 'There's no chance of that. Sergeant Noonan made it very clear last night that he didn't appreciate my help.' She laughed humourlessly but stopped when she saw the look on her father's face.

'Please,' he said quietly. 'Don't get involved. After last time, and everything you went through ...' He trailed off.

Emma reached across the table and took his hand. 'I promise.'

Sam nodded.

'Good. Because if Noonan is as useless as you say he is, and if I know Jimmy half as well as I think I do, he's going to be coming to you for answers.' He shook his head in disbelief. 'Colm Thornton, who would've thought?'

Emma silently reached for the jam, and they moved on with their morning.

Now, on her way to work, Emma looked over the side of the causeway. It was low tide, and the pond was empty. The whole harbour was dry. The sea had hiked up her dress, leaving the brown seaweed tangled up in the rocks and sand on her legs, the ropes and lines of the buoys all twisted up after the storm. The tide went out nearly as far as the pier, where the fishing boats waited for the turn. The morning light flashed in the water.

Emma's reverie was suddenly broken by the *click-clack* of sharp claws running on concrete from behind her. Before she knew what she was doing, she spun around and swung her rucksack out in front of her.

'*Gahharrrrrr!*' she shouted, trying to make herself look bigger than she was.

The fox, halfway across the footpath to her, stopped running. He looked at her and tilted his head. The two of them stared, both just as surprised by the other.

'You're not supposed to be here,' she said to the fox. This was unhelpful, of course, but she felt like somebody had to say it. The fox kept staring at her. 'You're not supposed to be here,' she repeated, as if maybe the problem was that he was a bit hard of hearing. 'You're not supposed to be here!'

The fox tilted his head to the other side now. Emma took this to mean *I could say the same to you.*

It wasn't baring its teeth, but she didn't trust that – she knew foxes could go from innocent to dangerous in a split second. Fox attacks were a constant feature in the papers. (The victims were usually puppies and small children, but still – her adrenaline was pumping.) She was close to the library; it was only just across the causeway. She might be bigger than a small child, but she wasn't faster than a fox. She'd have to reason with it.

'Are you hungry?' she asked.

The fox gave her what she thought was a hungry look.

Emma opened her rucksack and took out her brown bag lunch: a sandwich – ham and cheese on brown bread – and held it up to show the fox.

'Here you go,' she said, in a slow, calm tone. '*Heeere* you go.'

She put the sandwich down on the footpath, then backed away slowly. The fox still had his head tilted to one side, watching her curiously. When she'd gone a few steps, and he realised it wasn't a trick, he suddenly bounded forward. He tore the sandwich apart, gnawing and gnashing at the sliced ham. Emma looked at him again. He looked a bit skinny, a bit weary. She could hear the hedge rustling behind him – maybe a mate, or a cub. She wondered if Cordelia had flooded their den. She felt a wave of pity for the creature.

Then she turned and ran.

At the end of the causeway she turned around to see if he was still eating, but he'd disappeared. The sandwich was gone too. Maybe he'd brought it back to the hedge, like a good father. Or maybe he'd wolfed the whole thing down. Either way, anyway, she'd have to find something else for lunch.

Sam, a blow-in from faraway Dublin, loved to tell her a story about when he first moved to Kilcraven. As he stood in the old cottage for his first Sunday tea with his new in-laws, he spotted a large shadow pacing around outside behind the curtain. He poked his head out the window to see what it was and immediately pulled his head back in. Outside, in the front garden, was a bull. A large, escaped bull with no fence in sight. A large, escaped bull with a bone to pick it seemed, judging from the stomping and snorting. But that wasn't the strangest part. The strangest thing was the reaction inside: after he pointed it out to the rest of the family, they all peered through the window. 'Ah, sure, that must be Mike's,' someone said. And then they sat back down and went back to their tea. Sam, meanwhile, could hardly stay upright on his seat, he was so drenched in sweat.

It was one of the things Sam loved about West Cork, and why he stayed even after Emma's mum left – how the wild centre was always ready to burst its way through. And Emma loved that too. Sometimes, she told herself that was why she had come back, why she was still here. And sometimes, she almost believed it.

But now, it was time for work.

*

This morning, there was a surprise waiting for her at the front door – Maeve, her middle-aged colleague. It was a surprise because while Maeve was a good employee, she rarely made it in before the first patron; you could often hear the light tinkle of gin bottles in her voice until midday, and sometimes again in the early evening.

While Maeve waited for Emma to unlock the front door of the library, she was practically hopping up and down from excitement.

'You alright there, Maeve?'

But Maeve just waved her hands: *not out here*.

Emma pushed the door open and flicked the light on, and then they both went inside.

Kilcraven Library was small. Every surface was covered with books – but in a cosy, not chaotic way. It was something about the smell; fresh hardcovers mixed with worn paperbacks, the mixture of the high piles and the bright and airy windows. And of course, when you looked a little closer, you could see the meticulous organisation behind the layout (with corresponding signs in English, Irish and pictograms).

Emma chose every book in the library. She had to be magnanimous; she constantly reminded herself that the library was not an extension of her own tastes, and it was there to serve the community, not her. But Jesus, the community could have some awful rotten taste.

How many more novels about angry young men did they need, really? How much Hemingway could the world take? How many times could Jack Ryan save the world before he decided the world he lived in wasn't worth the saving? (It certainly wasn't worth the shelf space his books took up.) But that was what people wanted. And so, the books stayed.

There was a small section in the back right corner for newspapers and a few small chairs. That was the pensioners' section, and the site of heated battles each morning. Emma occasionally had to intervene (more often than she had to intervene in the children's section, it must be said), but a pot of tea or a well-placed word usually restored calm.

This, the library, was her sanctuary – the place where she did work that mattered. The place she had transformed from a glorified jobs centre into a genuine pillar of the community. The place that made her proud – of her work, of her talent and of herself. However briefly.

This morning, Emma had a pile of paperwork to get sorted before they opened, as well as a whole new shipment to catalogue. But Maeve was relentless.

'Did you hear?' she asked breathlessly, practically jumping out of her shawl. 'About the robbery?'

Maeve was kind and big-hearted, but her love of gossip and faint air of desperation could make her a bit of an acquired taste. To put it another way, when people learned that she was married to a failed barber who made the same three jokes about her cooking at the pub every night, they said, 'Ah,' and then raised their eyebrows knowingly. 'That makes sense.'

But Emma loved Maeve. She was a good friend. And her friend was absolutely bursting to tell her the news. Maeve would've heard every bit of gossip and stance on the matter before Emma even got out of bed that morning. Interestingly, though, from her question, it seemed like she hadn't heard about Emma's involvement. If nobody had got around to mentioning that, then there must be some truly exciting theories. Emma decided to play dumb for the minute. She could find out if the village agreed with her or the guards.

'Okay, I'll bite. What happened?'

But now that Maeve knew she had her audience's attention, she was going to take her time.

'Let me just pop the kettle on there.' Emma groaned, but Maeve waved her off. 'It'll just be two ticks.' And while they waited for the kettle to boil, Maeve told her the basics, rehashing the two bodies found, one of whom was Colm Thornton.

'Can you imagine?' she said breathlessly. 'Ran away in the night, thirty years ago – and now look at him.' She raised her eyebrows knowingly. 'He's clearly been busy.'

Maeve laughed, but Emma was frowning.

'Why'd he run away though, back then? And why'd he stay away so long?'

Maeve threw up her hands. 'Nobody knows. It was a big mystery at the time. There wasn't any trouble at home or with the law, no pregnant girlfriend. No trouble of any kind, it seemed like.' She lowered her voice. 'A lot of people thought he must've been taken.' She paused. 'His parents were devastated, of course. They put up signs every month for nearly fifteen years.' She lit a cigarette and leaned back in her chair. 'It was a big story, back then. Even where I lived, my mother always told me, *Don't stay out too late, or you'll end up the same as Colm Thornton*.'

Emma took the box from Maeve and lit a cigarette too. She frowned. 'I heard the opposite,' she said. 'When I was growing up; and this was about twenty years later, of course,' – she ducked as Maeve swung her hand at her – 'all the kids used to say, *Don't go out at night, or Colm Thornton will get you*.'

'Well, it seems like they were right about that.' Emma frowned at her again.

'We don't know he's guilty.' Maeve shrugged.

'Anyway, that's how these things go. The story changes, but the moral stays the same.'

The kettle began to whistle. As she watched Maeve get the teapot ready, Emma wondered. A teenager disappears from a small village, without a trace and presumably for no reason, as far as anyone can tell. Then he reappears thirty years later, in that same small village, at the scene of a violent crime.

'But what about last night – what do people think happened?'

Maeve was only too delighted to share the gossip she'd heard.

'Oh, there are lots of theories. Apparently, he'd been living up North, in Belfast. A *Catholic priest* in Belfast,' she added meaningfully. 'Naturally, a lot of people are thinking IRA.'

Emma frowned. 'Was Mr Hollis a Protestant?'

Maeve shook her head.

'No, he was as Catholic as they come – used to be, anyway, back when he still left the house. He was a big-time donor apparently.' She lowered her voice conspiratorially. 'Rumour is, the bishop used to come around his house twice a month for dinner.'

'Used to?' Emma asked.

'The money's long gone, apparently.' Maeve pointed in the air with her cigarette for emphasis. 'I met Trish at the shop there. She said that he would go into town every two weeks for a big shop. And he'd always pay in coins, small change, like. She said it used to take twenty minutes to count it all up. But the poor man only ever bought potatoes and butter and tea. Absolute mounds of the stuff, but that was it.'

Emma considered this.

'Paying in change doesn't make him poor, though – it makes him cheap. You can be cheap and still be rich.' She took a long, thoughtful drag on her cigarette. 'But why would Colm try to rob Mr Hollis? Why come all the way back from Belfast to rob someone? Surely there were plenty of rich people to rob up there?'

Maeve snorted impatiently.

'Are you listening at all? Of course he didn't rob him,' she said, lighting another cigarette. 'Apparently, Mr Hollis got on the wrong side of the IRA. Or maybe he'd always been on the wrong side, but his money kept him safe. Once the money ran out, so did his leeway.' She put her hands out, like a solicitor laying out her case. 'So they sent an old local boy down to take care of him.'

'But Hollis was Catholic.'

Maeve raised her eyebrows at her. 'When's that ever mattered?'

'And Colm was a *priest*.'

'And when's *that* ever mattered?'

Emma had to admit, it made a certain amount of sense. More sense than the guards' theory anyway. Maybe that explained their eagerness to go with the robbery angle – the only thing worse than an open murder was an IRA murder.

'Any other theories?'

Maeve blew smoke out of the side of her mouth. 'Apparently there were holes dug all over the garden. Somebody else at the shop – I won't tell you who – was saying that Colm was looking for where Mr Hollis had buried his fortune. Then he forced Mr Hollis to dig his grave at gunpoint—'

'Jesus Christ,' Emma said, shaking her head. 'When did this village turn into *The Godfather*?'

Maeve looked at her curiously. 'What'd you get up to last night, anyway?'

'Ah, well ...'

'You fell asleep at the desk again, didn't you?'

Emma considered telling her about how she found the body, and the scene at the garda station. But then Maeve wouldn't give her a second's peace the whole day, and Emma really did have a lot of work to do. She could tell her later.

'It wasn't that late,' she said finally.

'Because Sam came and woke you up?'

Emma didn't answer, but Maeve could tell she was right. She took a cigarette out and tapped it lightly on the desk. Then she looked at her friend.

'You know, Emma,' she said carefully, 'there is more to life than this library. More to life than this village, even. Go back to the city. You're too young to be stuck here.'

Emma laughed grimly.

'You're the second person to tell me that in the last twelve hours.'

Maeve lit her cigarette and looked straight at her.

'Because Sam and I know you better than anybody,' she said. 'And we know what you're capable of, and why you won't do it. But every so often—'

They were interrupted by a sudden, loud knock at the door. They had to squint to see who it was; the sun had burned off the last of the haze and was out in full force, splashing up out of the puddles and in through the windows. Another loud knock. They could make out three pensioners standing outside the library, pointing at their watches and looking concerned.

'Shit, we're late.' Emma snubbed out her cigarette and snapped into manager mode. She waved at the patrons, then turned to Maeve. But Maeve had beaten her to the punch and was already heading to the door.

'I'll unlock,' she said, over her shoulder. 'Oh, what'd you bring for lunch – I've got an apple if you want to trade?'

'Ah ...'

'What?'

But before Emma could explain that she'd given her lunch to a fox, the pensioners started rapping on the door again, and off Maeve went.

The day began.

Chapter 9

The pensioners weren't in a rush. They never were; they just liked things to be on time. Luckily, Emma had already put the papers out or they might've thrown a riot.

Nuala liked the *Echo*, and her husband, Connie, liked the *Examiner*. Philomena was in too – poor thing didn't read the papers, she just liked to sit there (with the papers, or with the people, Emma wasn't sure which). On a normal day, Frances and Jimmy would be with them, but Emma wasn't surprised not to see them. Sarah and Mary were just behind the rest.

Emma sometimes watched these elderly women and wondered what they'd been like at her age. What had they dreamt about? Did they have any ambitions back then? Were they ever curious? Or maybe this was what they always wanted – a life where they knew exactly what they were going to do every day, and who they were going to do it with and what they would talk about while they did it. They certainly seemed happy, in a distracted, apathetic sort of way.

Was this what her future looked like now? Would she turn into an old lady, talking about the rest of the world from a dusty, lonely corner? Seeing her life as a spectator, rather than a player?

There's only so much that happens in a small village, so you have to pick up the same old tired threads of conversation every day, unless you're vigilant. Was Emma being vigilant? Was she still curious about things she couldn't see? She didn't know, and that scared her.

When she lived in the city, training as an inspector, she'd had a future. One with hope in it. But then the incident with John Byrne came along and she lost that future, and she lost that hope, and now she was out of practice. She'd moved in with her dad, in her old village, temporarily. That was four years ago. And Emma was pretty sure, if she didn't start practising her hope again soon, that she'd lose the skill altogether.

One of the pensioners dropped her handbag and the sound brought Emma back to herself. She got back to her task list.

She sorted through the Returns bin, cataloguing and updating accounts as she went. She saw Maeve was heading to the back corner – she was eavesdropping on Nuala and Connie, but she had the trolley with her, so at least she'd get something done. And Emma had a few last forms to finish up before the post at eleven o'clock.

She was so caught up in her work that she didn't hear anyone come in.

'Sorry,' she said, when somebody tapped the desk with their knuckles. Then she looked up and her face fell. 'Oh – Jesus Christ.'

Charley Thornton grinned. 'Do I look that bad?'

She turned red and shoved the papers she'd been doodling on out of sight. 'No – no, you look great. I mean, you look fine. Under the circumstances, of course.' She bit her lip. 'Sorry, you just caught me a bit off guard there.'

Of course, she'd known ever since Frances said last night that Charley was coming back to Kilcraven, but this was quick, even from London. He must've left England as soon as he'd heard the news, and he must've come to the library pretty quickly after getting home. She tried her best not to think too hard about what that meant.

And to not think too hard about some of the stories she'd heard about his life in London – the girlfriend, for example.

And the worst part was that he looked good. Very good. And from the expression in his eyes, he clearly thought the same about her. After eight years, they took each other in for a moment.

Charley Thornton. Different, of course, but still so familiar. All the things, so many small details that she had put away like old boxes in the back of her mind. He'd grown stubble and his face had thinned out, but he still had the same hands, the same way of pushing his hair back off his face, the same way of biting the inside of his cheek when he was nervous. (Was he nervous?) The small scar on the bottom of his chin. The dimple in his left cheek. She could tell, just by the way he stood, that he was digging through those old boxes too. The way she felt when touched, the way she liked to be touched ...

Jesus Christ, she thought suddenly. *It's not even ten o'clock in the fecking morning. The man has a girlfriend. Pull yourself together*. But she couldn't help it, it was like the moon had suddenly swollen three times its size and pulled the ocean up through her throat, the waves tender and throbbing in her mouth ... *DAMN IT, EMMA!*

Charley finally broke the silence. 'How have you been?'

Emma shrugged. 'Oh, you know ...'

They both stood there, in the full knowledge that no, he didn't know – that was why he asked. But neither one of them said anything else. They just stared at each other.

In the last eight years, Emma hadn't dated much. There were a few men in college, but nothing special. Then, of course, there was John. And after him, in the four years after she left the guards and moved back to Kilcraven, there was no one. She didn't have time, she always told herself. If she was lonely or frustrated – she put that into her work, into building the library: more programmes, more grants, fewer books by Hemingway. *But maybe*, she thought as she looked at Charley Thornton, moving as if in slow motion, *maybe that wasn't the whole story*.

'I'm so sorry about your uncle,' she said, almost to fill the silence. 'How are your parents? How are Frances and Jimmy?'

Charley grimaced. 'I think they're all still in shock, to be honest. It's sort of like they're out of one limbo and into another. Dad's wandering around the place like a lunatic – I swear, I think he'd kill Colm himself.'

Emma exhaled.

'He's angry. It's a lot to process all at once. On the one hand, his brother came back, on the other hand ...' She trailed off, but Charley knew what she meant. He nodded.

'Yeah, I can't even imagine.' He leaned in across the desk and lowered his voice. 'And I'm sorry you had to be the one ... you know, that found them, and all that.'

There was a quiet fit of coughing from the shelf behind them, like someone had suddenly swallowed a large gulp of tea in surprise. Maeve was clearly listening.

'Oh, yes,' Emma said quickly, 'it was nothing. I'm glad I could help, anyway.'

'It was more than nothing.' His voice was warm, like a radio late at night, caught between stations. Emma found herself blushing again. He smiled when he saw it. Then he turned and looked around appreciatively at the library. 'I can't believe what you've done with the place. It looks incredible.'

Emma raised her eyebrow. 'You know, I don't remember you spending too much time in here back in our school days.'

'Well, I would've, if it looked half as good as it does now.' He frowned slightly. 'Except for the front door – the hinges are rusty, that's why it squeaks so much.' He turned back to her, returning her grin. 'Of course, if anyone could turn a place around, it'd be you.' He paused. 'But, Emma, what are you still doing here?'

And just like that, Emma stopped smiling. Her eyes narrowed. 'What's that supposed to mean?'

Charley hesitated. He had caught the tone of her voice, and it was his turn to turn red now.

'I just meant ... I mean, we used to talk about – you used to talk about – about—' He thought better about whatever he was going to say. 'Look, I'm sorry. Can we start over—'

'And did you travel the world, Charley?' Emma's voice was sharp. Whenever she had imagined this conversation (and in the last eight years, she had imagined it more frequently than she'd care to admit) she knew there was a possibility that it might go off the rails, but she'd imagined they'd make it a bit further. They hadn't even managed to say hello. 'Coming back home to a big parade, are you?'

Even as she said it, she regretted it. Charley winced – a full-blown, proper wince – and turned away.

'Charley, I'm sorry—'

'It's okay.' He coughed quietly, his cheeks flooding with colour. 'Maybe I'll see you around.'

And before she could say anything else or stop him, he was gone out the door.

As the bell above the door rang out, Emma sat and wondered why she had said that. Why did she have to get so defensive? Wasn't she always thinking the same thing? Wasn't she literally just wondering if she was wasting her life too, stuck in Kilcraven? He was right. And he hadn't meant anything by it, she knew that.

Maybe that girlfriend was bothering her more than she would've liked.

She sighed heavily, then without turning around, she said, 'You can come out now, Maeve.'

Judging from the angry sniff she got in response, Maeve felt the same about Emma as Emma did.

Before Maeve could start giving out, though, the library filled up with the mother rush – having deposited as many children in school as legally allowed (and possibly a few extra) the mothers came into the library at ten with the leftovers. Emma always told them not to worry about the kids making noise – the pensioners didn't mind, either out of kindness, deafness, or loneliness, collectively – but the mothers still gave out to their kids in hushed, strained tones.

'Johnny? Johnny! Keep your voice down ...'

'Bill Rutherford, you let that little girl go. Now!' Mrs Rutherford would turn to Emma and apologise. 'He's not normally like this.' (Bullshit. Bill Rutherford was *always* like that.)

Then a mother would hiss, 'Is that blood or ketchup?' And off they'd all go again.

Once they got their children quiet, it was the parents' turn to talk – at full, deafening volume.

Emma caught a wide range of conversations as she flipped through her paperwork. She tried not to – it was always the same alarming blend of tedious husbands and kaleidoscopic changes to their breasts – but they were just. So. Loud.

'He's had it for forty years, but he still has no idea how to use it ...'

'... the chafing, my God ...'

'... I feel like a flight instructor half the time ...'

'... like my tits are filled with nettles ...'

'... and the other half, like a captain solemnly going down with her ship ...'

'... you see *Dallas* last night? Jesus, they should've just left the poor man dead. At least *Home and Away* has Matt Wilson ...'

It faded into the background, though, as more patrons came in, dashing in and out, usually after a quick answer rather than a whole book. Just like the big shops used cheap booze to lure in shoppers, Emma used the encyclopaedias to lure in the village; they almost always left with a novel or a biography on whatever topic they were investigating. If you came in to find out if turtles were lizards or reptiles, you left with a biography of Charles Darwin. If you wanted to know where exactly Dorset Street was, you left with *Dubliners*.

Emma didn't see Jimmy Thornton until he was knocking on her desk.

'For feck's sake,' she said, dropping her cigarette on her lap. 'I'm going to get a bell for the lot of you Thorntons, I swear to God.' She furiously patted her lap until the cigarette fell loose, luckily leaving behind only a little ash, no burn marks. 'How are you doing?'

Jimmy shrugged. He had large dark rings around his eyes, and his skin looked paper-thin. 'I just need to talk to you for a second,' he said. 'If that's okay.'

From his expression, she could tell that he meant in private. She told him to follow her to the back corner of the library, behind one of the larger stacks, where nobody could hear them.

'Are you okay?' she asked, frowning. 'Is it Frances?'

Jimmy looked tired – exhausted, really. But there was something different about him this morning. He seemed nervous, or animated, even. And she quickly found out why.

'I want you to investigate the shooting,' he said plainly. As she started to protest, he held up his hands. 'I know, I know. I know you've got a million reasons to want to stay out of it—'

'A billion reasons,' Emma corrected. 'Starting with the main one: I'm a librarian. I'm not a guard.'

Jimmy looked at her fondly.

'I know that's not the main reason,' he said sadly. He saw her flinch, and he leaned over and put his hand on her shoulder. 'And believe me – I wouldn't ask if I had any other option.' He leaned against one of the shelves and stared up at the ceiling, tears forming in his eyes. 'But I know Colm is innocent. I know he is. But the guards won't listen. They say it's a robbery, he's guilty, open and shut. Adam won't listen either – I've never seen him so angry. And Frances ...' He paused, then the words seemed to rush out all at once. 'She won't visit him. She won't even talk about him. It's only me.' His whole body was shaking now, as he struggled to keep control of his voice. 'I'm sorry to ask, Emma, I really am. But I've got no other choice. If I don't try,' he took a ragged breath, 'it'd be like losing him all over again.'

Emma went over and pulled him close. He cried into her shoulder. He smelled like Old Spice and Brylcreem.

'I know, Jimmy,' she said quietly. 'I know. But what would I do? I tried to talk to the guards last night, and they wouldn't listen. I can't look at evidence, or interview witnesses – nobody would talk to me.'

'But everybody knows who you are,' he insisted. 'They know what you've done for the place; everybody loves the library.'

Emma looked at him sadly. 'That's not enough. I'd only just hear the same gossip everybody else does.'

Jimmy nodded; his shoulders slumped.

'I know, love,' he said, sighing deeply. 'I know. I just ... I just had to try, that's all.' He gave her a watery smile. 'I'm sorry to have bothered you.'

She waved it off, her throat tight.

'Of course, I understand. And I'm sorry, Jimmy.'

He nodded again. As he turned around to leave, his whole body dragged – his eyes looked vacantly around the room. *He was a good man*, Emma thought to herself. He and Frances were kind and gentle, always helping out people wherever they could. They'd had a hard life. And if she had a chance to help them, surely Sam could understand that. She just wanted to help.

Outside, through the front window, she saw Charley. He had a screwdriver and a small tin of WD-40 in his hand. And she remembered what had always drawn her to him. She, the girl who loved words and ideas, loved the opposite – the boy who might not be able to tell you what he thought, but would show you. The kind of boy who would help an injured bat or fix a squeaky door.

'Jimmy?' she called quietly. He turned around. 'Does Charley know? About ... about why I came back?'

Jimmy shook his head.

'No, nobody's told him.' He added quickly, 'Not because they're embarrassed or anything, mind you.' He hesitated. 'I think everybody just knows that's your story. And you'll tell him if you want to.' He turned around again.

Emma's heart sank. He was a good man. And like it or not, she owed something to the village that had taken her in and taken care of her the past four years – she owed it to them to help one of their own.

But maybe there was something more. There was another feeling, lying just below the compassion in her heart. It was anger. The guards had ruined her life four years ago – had left her looking just like Jimmy. And here they were, doing it again. Different guards, different place – same pitiless indifference. Here was a chance, maybe, to get them back. And also, maybe, to prove to Charley that she wasn't a failure.

And as a fishing village like Kilcraven knew all too well, there was nothing worse than a disappearance – a body missing at sea and never found. Here was a chance to right that wrong.

Did she think Colm was innocent? No, not really. But even learning that might help the Thorntons, if Colm died before he could explain for himself. At least it would give them some closure.

Besides, she didn't expect she'd actually find anything. As she told Jimmy, she was a librarian – she fully expected to learn nothing more than a few more rumours and tall tales. What was the harm?

In the end, she wasn't sure which emotion made her change her mind. She wasn't sure if it mattered. But she did change her mind. 'Okay,' she called to Jimmy. 'I'll do it.'

As he turned around again, relief flooded his face, and he quickly crossed the room and pulled her into a tight hug.

Jesus, she thought, *what have I done?*

*

After Jimmy left, Maeve nearly exploded out of the shelves to the left of her, a furious look on her face.

'Christ, Maeve, I thought I'd found one spot you couldn't hear me,' Emma said as she stormed over. 'Have you bugged the place or something?'

Maeve ignored her. 'For God's sake, Emma,' she said angrily. 'What were you thinking?'

But before she could say anything else, a fight broke out at the front of the library.

Nuala and Connie were shouting; Philomena had somehow got her hands on a pair of scissors and chopped through half the *Echo* before anyone – herself included – realised what she was doing. Emma ran over and did her best to restore order, but Philomena was quite upset.

'I don't understand what's wrong,' she kept saying, in a quiet whimper. 'Why is everyone so cross with me?'

Emma shot a withering look at Nuala and guided Philomena to a comfy chair behind the front desk, whispering, 'Nuala's just annoyed with the crossword. You know how she gets.'

Philomena looked up at Emma gratefully. Her eyes were bright. 'Thank you, love. Thank you.'

'You just sit here as long as you need.' Emma smiled. 'Put your feet up if you want. Just don't let Maeve catch you.'

Speaking of Maeve, she rounded on Emma as soon as the commotion was over.

'What are you doing, love?' she asked, her anger having slipped into concern. 'You can't go making promises like that to a grieving family. I know the guards are useless, and I know they've treated you shite, but—'

Emma held up her hand.

'I didn't promise anything,' she said calmly. 'I told him more than once that I didn't expect to find anything, and even if I did, I didn't expect it to make Colm innocent. The opposite, in fact.'

Maeve wrung her hands.

'I know, and I know you meant well,' she said anxiously. 'But Jimmy's not going to hear that. Grieving like that, he's going to—'

'I know what he's going to hear,' Emma said quietly. 'More than most, I know.' She could hear the library moving all around her. The murmur in the shelves. The bell above the door. The gentle shuffling of books taken down, examined and then put back again. Outside the door, the village gently flowed past – distant laughter and shouted *hellos*. Neighbours greeting each other, calling up the ladder to the men working on the roof of the old post office. 'He's going to hear that he's doing everything he can, rather than sitting around and waiting for something to happen. And he's going to hear that he's not alone.' Emma's eyes were bright. Maeve reached out and took her hand. 'It's not much, but it's all I can give them. And maybe that's enough. For now, anyway.'

Maeve took a deep breath.

'Okay,' she said finally. 'What can I do to help?'

The world outside Emma moved – but as the wheels in her head started turning, she stopped hearing it.

Colm might not wake up. He was probably guilty; Emma thought that revenge seemed like the obvious explanation. Revenge for something that happened between them when Colm was a child – something powerful enough to drive him away and then return thirty years later. It didn't take much imagination to figure out that motive. But either way, she had the chance to give the Thorntons an answer, one they desperately needed and more than deserved.

And maybe this was what Emma needed as well. A chance at redemption. A mystery that only she could solve – because nobody else would listen. She thought of the hundreds of men and women that arrived at 221B Baker Street, who begged Sherlock to help because nobody else believed them or cared. She might not be Sherlock, but she could try.

Emma rubbed her hands together. She looked at the clock. The game was afoot.

'What can you tell me about Mr Hollis?'

Chapter 10

The office of Flesk & Associates was designed to impress – a heavy front door swung open into a wide room full of dark wood and ornamental gilding. There were a few desks to create the impression, along with the name, that there were more than just Ian Flesk, solicitor, and his secretary, Mary Bennett. Everyone knew the truth, of course, but Ian insisted on keeping up the pretence anyway. To add to the illusion, he made Mary rotate to a new desk every two hours.

There was nobody at the desk when Frances arrived, so she went straight through to the back; she found Ian in his office, his feet up on the desk. It was not a good start to the meeting.

'There's not much in the way of assets,' he said now, his shoes firmly back in place and under his desk. 'Forgive me for saying this, Mrs Thornton, but there usually isn't with priests ...'

Frances winced. She had never liked Ian; as a child, he'd been cruel – the kind of child that pulled wings off butterflies. And now he was a man and he hadn't outgrown it. If anything, he'd graduated to pulling wings off birds. He hadn't asked once how Frances was doing, how Colm was doing in the hospital, or how any of the family was holding up. Instead, he just droned on about Colm's finances and the state of his estate.

'The state of his estate,' he chuckled to himself, running a large hand through his thin, greasy hair. 'That's a good one. I must remember that.'

'You're speaking about him like he's already dead,' Frances said sharply. 'I'm asking about his life – what you can tell me about what he was doing in Belfast all this time.'

Ian coughed quietly.

'Quite right,' he said, pulling papers towards him. 'Now, his parish in Belfast sent me all the details they had about his service and all that, and they were able to get me in touch with his bank, et cetera. I've had a scout through, and as I said, there's not much there.' He looked up at her. 'Normally, of course, there would be a fee for this sort of work. But I've decided to do this pro bono. Free of charge.'

He paused expectantly.

'Thank you,' Frances said, her teeth gritted. He beamed back at her.

'Don't mention it. Even with that generosity, however, there really isn't much here to distribute.' He tossed the slim folder to the side. 'There isn't even a will, I'm afraid.'

That was the real reason for Ian's 'generosity', Frances knew. He was giving up pennies – and presumably, cashing in a much larger favour in the future.

'Is that a problem? That there's no will?'

Ian shook his head, still shifting the papers around on his desk. 'Not in this case, no. If we were talking about a much larger estate, then it could be. The higher the amount in question, the more airtight you need the paperwork. In this case,' – he chuckled again – 'I think we'll be okay.'

If there was another lawyer, any other lawyer, within fifty kilometres, Frances would've stormed out. But men like Ian Flesk were a necessary evil – the greasy hair and paunchy middles that kept the world ticking and billing every tick. If Colm ever woke up, they'd need a solicitor. Ian was slimy, at best, but he was good. She considered asking him then and there if he'd do it, if he'd represent Colm. But she knew that he'd start billing her that very minute – and then he'd round that minute up to an hour, plus expenses. She decided to wait. What was the rush? She hadn't even been to see him in the hospital yet; she wasn't even sure she would.

There wasn't much to discuss after that. Frances signed the papers, declined Ian's handshake and left his office. In the main room, Mary Bennett was at her desk, the typewriter clattering away. And to Frances's astonishment, Mary smiled and waved at her.

Mary Bennett was younger than Frances, but she had a reputation around the village as ... well, as a woman who did not smile. Ever. Frances tentatively waved back.

Mary started to get up, but Frances hurried to the exit before she could get out from behind the desk. *For God's sake*, she thought, *another one*. Frances would never have thought of Mary as a gossip – she wasn't sure who she'd gossip *to* – but clearly, Mary could make an exception. She was just like the rest of the village, their curiosity masked as concern. Just that morning Frances had been approached by a woman who pretended not to know anything about the shooting – asking her how she was, and had she been up to anything interesting? Frances could see in her eyes, in the just-too-sharp edge of her voice, that she was fishing. Flying under a false flag, as one of Jimmy's books might put it. As she opened the door of the law office, she heard Mary call her name, but she didn't turn around.

Stepping back onto the street, she paused to gather her breath. *Jesus.* Even Mary Bennett was out for a story. And Frances knew it would only get worse if Colm woke up – if there was a trial. Or maybe it'd be worse if there wasn't – if he died and left behind a mystery, to be picked apart by the village until it was just bones left in the sand.

She looked up at the sky.

Jimmy and Frances had been grieving for a long time, ever since Colm ran away. But now, faced with the blank slate of the day, a new grief crept slowly into the room, filling up the empty space bit by bit, until it was wrapped up all around them.

It was an uncomfortable sort of grief – nothing like what they had carried around the last thirty years. With that grief, time had dulled the edges and turned the dark glass opaque. But now it was back, in a newer, uglier form. Her grief felt like an imposter; Colm was home now, after all. She should be happy. But what sort of homecoming was this? It was the contradiction – Colm had returned, but he'd never been further away – it was a grief that was so heavy, so empty, she didn't know if it was pinning her to the ground or hurling her into the air.

Frances should've stayed in town, gone around to the shops, tried to get back to normal – but she couldn't. She got back into her car and started for home.

She forgot that she had driven Jimmy into town as well.

*

Back in the office, Ian picked up Colm Thornton's folder again. Underneath all the pages Frances had just signed, was a small slip of paper that she hadn't seen. Or, to be more specific, that he hadn't shown her.

A deed. A property in Colm Thornton's name – a substantial property, enough to make him a rich man three times over.

And what was interesting – other than the fact that a poor man owned such a property – was who had sold him the property in the first place.

Ian leaned back in his chair and folded his hands over his stomach. He put his feet up on the desk once more and examined his shoes – old and scuffed. Second-rate, like most of his clothes. This deed had the power to change that. If he was smart. If he was careful. Very careful.

Because it could make him very rich, but it was risky. And not just because of Frances and Jimmy. He'd also be destroying evidence. The only evidence, it seemed, in the mystery of Colm Thornton's motive.

According to the deed he held in his hand, three days before he shot Mr Hollis, Colm Thornton had purchased the property.

From Mr Hollis.

Chapter 11

Adam sat in his kitchen, with his head in his hands. His brother, Colm, was back. And apparently, he'd only come back to murder an old man and get shot himself for the trouble.

Adam's stomach lurched. What was that emotion – anger? grief? hunger? He didn't know, and if Colm never woke up, Adam supposed he would never know for sure.

For the millionth time in his life, ever since the day his brother disappeared, Adam wondered what had gone wrong.

*

The sun had gone down long ago. A full moon hung above the old pier. The waves, pushed by some unseen force, quietly shuffled to shore. The night was quiet and still.

Two boys were sitting at the edge of the pier, their feet dangling high above the dark water below. The tide was in; it was safe to jump. But it was still a large enough drop that it called for a certain degree of self-reflection beforehand.

'C'mon,' the smaller boy said. 'You go first.'

'I told you, Colm, I've done it already,' the other one said. 'We're not here for me. C'mere, you scared or something?'

The smaller boy turned red. 'I'm not scared of anything.'

'Oh, yeah? You ran away when we were breaking the windows in Christy's shack.'

'But I broke the first one,' Colm argued.

'So? Then you ran.'

'Remember the bike race down the lane? I did it three times before you did it once.'

'But then I beat you nine times out of ten.'

'We're talking about first here.'

'And I only let you win that one time because you're my brother and I felt bad.'

The two boys volleyed accomplishments back and forth, listing off an entire summer's worth of adventure, meeting the other's small glories with a small glory of their own. It was clear to both of them that they were stalling, but neither could call the other out, for fear they'd be called out too. Until, finally, there was nothing left to argue about.

The smaller boy looked down at the water nervously.

'Why don't we just wait until tomorrow? Why do we have to do it at night?'

His older brother groaned.

'Do you really want to stand up here in front of everyone tomorrow, pissing your pants, like?' Adam shook his head. 'No, you've got to do it now, when no one can see. After the first time, it's easy.' He looked over. 'You just need to get the first jump out of the way.'

Colm shrugged, still staring down at the water. 'Why do I have to do it at all?'

'You know why. Because Abby's going to be there tomorrow.'

Colm turned bright red and mumbled something. His older brother laughed and slapped his back.

'You'll be fine. Once she sees you jumping off the pier, she won't be able to resist you, like.' He looked at his younger brother, who was shrinking even smaller into himself. He softened. 'C'mere, like – are you going to ask her or what? You know, I think she would—'

The smaller boy suddenly, and in one big sweeping motion, got to his feet, took a quick step back, then launched himself off the pier.

He fell through the wide, open night and hit the water with a splash; he came up gasping, spluttering from the cold.

His brother gave a whoop from above. 'You did it! You legend – you did it! Jesus, fair play, like!' His voice was cracking from the excitement.

Then Adam took a step back and flung himself into the water too.

*

Sitting in his kitchen now, Adam remembered every detail of that night. After they'd jumped in, as the two brothers sat on the pier again, the white moonlight stretched out across the black water like a bridge to somewhere. They lit match after match and threw them as far as they could – watching them streak through the night, before landing in the dark water, or on the moonlight bridge.

And with a quiet puff, they were gone.

Chapter 12

To get to Skibbereen, Emma had to borrow her dad's car. Rocinante, as they called her, had been well taken care of her entire life. Unfortunately, the car had been built sometime around the Civil War; she'd put a rag-n-bone cart or two out of business in her youth. These days, she sounded like a Brontë sister with a four-pack habit. Her brakes squealed at the merest suggestion of a foot; her engine whined on even the flattest road. But Emma and Sam loved her anyway. At least, that's what they said; they couldn't afford anything else, so the alternative was walking.

'Just a little bit further, girl, c'mon.' Rocinante made a noise just south of Yoko Ono. 'You can do it, girl.'

Emma was on her way into town for her first interview. That morning, Maeve hadn't been able to tell her much about Mr Hollis.

'Remember, I'm a blow-in,' she kept saying. 'I'm only here ten years now.'

Emma had done her best not to roll her eyes – Maeve was originally from Dunmanway, which was a five-minute drive from Kilcraven.

But she had one lead: a woman named Catherine Whelan, who had worked for Hollis before, as a housekeeper.

'A housekeeper?' Emma asked, remembering the state of his house. 'He didn't seem like the type who got hung up on the dusting.'

'This was a few years back. But then one day,' Maeve snapped her fingers, 'she was let go.'

Emma waited for the inevitable bit of gossip, a comment on any number of Catherine's shortcomings that might've led to the dismissal, or any of Maeve's usual colour commentary. But Maeve, uncharacteristically, was reserved. Generous, even.

'She's had a hard life, Catherine,' she said quietly. 'Her father was ... well, she was in and out of ... well, it was a hard life, all in all.' Maeve frowned. Then she added, 'And she didn't deserve it.'

Emma understood. Well, she didn't understand – she had no idea what Maeve was talking about, and Maeve genuinely seemed not to want to tell her. But Emma could sympathise with something that couldn't be talked about.

Unfortunately, Emma had known Catherine personally. Of course she had: Kilcraven was a tiny village. She just hoped that Catherine didn't remember her – or at least, that she was less angry now. But that didn't seem likely.

Eventually, Rocinante made it to town with Emma and most of its parts. And then, wheezing heavily, it collapsed into Field's car park, in a gentle sort of huff.

Emma checked her pockets. She had a pen but no paper. She considered. She could use an old receipt, but that might not look very professional. Sherlock never wrote on receipts – he never wrote notes at all. Emma decided to go with Sherlock and leave the pen behind.

As she got out of the car, her foot went through a mouldy patch in the footwell.

And with that, Emma's investigation had officially begun.

Chapter 13

Field's of Skibbereen was a large supermarket but had the atmosphere of a lively indoor village. Everybody met at Field's. You could spend all day there – and most people did.

After a brief bout of (purely decorative) shopping, the customers flung their carts away with reckless abandon and spent the rest of the day wandering the aisles or haunting the café, tracking down everyone they hadn't seen since their last big shop. The whole place was a strange mixture of a farmer's market, a hundred family reunions and a business conference, all at once – the baked-bean section of Field's saw more heated debate than the floor of the Dáil.

The oddest thing, to an outsider anyway, was that when the customers flung their carts away, the carts were full of paid-for shopping. Ireland was in its third decade of a recession in 1988, and here were endless rows of carts full of hundreds of pounds worth of food, left unsupervised, for hours. They even left frozen food. When children went into the HB freezer chests for a Choc Ice or Freaky Foot, they usually found the ice cream buried beneath large bags of oven chips and frozen chicken Kievs. And in fifty years of business, nothing had ever been stolen.

As Emma made her way to the back corner of the shop, she caught the edges of a hundred conversations – they were all the usual blend of half-truths and quarter-fictions that made up the gossip around here. And they were all about the same thing.

'God, it's shocking, isn't it? Absolutely shocking ...'

'... might've been an exorcism ...'

'... holes dug in the garden ...'

'... some sort of ritual, or something ...'

'... I heard the poor fella was right in the middle of his bath ...'

'... well, I heard there wasn't even any running water ...'

The futility of her mission began to creep in on Emma. Two or three times on her way over, she'd nearly turned around. She would have, maybe, but Rocinante wouldn't let her. Besides, she remembered the look on Jimmy's face and the third man out there somewhere. She kept going.

Emma made her way out the back of Field's and into the loading area. She found Catherine Whelan having a smoke on one of the empty crates. It was immediately clear from the look on her face that Catherine remembered her.

'Are you here with an apology?' she demanded, before Emma even said hello. 'Maybe a new boyfriend you haven't gone and slept with? Only a few years too late, I suppose.'

'Well, I was hoping—'

'Jesus, another favour.' Catherine snorted. 'Did you not hear what I just said?'

'I didn't sleep with him,' Emma protested. 'It was an accident—'

'An accident, Emma?' Catherine laughed bitterly. 'How exactly did you manage that?'

She got up off the crate and resumed breaking down the cardboard boxes. Clearly, the interview was over.

Emma had known it wouldn't be easy, but she hadn't expected it to be this hard either. Sherlock certainly never had to defend himself like this, against accusations that he'd slept with one of his client's ex-boyfriends. And Emma, of course, had done nothing of the sort. It had been an accident.

Five or six years ago, Emma was in her third year of university. She needed a place to stay in the city. Catherine, a few years ahead of Emma at school, kindly put in a good word to her aunt, who had an empty flat near Blackrock. It was a nice flat, in that it was usually dry and it didn't have roommates. So Emma moved in.

And yes, she went on a few dates with the good-looking neighbour. Who, it turned out, already had a girlfriend. Whose name was Catherine Whelan. But he had told Emma he was single – as soon as she found out he wasn't, she ended it. And besides, they hadn't slept together. He'd only told Catherine they had because he was a prick.

Standing in Field's now, Emma tried to explain this to Catherine – but judging from her expression, it would be an uphill battle. So, she decided to pivot.

'C'mere to me,' she said conspiratorially, 'Settle a bet for me. You used to work for Mr Hollis, right?'

Judging from Catherine's expression, moving swiftly from sullen to furious, that approach was not going to work here.

'For feck's sake, Emma,' she said angrily, flinging aside her box cutter and elbowing past her to the door. 'The man's barely dead a day, and you're here making bets on it.'

Emma grabbed her arm as she went past.

'I'm sorry,' she said honestly. 'I'm just trying to help the family.'

Catherine frowned. 'Well, what do you want to talk to me for? I only worked there a few months.'

Emma shook her head. 'I know it's a long shot. They're desperate – they just want some answers, that's all.'

Catherine's eyebrows furrowed. She looked Emma up and down suspiciously. 'And what do you get out of it?'

Emma let go of Catherine's arm and slumped against the wall. 'Nothing. I just ...' She struggled for the words. 'I thought I could help. They helped me when I ...' She shrugged helplessly. 'I just thought I could help.'

Catherine was quiet for a moment. Then she nodded. 'I heard a bit about that,' she said, not unkindly. 'For what it's worth, I was sorry to hear it.'

As Catherine lit another cigarette, it was Emma's turn to look closer at the woman in front of her. Catherine was only five or six years older, but her face was full of deep lines. Her eyes were coal black – they had no reflection, even in the harsh lights of the loading area. A tremor ran through her hands; there was a whiff of old beer and a sweat-stained shirt. But Emma didn't feel pity or revulsion. She felt understanding – and the closer she looked, the more she understood. Here was a kindred spirit, with a similar First Act; they'd just made different choices in their intermissions.

Emma lit a cigarette of her own and inhaled deeply. *Focus on the task at hand.* On the life she could save.

'Look, I just want to give them some answers. And I need your help.'

Catherine considered it for a moment.

'You sure you didn't sleep with my boyfriend?'

Emma laughed.

'Promise.'

'Okay,' Catherine said. She reached over and took one of Emma's cigarettes, tucking it behind her ear. She raised an eyebrow. 'What do you want to know?'

'Do you know anything that Hollis was mixed up in? Or, no, actually – why were you fired? Not that I think you did anything wrong,' she added quickly. 'But a sudden change in lifestyle or circumstance could be significant.'

Catherine lit her cigarette. 'I don't know where people got that story from,' she said, shaking her head. 'I wasn't fired. I quit.'

Emma leaned in. 'Did he—'

But Catherine held up her hand.

'Before you ask – it wasn't anything he did either. The hours didn't suit me anymore, that's all. I'd started seeing someone, and sure, Hollis was nice enough, but it was getting clear he needed someone more full-time. A carer, like.' She shrugged. 'I was fine with cleaning, but I wasn't going to be a nurse.'

Emma frowned. 'You said ... he was nice?'

Catherine snorted in disgust. 'I know what the village said about him. But that's the village for you. It might be true, it might not be – they don't care, so long as they have something to talk about and someone to look down on. All I know is that he was kind to me. Kinder than the village was, anyway.'

Emma didn't know what to say to that.

*

As she made her way back to the front of Field's, moving through shelves of tinned sweetcorn and fridges filled with a hundred different types of sausages, Emma thought about everything Catherine had told her.

By her account, Mr Hollis had always been polite and accommodating, far from the angry old man Emma had heard about. And she hadn't been fired, which meant the only change in circumstance was that he was getting older – and less likely to be mixed up in something shady.

Was it possible that the village was wrong about Mr Hollis? Or was Catherine wrong about the village? Emma knew from personal experience that a village could shelter and protect one of its own – but that didn't mean it couldn't also have a limited definition of who, exactly, was 'its own'.

If Mr Hollis had actually been a decent man, that threw a wrench into her investigation and her theory about Colm. It was unlikely that Colm had been at the Big House by chance. Everything pointed to revenge for a long-standing dispute or an injury done to a young boy, long ago. The gap of thirty years, the distance Colm had travelled to take that revenge, pointed to something unforgivable. It wasn't pleasant, but it made the most sense. And it meant that, while Colm was technically guilty, karmically, he was the real victim.

But if Hollis was a decent man – then it was cold-blooded murder, plain and simple.

All of a sudden, Emma wasn't sure she wanted to find out the truth anymore.

And of course, that was the precise moment she bumped into Jimmy Thornton, hunched over his shopping cart, examining the underside of a turnip with a dedication that bordered on the obscene.

'I'd say you're better off planting that one,' she said. 'More return on your investment.'

Jimmy tried to smile, but his face was heavy. 'Any luck?' he asked hopefully.

Emma considered lying – after all, it'd only been a few hours. And she hadn't really found anything. But she couldn't lie – not to Jimmy.

'I was just talking to Catherine Whelan there,' she said. Jimmy leaned in to hear better. 'According to her, Mr Hollis was a pretty good man, at least from what she saw.'

Jimmy turned back to his turnip.

'What you've got to understand about Catherine Whelan – with what she's used to, she'd call a man a saint if he so much as said "thank you".' He put his hands up. 'I'm not saying she's wrong. She's just got a different definition of what a decent man is, that's all.'

'Mmm,' Emma said noncommittally. 'So, I haven't accomplished much of anything, is what you're saying.'

Jimmy laughed.

'I'm saying you need to go down to Nolan's.'

'What?'

'Nolan's, girl. If you want to know anything about anyone, you'll learn it there.' He winked. 'Now, if you'll excuse me, I'm going to get a cup of tea. My wife seems to have forgotten all about me.'

Chapter 14

Until six years ago, Jimmy had been a carpenter. Then one day, his boss called everyone into the office. There were rumours of a big project coming up, and they were expecting good news.

Instead, the boss told the seven men they were being made redundant. Immediately. There would be no redundancy payments or pension either. The company was bankrupt; the boss hoped there would be enough for everyone's last pay cheque, but he couldn't promise anything.

Of course, all hell broke loose. But there was nothing that could be done and besides, the guards were on hand. Jimmy, for his part, just sat down on an old toolbox – he wasn't angry, at least not yet. It was a numbness, a crushing numbness, like a finger caught in a vice grip. His hands shook as he stared at them. He had worked for the company for thirty years, and in the blink of an eye, it was gone. He didn't tell Frances for three days.

He was sixty-four years old, just a year shy of a state pension. Ever since, they'd been barely scraping by. All it would take would be a small shove. A small shove like, for example, having to pay for a solicitor to defend their son on murder charges.

But maybe, Frances thought desperately as she drove home from town, *maybe Colm wouldn't wake up*. And then just as desperately, she hated herself. She thought to herself, *How could you say that?*

But the reply came instantly, angrily – *how could you not say that?*

Frances was halfway home, on the back road just above the Doctor's Hill, by Mossie Black's field. She pulled the car over and got out. She stood in the hedgerow and looked out across the low valley; it slowly filled with mist from the sea.

For a long time, she didn't say anything. She tried to clear her mind – focus on what she could see, what she could hear.

She stood listening to the whimper and moan of the wind all around her – the shudder and the scrape of the corncrakes and the cows. She could slip away, slip under, and the world wouldn't notice. She wondered – a twig cracked in the hedgerow behind her, and she spun around.

A small fox cub froze halfway across the road, with one foot still in the air.

They stared at each other. The fox cub tilted his head at her, then lost interest and continued on down the road. He disappeared into a small shrub around the corner.

Frances slumped and curled up into the hedgerow. And she cried. She cried for the life they were promised, whatever it was and wherever it had gone. She cried for Jimmy, who had worked so hard for so long, only to have it ripped out from underneath him. Only to watch that same boss start a new company less than a year later – the same boss who slapped him on the back anytime he saw him down at Nolan's and asked about his family. The new company was really the same company, with newer, cheaper workers.

She cried for Adam, desperate to help the people who should be helping him.

And she cried for Colm.

And then she remembered that she had dropped Jimmy off at Field's to do the shop while she talked to Ian. She was his lift.

Cursing herself, she got into the car, heading back to town.

*

It could have gone on like this forever. Frances and Jimmy could have kept on hurtling through the black, just barely holding on. Or, they might have let go, as Frances almost did, until the fox cub broke through to her.

But that afternoon, something unexpected happened.

Cordelia hadn't just uncovered a crime scene. She uncovered something else – a wheel, buried underneath Kilcraven, that was just now starting to turn. That was just now starting to roll down the hill, crashing its way towards Frances and Jimmy and Emma and Kilcraven.

Mary Bennett, who had been acting so strange all day, knocked on Ian Flesk's door. She had her black bag clutched tight to her side, and her jaw was set.

The wild centre was breaking through. And it had a gun.

Chapter 15

All across West Cork, the old clocks chime, deep in the ground and far beneath the sea.

Every year, in late summer, the nettles and gorse shrubs fill up with small white eggs and then little black caterpillars. The caterpillars eat the green leaves and yellow flowers and grow longer and fatter. By late autumn, the caterpillars have blossomed and emerged with wings and the sky over Kilcraven fills with butterflies.

And every year, at the same time, the trees erupt into colour. The silver birch and the blackthorn, the alder and the ash; the leaves burn red and yellow and orange and then fall away.

In the harbour, the lobsters moult. Their shells strew the ocean floor like strange leaves and the lobsters are left in their soft flesh in the cold water. They hide among the rocks and the rubble of old shipwrecks; they huddle in fear as dark shadows circle above them, like birds of prey, waiting to strike. They wait for their shells to harden again.

It was 1988: of course, the village wasn't all farmers and fishermen anymore. But it was still *mostly* farmers and fishermen – and those who weren't were only a generation removed.

They felt the old clocks chime in Kilcraven and made their peace with it: this was how the world worked. It was all just a great wind, a big wave – and you couldn't hold back either one.

But still, they made their plans. They met in Nolan's, they met in the shop, they met in their fields and on their boats, and they made their plans – big nets to catch the great wind.

And sometimes, those plans were made in dark rooms, with dark words and even darker hearts.

Somewhere in Kilcraven, two people sat across a table from each other. One of them, who had lived in the village his whole life, was scared. Not in a trembling, wide-eyed sort of way – and certainly not of the man who sat across the table – but scared in a feral sort of way, a wild-animal-backed-into-a-corner kind of way. It was the sort of fear that made a man dangerous.

The man across the table, on the other hand, was in the room for a simple reason: he needed money. Well, he didn't need it. He *wanted* it, more of it – always more.

And each man was the answer to the other's problem.

The scared man looked at the stranger's rumpled, dirty clothes. 'You look like hell. Rough night?'

The stranger returned his gaze placidly. 'Do you really want to know?'

The scared man considered what he knew about the stranger and his line of work, and decided that he did not.

'Did he explain the situation to you?'

The stranger nodded. 'There's someone asking questions, and you want them to stop.' He waited for the scared man to nod. 'Do you have a picture?'

The scared man slid a piece of paper across the table. The stranger read it and frowned.

'Means nothing to me.' He looked at the scared man. 'A picture would work better than a name.' He tossed the paper on the table. 'A name, a name I don't know, means asking questions. Knocking on doors. Pretty visible. People see that, small village like this – and they start asking questions about me.'

The scared man waved him off.

'Better you than me. After it's done, you can disappear into the background. I can't.' He tapped the paper. 'Small village, like you said.'

The stranger raised his eyebrow, a bemused expression on his face. 'After what's done, exactly?' He leaned in. 'You haven't told me exactly what it is you want done.'

This was the part the stranger enjoyed – watching his client squirm, trying to dance around the word. Like maybe if they didn't actually say the word, didn't give the order out loud, then they wouldn't be responsible for what happened next. As if they hadn't called him precisely because they knew exactly what he did and they wanted it done.

The stranger hated his clients. He hated that they thought guilt was something you could scrub out of a sheet, like virtue was something you could put down and pick back up again, whenever you wanted. But he was a businessman, first and foremost. He wanted their money, so he had to play the game. So, he took pleasure where he could – watching them squirm in their seats, like an insect pinned to a card. But the scared man surprised him.

When he answered, there was no squirming, there was no trace of guilt – his words were hard and clear.

'When you find her – kill her.'

*

And somewhere in Kilcraven, a tree erupted into coloured wings – tortoiseshells and common blues and moth eyes – even a monarch or two.

Chapter 16

It was Tuesday night down at Nolan's pub. Emma stood in the doorway and looked around the room. In the corner, a stove cracked and popped behind a grate; a ship's clock made quiet sounds like little licks; a conversation balanced in the air among the glass.

If the pub was a harbour, the tide had run out; the usual sea drift was left scattered around the bar. Great boulders turned to rocks, to pebbles, to sand. In other words – it was the regular crowd.

Jimmy had told Emma she'd find answers here. Emma, looking around at the customers, red-faced and top-heavy, was ... unconvinced. But Sherlock had his Irregulars; these would be hers. The Incontinents, maybe.

At the front of the bar were Paddy and Noel, the two brothers who had lived in the same house their whole lives and had probably never gone farther than the end of the road. They could explain, in inexorable detail, the poetry of a sheep's placenta – when it's a bubble, and when it's a burst – but they'd blush and stammer if a woman so much as looked towards the toilets.

Oisín and Nora sat in the far corner. An elderly couple who seemed to live on sherry, orange slices and resentment. They would be helpful in that, together, they provided a nuanced take – if Nora opposed something, then Oisín would agree with it, and vice versa. They each always argued the opposite, whether they believed in it or not.

Nobody knew much about Tito, which in a small village meant that nobody wanted to. He was peculiar, and he kept to himself. He had a Liverpool accent. He was nearly sixty, and he'd lived in Kilcraven for at least thirty years. He didn't follow soccer. And that was it – the grand sum of what the village knew about him. Even the regulars couldn't say where he worked, or what he did with his time when he left his bar stool.

Emma looked around for Danny, but he wasn't there yet. He would be, though. Danny Angelus, they called him – he was as regular as clockwork. He lived next to the pub, on the far side from the shop. So, every night, he told his wife he was going down to the shop. On the way back, he'd slink into the pub, where he'd down two pints as quickly as he could, his bags of shopping around his feet. It was unclear whether his wife actually fell for this charade, but maybe she just appreciated the effort. Or the quiet.

It was Danny that Emma most wanted to talk to – he was the youngest of the crowd, about the same age as Adam and Colm, so might be able to tell her what Colm was like before he left, when he was a kid. She couldn't ask Adam – from what Jimmy had told her, the subject of Colm was off limits as far as Adam was concerned. Emma checked her watch. Danny should be here soon. She had enough time for a pint anyway.

All the regulars were talking about the murder, of course. Words of sympathy and confusion mixed with the woodsmoke in the air. And as she made her way to the bar, she thought that maybe Jimmy was right about coming to Nolan's. There was an advantage to being underestimated – it became a sort of disguise.

Nobody ever looked at this group twice, or even once for that matter, and no one ever held their tongue around them. If anything, they probably spoke more freely to this lot than they ever did to anyone else in their life. *What did it matter*, they thought. *Who would this lot tell? Who'd believe them if they did?*

Between them, what this ragtag bunch of barflies knew could probably topple governments. Or at the very least, end half the marriages in the county.

Maybe they'd sense that she was one of them: a collection of bad luck and missed chances – a fellow write-off. But if not, how could she get them to talk? Sherlock used to pay his Irregulars with coin – what they wanted most. She'd start there.

'Murphy's, please,' she said, when Fintan came over. 'And a round for everyone else too.'

The regulars all straightened up; even Fintan looked dumbfounded. People didn't buy rounds for the house in Nolan's. Even during the run-up to elections, when TDs hastily arranged visits, pretending they hadn't completely forgotten about West Cork for the last four years, the most they'd offer were a few packets of crisps and a handshake. Fintan raised his eyebrow at her.

'You after winning the Lotto or something?'

Emma shook her head. She turned to the rest of the bar. 'Who here knows something about what happened with Colm Thornton?'

A cloud of unease settled over the bar. It was one thing to talk about the gossip, it was another thing to come right out and ask for it. The two brothers looked at each other. Nora fiddled with her sherry glass. Emma couldn't make out Tito's expression; he was slightly removed from the group. But he seemed to be staring right at her. Oisín, though, seemed to take his wife's silence as a point of view. Naturally, he took the opposite. 'Sure, we know the same as anyone.' He took a sip of his drink. 'But from what I hear, you know more about that business than we do.'

The pub was completely quiet now. Even Fintan had stopped pouring. Every eye in the room was trained on Emma.

She nodded. 'I found the bodies.'

There was a restrained sort of gasp in the room. The whole pub fell silent, ready to hang on her every word. And suddenly, Emma knew what her Irregulars wanted more than coin, more than drink, more than anything in the world, really.

This group were lonely and nosy – in equal measure. Which meant they'd talk, but they would ramble – the nosy ones veering off into gossip at every opportunity, whether it was relevant or not; the lonely ones talking just to talk, long past the point they ran out of facts. Trying to get a fact out of them would be like trying to take a sip from a waterfall.

But if Emma could give them a carrot at the end of the stick, to keep them on course, she might get something useful. And, as it turned out, she had a prize any one of them would give their left butt cheek for – the chance to hear the story of what really happened at the Big House. Straight from the horse's mouth. They wouldn't have to buy their own pints for two weeks, at least.

'So, what do you say?' she asked. 'If you help me out, I'll tell you what really happened.'

There was a general grumble of approval, so Emma pulled up a stool. She checked her watch again. Danny, strangely enough, was running late. She'd have to start with the victim.

'Mr Hollis. What can you tell me about Mr Hollis?' The Irregulars all stared at their feet uncertainly. Emma realised she'd have to be more specific. 'What was Hollis like?'

Paddy piped up. 'He was a big man for the church, wasn't he?'

His brother, Noel, agreed. 'He must've been a big man alright; he had the bishop round his place once or twice a month.' He chuckled. 'It would've driven Ma spare if she'd been alive to see it – all the trouble she had, just to get the priest in for the Stations. And himself, having supper with a bishop.'

Emma nodded – as far as she knew, Paddy and Noel had heard it from Maeve, same as her.

But Nora was shaking her head.

'Sure, that's not true.' She straightened up and looked around at the group knowingly. 'I was talking to Father Westwood this morning, after confession.' Oisín muttered something under his breath, but Nora shushed him. 'I asked the priest, was it true what they said about Mr Hollis, that he'd had the bishop around the place all the time? And do you know what he said?' She paused dramatically, taking a long sip of her sherry.

'Oh, for God's sake, woman,' Oisín snapped, 'we're not playing Twenty Questions here.' He clearly wasn't happy his wife had beaten him to a good story.

Emma ignored him. 'Go on, Nora,' she said. 'What'd the Father say?'

Nora put down her now-empty glass. 'He said it was all hogwash. According to himself, nobody north of Skibbereen has heard of Hollis – certainly not the bishop.'

Emma frowned. 'So, he never visited Hollis?'

Nora shook her head. 'He might've stopped in once or twice, but that would be on a fundraising appeal, not a social call.' She rattled the melting ice in her glass, then fished the orange slice out with her finger. 'All that talk about secret meetings – it's just the usual nonsense you hear in a small village about the man in the Big House, making them out to be more important than they are.'

As Nora bit triumphantly into her orange slice, watered-down sherry and pips running down her chin, Emma considered this new information. She still thought that revenge made the most sense. But what if ...

Maybe it wasn't just the bishop who paid house calls to fundraise. Maybe Colm was in the wrong place at the wrong time. Stranger things have happened, surely? But before Emma could go any further down this train of thought, Oisín started laughing.

Well, it wasn't really laughter – he was glaring at Nora. But it was clear that he was now going to take the opposite view.

'Yes, and why would Father Westwood lie?'

Paddy and Noel frowned. Nora crossed herself. Even Fintan suddenly busied himself wiping glasses. Oisín saw that he had their full attention and started to enjoy it, preening in the limelight, just as his wife had done. It took all of Emma's strength not to snap at him.

'Well, Oisín, why would he?' she asked. 'Why would Father Westwood lie?'

Oisín leaned back in his chair, lacing his fingers together on his belly. 'Well, as Nora here failed to tell you – or maybe she just forgot – the bishop was here, in Kilcraven. A while back. But he wasn't exactly down here on a social call.' He looked around the group. 'As some of you probably remember, Mr Hollis wasn't exactly a pillar of society.'

Emma's pulse quickened. But before she could say anything, Noel groaned.

'Ah, God – little James O'Donovan.'

Oisín nodded grimly, any trace of a smile gone now.

'One afternoon, nearly ten years ago,' he explained to Emma, 'Hollis went out for a drive. Steaming drunk, apparently. Little James there, he ran out on the road, and Hollis didn't see him. Just barrelled on through.' Oisín's face darkened. 'That bastard didn't even stop.' Nora protested half-heartedly, saying not to speak ill of the dead, but Oisín slammed his hand on the table. 'I'll speak ill of him, damn it! The bastard just kept driving up the hill. When the guards came, he was pouring himself another drink.'

'Poor James was in a bad way,' Noel said quietly. 'It was a miracle he survived, but he never walked again.'

A heavy silence settled into the corners of the pub. The old ship's clock chimed out the dogwatch, and a radio behind the bar whispered warm static. Dust fell, dust collected.

Finally, Emma spoke. 'And what happened to him? To Hollis, I mean.'

Oisín snorted. 'Nothing. Absolutely sweet fuck all.' He drained his glass. 'The bishop turned up that night. Two days later, Hollis was back on the road.'

Emma shook her head in disbelief. 'That's impossible; not even a bishop could swing that, surely?'

There was grim laughter around the pub. Even Nora smiled.

'Jesus, Emma,' Oisín said, 'did you come down in the last shower?'

Emma flushed, but one of the brothers leaned forward and patted her knee kindly.

'What he means to say is,' Noel said, 'the family was paid off. Handsomely, I imagine. They would've known there wasn't any point fighting. Not against the Church. But also, they were devout. It was the best they could do, to get James what he needed to recover.'

Emma looked around.

'So, Hollis was a bastard, you'd say?'

Everyone nodded – even Nora, although she crossed herself at the same time.

And just like that, Emma thought, Colm might be innocent again.

Well, morally, anyway.

There was a small break in the interview, as it were, and everyone refreshed their drinks and shook off the heaviness that had crept into their bones. Emma noticed Tito sitting by himself, off to the side of the bar, holding a book in front of him. His alert expression made it obvious that he had been listening intently, rather than reading. His ears were practically quivering. She made her way over.

'Hey, Tito. Why the long face?'

He looked up at her over his book. He shrugged. 'No long face. Just reading my book, minding my own business.'

His voice was soft and full of gravel, or rust – like it didn't get much use. But the edges of his Liverpool accent were still sharp, and his point was clear. Emma ignored it.

'Is it any good?' She gestured at the book. A Maeve Binchy, interestingly.

He turned it over and studied the cover, like he'd never seen it before. Then he looked back at her. 'You want to know if I know anything about Mr Hollis,' he said simply. He gestured at the rest of the group around the bar. 'Why I'm not joining in with the rest of them.'

The Irregulars hadn't noticed her absence – if anything, they'd gained their own momentum. They were feverishly discussing their own private theories, all notion of Emma's prize forgotten. Oisín and Noel argued their case loudly: it was the Church – they'd helped to get rid of the O'Donovans, but now Mr Hollis hadn't held up his side of the deal. Fell behind in payments, maybe. Paddy could swear on a Bible that there were holes all over the back garden, like someone was looking for something, and Nora suddenly remembered two people who went missing a few years ago, and ... well, it was a variation on the blackmail plot, but this time it was the IRA responsible.

'No, that's not much of a mystery.' She gestured at the seat across from Tito, and he shrugged again. She sat down. 'Is it true, about the boy?'

Tito nodded. 'The basics, anyway. Hollis did knock down a boy, and he was drunk. And apparently, the bishop did intervene in some way – I don't think it was as sinister as all that, though. From what I heard, Hollis paid the family himself.'

'And what do you think of revenge as a motive? For the killing?'

Tito raised his eyebrow over his pint.

'Ten years later?' He shook his head. 'The O'Donovans are long gone – Australia, apparently.' He took a sip. 'Besides, the parents are elderly, the boy is in a wheelchair – they don't sound much like your third man, do they?'

Emma started. She hadn't told anyone in the village about the third man. 'How did you – did you talk to the guards?'

Tito didn't answer for a moment. 'I hear things,' he said simply. 'Now, speaking of the guards, why are you down here, asking questions? Why is a librarian sticking her nose where it doesn't belong?'

And suddenly, Emma understood why the group kept Tito at a distance. It was impossible to judge his inflection – to tell what message, exactly, he was trying to convey. If he was being friendly – or threatening. But it was clear that he was definitely sending a message.

Before she could answer, however, the front door opened behind her. Emma looked at her watch. This must be Danny; she could finally get some information about Colm. But when she turned and looked at the door, she didn't see Danny standing there. She saw Charley Thornton, looking as surprised to see her as she was to see him.

*

'I swear to God, every time I turn around these days, there's a Thornton.' Emma laughed later, as Charley took two pints from Fintan and handed her one. 'I'm used to a few here and there, but this is getting too much now.'

Charley grinned.

'Well, there are about twenty people in this village. It'd be strange if you *didn't* see me.'

Emma flushed and gulped down some stout. 'Fair enough.'

Charley took a sip, then leaned against the bar. He looked at her, like he was just a few jigsaw pieces short of a full puzzle.

'But what about you? In a pub, on a Tuesday night with the old fellas – it's not exactly the Emma Daly I remember.' There was an awkward pause, as they both remembered their argument from earlier. 'I just meant that you were never a big one for the pub.'

Emma conceded the point and explained what Jimmy had asked her to do. Charley nodded grimly.

'It's all he talks about: how Colm must've been framed or been caught up in something that had nothing to do with him. The rest of them are just quiet, like they're pretending it never happened. Like he never came back at all.' He lit a cigarette and held it out to Emma. 'So, what've you found so far?'

Emma looked at him curiously, taking the cigarette and quickly inhaling. 'You're not curious why Jimmy asked me?' The smoke curled up around her jaw and down through her nose. 'Why he'd ask a librarian to investigate something even the guards don't want to touch?'

Charley looked at her.

'We both know you're much more than a librarian,' he said quietly. 'You're the first person I'd ask.'

Their eyes met, and it was like the whole room quieted down, and they could feel each other's slightest movement. Then a few patrons stumbled between them, and the spell was broken.

'What do you think?' Charley asked, finding a seat. 'Do you think he's innocent?'

Emma berated herself inwardly. She was here for a reason. Someone was dead. And, of course, the girlfriend. Whom he hadn't mentioned yet, but only because he clearly didn't feel the need to. Maybe this chemistry was only one-sided.

'I don't know, Charley,' she said honestly. 'But to tell you the truth, I think the simplest answer is probably the right one.'

'And what's that?'

'That Mr Hollis did something bad to Colm thirty years ago. Colm came back for revenge. He killed Mr Hollis, but not before Hollis got in a shot himself. And the other man, most likely Hollis's guest, ran off.'

Charley was nodding, his shoulders slumped. Emma imagined it was one thing to believe something, quite another to be confronted with it as truth.

'So, when you say, he did something bad to Colm,' Charley said slowly, 'you mean ...'

Emma nodded.

'He was a powerful man back then. Able to get away with murder – and didn't seem too affected when he did. I think—'

She had to cut off; someone roughly edged in between her and Charley, nearly spilling their drinks. It was Tito, looking supremely unconcerned as he raised a finger to Fintan for another pint. The way he had positioned his body, he blocked Charley out, but it could've been accidental.

'You're wrong,' Tito said, in his simple way.

'Excuse me?' Emma asked, unaware she'd been speaking loud enough for anyone else to overhear. In fact, she was quite sure that she hadn't been. If he had overheard, it was deliberate.

'You're wrong,' he repeated, as Fintan set a pint down in front of him. Tito took his time counting out the change. Behind him, Charley silently mouthed to Emma: *what the hell?* Tito set down the coins, then, without looking at her, said, 'That accident with James O'Donovan. Hollis had only been in Kilcraven for five or six years when it happened.'

Emma frowned. 'And?'

'And – the accident was eight years ago. Eight years, next week, actually.' He took a sip of his pint, then started back towards his table. 'Surely, a smart girl like you – you can do the maths for yourself.'

Emma stared after him. Charley frowned at her. 'What the hell was that about?' he asked.

Emma shook her head, still muddled. 'I was wrong.'

Colm Thornton ran away from Kilcraven thirty years ago. Hollis only moved to the village later. Nearly fifteen years *after* Colm had left for good. They'd never met.

Once again, Emma was in the dark. If Colm had killed Hollis, he had no discernible motive. It was cold-blooded murder, pure and simple. And with no motive in sight, she wasn't any closer to proving him ... anything at all. Innocent or guilty.

And the third man was still out there. It might not be over yet. Suddenly, for the first time, Emma felt scared.

Chapter 17

'Could yeh maybe talk to somebody else about your damn birds?'

Charley was still at Nolan's pub. Emma and the group of regulars had left hours ago. Outside was damp. Outside was cold. The pub was warm as he overshot 'a couple of pints' by a couple of pints, patiently drinking his eyes into his coat pocket. He'd been pouring out his heart (or at least his mouth) to the elderly gentleman named Connie next to him.

He was a fuck-up, he explained. He had no direction whatsoever. Not like his dad. Adam knew what he wanted to do since he was a kid, and he was fecking brilliant at it. For a long time, Charley had wanted to be a doctor too. He'd tagged along with his dad on his rounds; for his tenth birthday, his dad gave him his own lab coat. But somewhere around sixteen, he realised something – he didn't actually want to be a doctor, he wanted to be his dad. And he was nothing like as good as his dad.

His dad was disappointed in him, Charley continued. And he doesn't even know the half of it. If he knew ... Jesus. He'd hate Charley more than ... well, more than Charley hated himself at that moment.

Charley talked through the better part of four pints. But Connie clearly didn't understand a word.

'C'mere to me. Would you leave me alone about the birds?' Connie said again. 'I don't give a damn about no birds.'

Charley blinked at him. 'Birds? What are you on about, birds? I'm talking about ... well, I'm talking about myself and my problems here.'

'Are you trying to be funny, like?' Connie spoke with a hard shove. 'You've been talking my fecking ear off about birds the last two hours.'

Charley assured him he hadn't been. He tried to jog his memory, but it was a bit unsteady on its feet – more in the hedges than the footpath. 'If you follow me.'

'No, I don't follow you,' Connie said.

Charley nearly dropped his glass. He hadn't said anything out loud. The words were clearly tipping out of his mouth; he was losing the quotation marks somewhere. He tried to make sense of it. After what felt like three uncomfortable minutes of his slack-jawed stare, Connie raised his eyebrows to Fintan behind the bar. 'Absolutely scuttered, he is.'

Damn it. He must be, so. Connie was an old farmer, from out in the country where they rarely got visitors; he was a man who kept his livestock nervous. You'd see him at the bank, standing in the marble foyer – he'd be absolutely drenched in cow shit and slurry. Like he'd been dipped in up to his armpits. The bank staff running around frantically, opening windows and gasping; and Connie standing happily in the middle, patiently complaining about the queue. And Connie was a lot of things, but he was rarely wrong. If he said Charley was colouring outside the lines, then Charley was inclined to believe him.

And just as he grasped this fact, his father walked in. 'Hello, son.'

'Hello, Father.'

They were silent for a few moments, then Charley started giggling. 'Forgive me, father, for I have sinned ...'

Then he burst out laughing and fell off the stool.

*

As they walked home, Charley clung onto Adam's arm. 'Da?'

'Yes, Charley?'

'Have you ever heard of a bird – it's a white-throated ... white-feathered ... sparrow or something.'

Adam exhaled. When he walked into the pub that night, he'd been furious. His son, getting pissed, at a time like this? With his grandparents nearly catatonic with grief, with his father out of his mind with worry ...

But that was when he saw Charley, in the middle of all his confusion, and realised that he was grieving too – the wrong way, to be sure, but he was still young. Besides, Adam would have more luck talking sense into a concussed goose, for all the good it'd do, with Charley in such a state. Adam could afford to be patient.

'Have you heard of them?' Charley asked again. 'The white, whiteish bird?'

'I don't believe I have, son,' Adam said gently. Charley looked up at the stars.

'See, it keeps doing this thing, Da. Apparently, it keeps forgetting how to fly. Just every so often, out of nowhere. Just forgets how to fly. Are you with me?'

'I'm with you.'

'But the damn bird lives on a beach. And it's a strange beach. Every so often, apparently – am I saying "apparently" too much, Da?'

'Not at all, son,' Adam said gently. 'Keep going. We're almost there.'

'Right, so. *Apparently*, the sea level keeps rising. So, all the birds, these white-feathered ones, they all die out. They go extinct. End of story. Right? Right, Da?'

'Well, if you're saying—'

'No, no, no – just wait. Because the weirdest thing happened then. The birds, the white-throated seagulls or whatever, they came back. Back from extinction.' He tried to snap his fingers. 'Just popped up out of nowhere. And suddenly, they could fly again.'

'Huh. Well, that's an odd one, I suppose. Here we are.' They were at their house, standing at the door.

'Wait. Wait, Da. Let me finish.'

'Okay, son.'

'Right, so. Because the ending is the best part.' Charley laughed, his voice slightly wild. He looked up at the stars again. 'The damn things went extinct all over again.'

Adam frowned. 'What?'

Charley grinned. 'Yep. For the same reason, too. The damn things forgot how to fly again.' He was still grinning. But there were tears in his eyes.

Adam looked at his son, his only son, crying on the doorstep. His eyes, blue and green, unchanged after all these years. Suddenly, Adam saw his son as he was when he was just a little boy. When all he ever wanted, all he ever needed, was something simple. And then he thought of all the times he hadn't given him that simple something, in pursuit of some long-forgotten lesson. Maybe, just maybe, there were second chances after all.

He pulled Charley into a hug and whispered urgently in his ear. 'You've got to remember, son.' He shook him slightly, pleading. 'You've got to remember how to fly. Or go somewhere where the water can't reach you.' He squeezed him as tight as he could. 'Just because you can't fly, doesn't mean you have to drown.'

High above, the stars quietly felt their way home through the dark.

Chapter 18

Across town, in the hospital, Colm Thornton hung somewhere between consciousness and dream. He couldn't move, he wasn't awake, but he could hear the shuffle and murmur of doctors' voices all around him.

He knew he was in trouble.

*

In 1981 there were eighty-three priests ordained in Ireland. They all had their reasons.

For thirty-three of them, it was a lack of prospects. For another twelve, a lack of imagination. For eighteen of them, it was something to do with faith. And for the rest, it was something to do with power.

That year, there were also five priests who left the cloth. They had all died. But now, there was going to be one more, a sixth – a priest who left without dying. Colm.

In 1981 Colm had been a priest for twenty years in a little town on the outskirts of Belfast. And now, he was leaving.

A man named Henry Farrell was also leaving, leaving Ireland behind, and Colm was coming too. They'd start a new life in London. They were leaving together.

Tonight.

Henry sat quietly, smoking cigarettes one by one, watching the sky grow dark above the sea. He was sitting in their spot – a hidden cove they called Gobeen. After twenty minutes the adrenaline was beginning to wear off, making way for the anxious knot in his stomach. The waves shuffled along the shore; sandpipers stepped quietly along the stony beach. A grey heron stood still, not moving, looking deep into the water.

And then, a familiar voice rang out. 'You going to swim, or what?'

Henry turned around, grinning. 'Fancy seeing you here.'

'I nearly didn't make it,' Colm said, panting slightly as he clambered over the slippery rocks. 'I got stuck with two of the officiants. Jesus, they'd talk your ear off just to see something happen.'

Henry didn't say anything, but his stomach had dropped. Colm didn't have a bag.

When Henry didn't move to get up or even say hello, Colm sat down next to him, side by side on their usual seat, a large oak tree that had fallen in a storm a few years ago. They both stared out at the water. There was a heavy current in this part of the harbour; where it met the mouth of the cove, there was a riptide. In living history, eight people had drowned in the rip. None of them was ever found again.

'So – you did it?'

Henry nodded. Colm whistled quietly. 'How'd he take it?'

'My da?' Henry laughed darkly. 'He pretended I hadn't said anything. Went back to his paper.'

'Your mam?'

Henry sighed. 'She told me if I was to disgrace the family, it might as well be far away.'

Colm reached over to take his hand. Henry flinched. 'Don't,' he said.

'Henry—'

'You didn't do it, did you?' It came out in a sort of rush, all at once, but clipped – like startled cattle running through a gate Henry forgot to close. Colm let his hand drop.

He put his head in his hands. 'I can't, Henry. I'm sorry. I just can't.'

Henry blinked hard. He looked all around him, for something to latch on to. 'I know.' His jaw was clenched, and he tried to keep his voice from pleading. 'I know. But we'd be safe in London. Nobody knows us there. And it's different—'

Colm shook his head. 'It's not that. It's not because of any of that—'

'Is it me?'

Colm looked up. He reached over and pulled Henry's face towards him. 'No,' he said firmly. 'It's not because of you.'

Henry was still blinking hard. But now he made himself meet Colm's eye. 'Then why won't you? What are you so afraid of?'

Colm held his gaze a minute longer, then pulled away. He put his head down into his hands again.

'For all our talk,' Henry said quietly, trying to keep his voice under control. 'I always knew this would happen. I only bought one ticket.' He started to cry then. 'I didn't buy you a ticket because I knew you weren't going to come. I could tell that it was all a fantasy, a dream, for you. Not real life.' He looked over at Colm. 'But then I came here anyway.'

'Henry, if I could do what I wanted, what I knew was right – then I'd be on that ferry with you. But I can't. I can't.'

'Why?' Henry pleaded. 'If you just told me, I could help—'

'I'm sorry,' Colm cried. 'I just can't.'

Tears were still streaming quietly down Henry's face. But, after a minute, he took a deep breath, and he reached over and rubbed Colm's back. 'It's okay.'

Colm let out a muffled sob. 'I'm so sorry.'

'You don't have to be sorry, Colm.'

'That doesn't mean I'm not.'

'I know.'

Henry and Colm sat there, talking and crying and eventually, laughing, late into the evening, the daylight quickly draining out of their corner of the sky. They didn't care. This was the last time they would look out into the same corner of the sky; they stayed even as their breath became visible.

They held each other, collapsing into one another, there among the bending and broken pines. Eight people had sat there before, then gone mad and disappeared into the mouth of the cove, out where the current was a riptide. They all drowned. There were no gravestones, but Henry and Colm sat in a graveyard. A graveyard that could easily have held two more.

They sat, side by side, as friends. As lovers. As two bodies in a constellation.

The two drowning men held each other, and held each other up out of the water, somewhere above the waves. Where the light is, and was, and always will be.

*

As Colm slept in his hospital bed, even though he couldn't speak, he could feel. He could feel the same question coming back to him over and over: *why?*

Why didn't I listen to you, Henry? he cried out in silent pain. *None of this would've happened then. I'd be safe.*

I'd be home.

Chapter 19

The next morning, Emma did something she had never done before – she asked Maeve if she could take off early.

Maeve frowned.

'You're the boss,' she said. 'If anything, I should be asking you. But why – what's wrong?'

When Emma explained what happened at Nolan's the night before, Maeve shook her head sadly.

'This is not what I meant by a life outside of the library, Emma. I meant boys, cinema, *Charley*. Not more work.'

'This is different,' Emma replied. She stamped a book emphatically. 'I'm helping a friend.'

'Are you?' Maeve raised her eyebrow. 'Or are you trying to prove the guards wrong?'

Emma flushed and continued stamping. 'I want to help.'

Maeve nodded. 'Sure, I know you do – you're a good person.' She reached out and took the stamp out of Emma's hand. 'But I also know it goes deeper than that. I think you'd like to be the one outside the tent, pissing in, rather than inside the tent, getting pissed on.'

Emma stared at her. Then she burst out laughing.

'Feck's sake, Maeve,' she said. 'Where the hell did that come from? What does that even mean?'

Maeve shrugged. 'Something my da used to say. I'm not even sure he fully understood what it meant either.' She turned back to the books she was sorting. 'But, yes, I know you want to help the Thorntons. And that's a noble goal. Just make sure you don't run yourself into the ground trying to right all the wrongs in the world.' She lit a cigarette and looked back at Emma, frowning. 'Besides – do you actually think he's innocent?'

Emma considered the question. Before last night, she had one theory: there was clearly a powerful reason for Colm to run away as a kid – and it made sense that it was the same reason he came back. Revenge was the most likely explanation.

But now, that theory was shot. Colm was long gone before Mr Hollis ever set foot in Kilcraven. And to make matters worse, apparently Kilcraven – the quiet, peaceful village she'd lived in her whole life – had a closet bursting with skeletons. And she'd gone and opened the door. Blackmail plots, disappearing strangers, conspiracies around the church and the IRA; she was dreading what she'd find out next. A swinger's club? A sex cult? Rod Serling? Maybe Sherlock was right when he said the country was more dangerous than the city. Or they just had more imagination.

Either way, Colm and Hollis hadn't met before. That much was true. But did that mean she thought Colm was innocent?

If he was innocent, then he was unlucky – unlucky on a cosmic scale. Unlucky to a ... well, an improbable degree. Was it possible that Colm had returned home thirty years later only to immediately stumble into a robbery or argument gone wrong? And if that was the case, then what the hell was Colm doing at Mr Hollis's house in the first place?

According to this morning's papers, Colm's church up North was as mystified as anyone else about why Colm was in Kilcraven. And the guards up there couldn't find any link to organised crime. Mr Hollis still had a few old business associates in London, but he never did business in the North. They'd been trying to track down an old business manager of his but had been unable to find him. But that was just protocol – they didn't suspect Hollis of anything criminal.

Which meant that Mr Hollis and Colm Thornton had met for the first time that night – the same night they were both shot. It was unlikely, improbable even, but as Sherlock always said: follow the facts. Once you've eliminated all the other possibilities, whatever is left, however improbable, must be true.

So, they hadn't met before. But then what the hell was Colm doing there?

Emma realised that she'd started with that question, and that she'd just gone in a big circle. She sighed heavily and sat down.

'I don't think I can do this, Maeve.'

Maeve looked at her. Then, she quietly went over to the front door and flipped the sign over to Closed. The library was quiet. There were only one or two pensioners in the back corner. As Emma sat and stared into space, Maeve busied herself getting the cups and the kettle going.

'I just ...' Emma began. 'I just wanted to help. And I know – I know I was never going to solve it or anything. But at least I'd be doing something. At least I'd be helping. I know what it feels like to just be stuck in it, every day. How it fills you up if you stop moving, how every day feels like you're being buried alive. And every so often ...' She trailed off.

Maeve was watching her closely.

'Then don't give up,' she said simply. Emma looked up at her, confused. Maeve continued. 'If that's the only thing you can give them – that you tried, and you didn't give up on them – then give them that. Whatever happens, whatever you find or don't find – that'll be enough.' Emma stared at her for a second, then jumped up and gathered her into a hug. Maeve, for all the things she was, was not a hugger. But today, she hugged back. After a minute, they pulled away, both blinking hard.

Maeve handed Emma her cup of tea and they both blew extravagantly on their mugs to cool them down.

'So, where are you off to now?' Maeve asked.

Emma thought about it. She could go to the church and talk to Father Westwood. It was possible, at half ten in the morning, that he might even be sober. But she dismissed it; she believed the papers, that it had nothing to do with the Church. Besides, if it did, Father Westwood would be the last to know. She hadn't been able to track down Danny Angelus, and Adam was definitely out of the question.

'Do you think anyone's gone to visit Colm yet?'

Maeve started to say something, but then remembered she was meant to be positive. She pretended to blow on her tea again. 'It's worth a try. As far as I've heard, he's still in the coma, but the guards might be keeping it under wraps.' She nodded. 'Yes, I think it's worth a try.'

At the mention of the guards, Emma deflated again.

'They won't let me anywhere near him,' she said bitterly. 'He'll have a guard at the door.'

Maeve waved her hand, as if to say, *that's nothing*. 'You're a young woman, Emma, and a good-looking one at that,' she said confidently. 'And if you've never learned how to use that to your advantage, I'm afraid I can't help you.'

Chapter 20

Charley woke up in his bed. It was still early; the light behind the curtain was blue and cold.

God, his head hurt. He closed his eyes and rolled over onto the cool side of the bed. His mind walked slowly down a staircase, with the feeling of bare feet on a marble floor, towards a memory. In this very room, eight years ago.

It was Emma and Charley's last goodbye. Emma's bus to the city was leaving in two hours, and by the time she came back on the weekend, Charley would be gone, disappeared into London as an apprentice on one of his granddad's old building crews. They had a brief window of time together, for the last time.

He'd been up crying the three nights before. It was her with the bright future; he didn't want to hold her back or look weak. So, the whole last day with her, he shrugged around, playing it cool, he thought. Playing tough. As if it wasn't important, like it wasn't everything he'd been daydreaming about for weeks – the *what if*. *What if* it didn't have to end?

They were eighteen years old – neither of them knew how to handle it. They barely knew who they were, let alone who they'd be without each other. Maybe they had to fight. To make it easier to separate.

Charley rolled over, the bedroom ceiling coming into focus as the memory receded. The light was now clear and warm.

The walls in his parents' house were thin, so he could hear the murmur of his dad talking to someone in the kitchen below. It sounded like Frances. He quietly crept out of bed, careful to avoid the squeaky floorboard (third from the left). From the top of the stairwell, he could hear their voices easily.

'It's probably just a lot for him to process,' his granny was saying. 'It's upsetting for him too. And clearly something has happened in London that he's not ready to talk about yet.' A cupboard closed loudly. 'You're not angry with *him*, Adam. He seems a bit lost—'

'He seems a bit drunk,' Adam retorted angrily. 'Your man, Donal, he said he was in and out of every pub in town.'

There was a long pause, and Frances murmured something Charley couldn't hear. Then, Adam's voice, choked with emotion now: 'I just wish he would come home. Talk to me – not like that, last night, rambling about birds. But like he used to.'

Charley couldn't listen to any more. His throat was in his mouth as he crept back up the stairs, into his room. And then he slid open the window.

Can't you see, Dad? he thought, as he eased himself down onto the footpath. *Can't you see I want to? That I would give anything to talk to you? To tell you the truth?*

He couldn't, though. And that was the problem. Because the person he would hurt most would be Adam. Frances and Jimmy too, but mostly Adam. And he couldn't do that. His whole life, growing up in a small village as the son of the doctor, Charley had resented his identity. He'd hated that everyone expected him to grow up and take over his dad's life – like his childhood was just the waiting room of a much bigger destiny.

And what about his mother? She might've died when he was young, but he was still half hers. From the stories he'd heard, she was nothing like Adam. Where he was serious, she was fun. Where Adam was solid and predictable, she was fire and passion. So, why did everyone think Charley would be just like Adam? It was like they all forgot about her.

But then he moved to London, and he realised that having an identity – any identity at all – was a privilege. And suddenly, he'd missed being the doctor's son. He missed being Charley, not Mick or Paddy or you.

But it wasn't as easy as saying he wanted to move home, or that he actually did want to study as a doctor (he didn't).

So, Charley decided to head back to town. The village had fewer people, but they all lived in each other's pocket. In town, you could disappear. If he couldn't keep from falling apart, in town he could at least do it without an audience.

Chapter 21

'What do you mean, you're an investigator?'

'Colm's family has hired me to look into—'

'Oh, so you're a solicitor?'

Emma had been talking to the guard stationed outside of Colm Thornton's hospital room for nearly twenty minutes. She was getting nowhere. He had proven impervious to flattery and flirting and was now proving to be underwhelmed by her credentials.

'No, I'm not a solicitor,' she repeated for the third time. 'His family has hired me to investigate what happened that night.' The guard stared blankly at her. 'They think he's innocent,' she added.

'Well, that's got nothing to do with me,' the guard said. 'I'm under orders from the sergeant not to let anybody in that doesn't have a badge. Do you have a badge?' The tone in his voice clearly implied that he knew the answer already: no, you don't, so feck off.

Emma sighed and fecked off.

It was there, in a badly lit corridor with the smell of old plastic sheets and pine disinfectant all around her, that she felt a tremor running through her. An echo. She'd been so caught up in the excitement that it had only just now sunk in where she actually was. It was the same ward and everything. A wave of nausea came over her.

A flash of images. The stretcher. Bright eyes, red and scared. Alarms ringing, nurses shouting. Small, hot breath in her ear, a small arm around her neck. His hand in hers, then pulled away.

She felt a hand on her shoulder.

'Are you okay? Excuse me, are you okay?'

An elderly woman was squeezing her shoulder gently, a look of concern on her face. 'Do you need to sit down?'

Emma shook her head. 'I'm okay,' she said, wiping her eyes with the back of her sleeve. 'Thank you, though.' She looked at the woman properly now. She recognised her. It was Mary Bennett; she worked in town, at the solicitor's office, but she lived in the village. 'Mary – thank you.'

Mary Bennett was wearing the same outfit she wore every day, even in the summer – a heavy quilted coat and a hat that resembled a tea cosy, and always, always a large black bag on her shoulder.

'Are you okay?' Mary asked again. 'You looked like you were going to faint.'

Emma was confused. Mary Bennett had a reputation around the village, and it wasn't for acting sweet and concerned. She had a reputation that made her lucky she wasn't around during the witch trials. But Emma was more confused about what she was doing here. There was only one patient in this wing.

'Are you visiting Colm Thornton?' Emma asked.

Mary's face fell. Then, she drew herself up with a sharp look. Despite her size, it was enough to make Emma nervous.

'I can't imagine how that's any of your business,' she snapped. 'And I'll ask you to remember that.'

And then she stomped down the corridor, her black bag swinging at her side.

Emma frowned and looked around. As far as Emma knew, Mary didn't have any friends, let alone any friends in this wing – there was nobody else in this wing. There were no other patients, and nobody in the examination rooms either. Mary was clearly visiting Colm, that much was clear.

But why?

And just like that, Emma had a new lead. She waited until Mary had turned the corner, then hurried after her. She'd learned how to tail a suspect at Templemore – at least, she'd read the basics in a textbook. It couldn't be that different in real life, could it?

Chapter 22

It could, it turned out, be that different. For one thing, Rocinante didn't exactly blend in. The car whooped and wheezed down the road – the smoke could be seen from Dublin. For another thing, Mary drove impossibly slow – it was only supposed to be a fifteen-minute drive from the hospital back to the village, but it took Mary nearly forty minutes. Emma had to pass her half a dozen times, then wait for her to pass again. Her only hope was that Mary was too focused on the road to notice the same 1962 Ford Cortina, bonnet ablaze, drive past her repeatedly.

Eventually, Emma gave up and drove on ahead of her. She guessed that Mary was going to the village, and she was right. Five minutes later, Mary's car toddled past, and Emma fell back in behind her.

She followed her past Mary's house, through the village centre and out towards the townlands. With a quickening pulse, Emma realised they were headed in the direction of Mr Hollis's house. And sure enough, ten minutes later, Mary slipped off into a small drive that led up to the Big House. Emma drove a little further out of sight, then parked Rocinante, quietly belching acrid smoke, in the field behind Mossie Black's house. She stealthily walked up the hill, until she was almost in the same spot she'd been that night when she saw the murder. It was the early afternoon now, though, so she hugged close to the tree line. She peered out over the ledge, towards the house.

There was nobody there.

She frowned. What the hell? Where was Mary?

And then she heard a branch break behind her. Her blood ran cold. The third man. Emma cursed herself for being so stupid – following an old woman when there was an actual murderer out there. Slowly, carefully, she bent her knees, like a spring winding taut. She'd go down swinging, anyway.

All at once, Emma spun around, then froze – her fists clenched, uselessly, in front of her.

'What the hell?'

She wasn't sure what she'd been expecting. But whatever it was – it certainly wasn't Mary Bennett, standing alone, with her black handbag at her feet.

Pointing a large gun at Emma's head.

Chapter 23

In a hospital thirty kilometres away, a series of lights started flashing across a black screen. A minute later a man opened his eyes, blinking hard.

Colm Thornton was awake.

*

Maeve was right; Sergeant Noonan had left specific orders at the hospital that the Thorntons should not be notified that their son was awake. He said it was to do with security and due process. He was very clear on the matter – nobody would talk to Colm until he had.

But of course, it was West Cork. Even without the help of phones, it took less than an hour for the news to get to the village. And of course, it arrived at Nolan's first.

'I ran all the way here,' Fintan told Frances, panting slightly at the Thorntons' front door. 'But I'd be happy to drive you and Jimmy in to see him. I can go get my car now, if you'd like.'

Frances thought for a moment. Then, as politely as she could, she shut the door in his face.

*

After Sergeant Noonan put the phone back down, he waited for the man sitting across from his desk to speak. To ask what the news was. But the other man just stared at him expectantly – like a headmaster might stare at an uneasy schoolboy, waiting for him to crack. It was the sergeant's office, he was the one sitting behind the big desk, and yet, he felt like he'd been caught with his hand in the cookie jar.

Noonan ran his hand over his tie, adjusted his belt buckle, kept his eyes trained on the ground. 'That was the hospital,' he said slowly. 'It's not good.'

The other man nodded. 'Colm Thornton is awake.'

Noonan frowned. 'You knew already?'

'I knew that you should've taken care of it before it got to this point.'

Sergeant Noonan leaned back in his chair, lit a cigarette, ran a hand through his hair.

'Jesus Christ, you're talking like I should've put a pillow over his head.' Noonan glanced at the other man out of the corner of his eye. From the other man's expression, it was clear he'd expected Noonan to do exactly that. 'Look, I know there's a lot of money on the table here, but you're talking about murder—'

'It's not just money, you moron,' the other man snapped. 'If this gets out, if Colm talks, the whole thing comes undone. People start asking questions, and it's a short leap from this property to the whole damn thing. Every bit of grease I used, every dirty trick you pulled – it'll all be there, out in the open.' The other man's eyes hardened. 'And I won't hang alone.'

It was like he'd slapped Noonan across the face. Like he'd let him run around in the garden for a bit, then suddenly stomped on the leash. It was true that the Hollis property was a single ace in a whole house of cards. And if it fell, if anyone pulled one card out, the whole house would fall on Noonan. The other man was a weasel; he'd wriggle his way out of it one way or another. He'd pin the whole thing on the sergeant.

Noonan was in too deep. His shoulders crumpled; he slid open the bottom drawer of his desk and reached for the bottle of whiskey he hid there.

'I'll give you one warning, Noonan.' The other man spoke quietly, but it was like a knife thrown suddenly across the room, inches from Noonan's hand. 'If you fall apart now, I'll bury you myself.'

Noonan froze, his hand hanging in the air. Then, he took it back out and slowly closed the drawer. 'What would you like me to do?' he asked.

When the other man saw the way Noonan kept his eyes down, he leaned forward. 'I would like you to take care of the situation.' His hand shot forward suddenly, and Noonan flinched. The other man smiled as he took Noonan's box of cigarettes and slowly lit one, exhaling luxuriously before continuing. 'I don't care what you do. But there *will not be* a trial.'

Sergeant Noonan frowned. 'Surely that would look more suspicious. If he suddenly dies in the hospital, under my care.'

The other man waved his hand. 'Then take your name out of the equation. Make sure he gets transferred to the jail as soon as possible, and once he's there ...'

The other man trailed off. He didn't have to say it. Once Colm was in the general prison population, there were always a few men who could be persuaded to do the dirty work. Make him go away, for a price.

Noonan's hands trembled; his stomach ached. He had been loved once, long ago – held in the arms of a woman who would only ever remember him as good, as gentle, as her whole world. But she had died too young, and as he fought his way upstream, he put his goodness down for a little bit – to swim a little easier, a little further, to help make ends meet. It was supposed to be temporary. He thought he'd be able to pick it back up again. But, of course, life didn't work like that. Everything he let go of was swept away in the current and gone for good.

And now, he was here, in waters too deep, too far from shore – chained to a man who would stop at nothing to save his own skin. Deciding whether or not to help kill an innocent man.

If Noonan stopped now, he would go down. All of the bribes, all of the strong-arming and blackmailing and gun-pointing he had done on this man's behalf, would send him away for a very long time. If Noonan stopped now, he wouldn't have killed anyone, but his life would be over. And with a man like this one as an enemy, he'd be as good as dead.

Noonan thought the way all gamblers think – *I'm this far already, a little bit further isn't going to make it any worse. And it might just mean I get away with it all. In for a penny, in for a pound.*

'Okay,' he said. 'Once he's transferred from the hospital, that's when we'll do it.' He picked up the telephone and called the hospital. While he waited for it to ring, he looked at the other man. 'You know, this business with Hollis ...' He hesitated. 'You weren't involved in that, were you? The murder?'

The other man's face split into a wide, cold smile. 'Of course not, Sergeant,' he said, in a voice like a razorblade. 'No – if I'd wanted Hollis dead, I would've had you kill him.' As Noonan's face turned pale white, the other man stood up to leave. 'Besides, the last thing I wanted was attention – anyone looking anywhere near this.' He shook his head. 'No, Sergeant, I had nothing to do with that murder. Whoever killed Hollis is still out there, somewhere.'

Noonan could barely hear the operator's voice through the ringing in his ears.

Chapter 24

Frances and Jimmy Thornton's house sat at the end of a row of houses, all painted different shades of pastel. Each house had a small garden outside the back, surrounded by Connie's field and fenced in by wooden posts and wire mesh to keep the cows back. Between the wooden fence and the field, there was another, smaller fence – an electric fence. And in between these two fences, there was a sort of no man's land – not quite a field, not quite a garden. This had been taken over long ago by all kinds of sweetgrass and crabgrass and bluebells, turning it into a jungle of sorts.

As they made their way up the front steps, Mary Bennett and Emma could see Jimmy in the no man's land out back – it was unclear what he was doing, but he looked busy.

'Are you sure you want to do this?' Emma asked Mary.

Mary nodded. 'It's now or never.' Then she knocked on the door.

*

'Can I tempt you to another biscuit?' Frances held out a tin of digestives to her two guests.

'No, thank you,' Mary said. 'One is more than enough for me.'

Frances waved her guest off. 'Ah, go wan,' she said, 'sure, they'll only go off if you don't—'

Mary Bennett stopped Frances with a stern look. 'I said no,' she said sharply, 'and when I say no, I mean it.' The tin hung limply in the air as Frances gaped at her.

'I'll have one,' Emma said quickly. 'Oh, Frances, they look lovely.'

'Thanks, love,' Frances said weakly. She considered offering more tea but thought better of it. She sat back down and assumed a forced cheeriness. 'I wish I had your restraint, Mary. They never last more than a day in this house.'

Mary was unimpressed. 'Sure, that's what the whole world is like these days.' She sniffed. 'Nobody has any restraint. And we've seen what that leads to, haven't we?' She emphasised this last point with a raised eyebrow – it was unclear if she was inviting Frances to join in with her condemnation or to receive it. (Which, Frances thought, was probably exactly the effect she was going for.)

It should be pointed out that Mary was trying her best; she just wasn't very good at this sort of thing. She was the sort of woman you only found in a small village – an elderly woman who people laughed at and grovelled to, in equal measure. She had worn black for nearly forty years now, and people said it suited her far more than the marriage ever did. Not that anyone could even remember her husband or her marriage.

They didn't know what to do with her, so they just forgot about her. And Mary forgot what it was like to be invited in for tea, and how to keep certain opinions to herself.

Even Frances struggled to keep the small talk going. And the scene outside the back window wasn't helping either, where she could see Jimmy running around in a lightly hysterical jog. He had been upset by the news about Colm waking up and handled it by convincing himself he heard a fox cub crying in the garden. But Frances wasn't sure Mary would understand that.

'They keep me regular,' Mary was saying, as she rummaged through her black bag for a boiled sweet. 'As I'm sure you know, Frances – at our age we need all the help we can get.'

Frances didn't know what to say to that. Just like she hadn't known what to say when Mary explained how many dog shits she had seen on the footpath outside.

'Seven! Seven different dog turds!' she cried. 'Do you know how long it takes for a single dropping to disintegrate? Ten days, at the minimum. At the absolute minimum, with plenty of rain.'

Emma kept trying to interrupt, and get Mary to explain why they were there, but Mary would not be hurried towards her destination. Unfortunately, she only had four topics of conversation – the benefits of boiled sweets, the moral collapse of Western civilisation, dog shit and her job. They moved quickly through the boiled sweets – Frances didn't like them, for which Mary blamed Western moral collapse – and then into the topic of her job.

'It's a great job, sure it is,' she said fondly, staring out the window wistfully. 'In twenty-eight years, I was the only girl there.'

Frances wondered when she had ever been a girl, but instead asked, 'And what sort of work do you do?'

'I started as a typist,' Mary replied, 'but they quickly realised I was too valuable to waste on typing. I remember, one day, Will – Will O'Donovan, the old partner – lost the run of himself altogether, going on and on about my work.' She leaned in conspiratorially. 'Well, I don't mind saying that I'd caught a few mistakes: an incomplete filing here, a faulty deposition there – brought us back from certain ruin more than once. And myself just a typist – can you believe it?'

'No,' Jimmy said brightly. He had just come in from the garden, his face bright red and the armpits on his shirt ringed with sweat. 'I simply cannot believe that, Mary.'

Frances quickly jumped in.

'My goodness, Mary, that sounds an awful big responsibility. So, you must've had a good nose for it all. And then you moved on to ... secretary, was it?'

Mary turned to her and drew herself up. 'No, dear, it was not secretary,' she said incredulously. 'I was the office manager, reporting directly to Will O'Donovan himself.' She smiled at the memory. 'I worked under him for twenty-two glorious years – he barely made a decision without asking me first. Until that other man bought him out.' Her face darkened. 'Nothing's been the same since.'

Jimmy sat down on the couch next to Mary and slapped his knees. 'So, what brings you to our doorstep, Mary?'

Frances shot him a warning look. 'You know, I've always wondered what it would be like to work in a solicitor's office,' she said, with as much enthusiasm as she could muster. 'What did you do all day? It was some sort of—'

Mary held up her hand to cut her off. 'I apologise, I don't believe I've made myself clear,' she frowned sternly at Frances, 'but I'm not here for idle chit-chat.'

Frances, who, of course, had no idea what she'd done wrong, looked at Emma, bewildered. Emma looked at Jimmy. Jimmy, in turn, stared determinedly at the biscuit he was holding.

'I've always wondered why they call it a digestive,' he muttered. 'They certainly don't help with it, that's for sure.'

'I'm here about Colm's estate,' Mary said, frowning at Jimmy. 'I've seen the paperwork myself.'

Jimmy leaned back heavily on the couch with a sigh. 'We know all about it. What there is to know anyway. We understand he didn't have a will, sure, but I can't imagine anyone's going to fight over the few pennies he had.'

Mary shook her head vehemently. 'Ian Flesk lied,' she said. 'Colm might not have a will, but he does have an estate. And without a will, the estate passes to you, Frances. But Ian figures he can claim it if it goes into probate, or if Colm is sentenced—'

'Hang on,' Frances interrupted. 'What do you mean, he can claim the estate? What estate? What are you talking about?' She looked at Emma, who had been unusually silent the whole time. 'And I'm sorry, love, but what on earth are you doing here?'

Emma looked at Jimmy again. By his flushed face, it was clear he had not explained her investigation to Frances and he had no intention of doing so now. She turned to Frances.

'I was looking into what happened,' she said simply. 'The guards wouldn't listen to me, but there's another man out there, and I don't think they have the full story.'

All the colour drained from Frances's face. She closed her eyes. 'I don't want to hear about this,' she said quietly. 'I don't want to know—'

Jimmy interrupted her, coming over to sit next to her on the other couch. 'I know you don't, love,' he said, taking her hand. 'But you have to face it – we have to face it. Emma thinks Colm might be innocent, don't you, Emma?'

Emma froze, a biscuit halfway to her mouth. 'Well, I ...'

Frances pounced on her hesitation.

'You see? She doesn't think he's innocent any more than I do. Any more than anyone else does.'

Emma and Jimmy started to protest, but a quiet cough interrupted them. They all turned to Mary, sitting primly on her chair, another boiled sweet tucked into her cheek.

'Now, if you're done with all that,' she said sternly. 'I'll tell you why I'm here.'

Chapter 25

Earlier, in the offices of Ian Flesk, something rather out of the ordinary had happened: Mary Bennett had knocked on Ian's office door.

Mary Bennett hated Ian Flesk. She hated his greasy hair, she hated his greasy smile, she hated the way he leered at her. She hated the way he treated her, and she especially hated the way he treated other people.

She was sixty years old and had been Will O'Donovan's secretary for over twenty years. But after Will O'Donovan retired the year before, he sold the business – as well as his half of the partnership – to Ian Flesk. Will O'Donovan's last day was the last time Mary had been happy in the office.

Now, when she didn't get an answer to her knock, she opened the door quietly and sat down in the chair usually reserved for clients.

'Ms Bennett—' Ian began, but Mary cut him off.

'Excuse me, Mr Flesk,' she said sharply, 'I believe I'll have my say now.'

Ian tried to mask his surprise, quickly lowering his eyebrows back into a furrow. He'd always heard that Mary had a reputation around the village, but in the office she was the picture of decorum – never a stray word or hair out of place. You could scream at her for an hour (and he often did) and she'd sit there and wait patiently, like she was waiting for the bus to arrive. But now, her eyes were hard; her voice was like a flint and whetstone, leaving a trail of sparks in the air.

'I just saw Frances Thornton leave the office.'

'Yes, and?'

'And she left empty-handed.' Mary pointed at the sheaf of papers in front of Ian. 'You didn't give her the property deed. You didn't tell her about it, did you?'

Ian's mouth hung open, but his cheeks were turning blotchy and his eyes were narrowing. 'Excuse me, Ms Bennett, how dare—'

Mary held up her hand.

'Don't lie to me, Mr Flesk. Every piece of paper in this building goes through my desk first. I know more about this business than you do. I know exactly what you have on your desk there – and I know why you haven't told Frances about it.' She crossed her legs and folded her hands together in her lap. 'So, what are you going to do about it?'

Ian struggled to take deep, calming breaths. He frowned and pretended not to understand. 'Do? What do you mean, do, Ms Bennett? It's my business, my name on that door, not yours. That will be all.' He gestured at the door, a bit more impatiently now. 'Now, if you don't mind.'

She narrowed her eyes. 'I've been in this office for thirty years, Mr Flesk. Even if I hadn't, I'm a quick learner. The Thorntons are good, decent people and if you think—'

'That will be all, Ms Bennett!' Ian shouted. 'The door is behind you, and for your sake – if you want to keep your job – I suggest you walk through it immediately. Immediately!' His face was purple from the strain, his neck bulging over his collar.

Mary stared at him a moment longer. Then she grabbed her black bag off the desk and marched out.

*

'The property is substantial,' Mary said now, in the Thorntons' sitting room. She paused, taking in their puzzled expressions. 'And it doesn't matter if Colm didn't have a will – if there are no dependants, then the estate goes to the parents.' She added, 'To you, Frances and Jimmy.'

As Jimmy slumped heavily onto the couch next to an equally confused Frances, Mary explained Ian's plan, as she saw it. He was trying to hide the estate from the Thorntons. If Colm died during a crime, or lived and was sentenced, the contents would disappear into the mysterious, nebulous 'possession of the state and creditors to the estate'. Ian could claim himself as one of those creditors, as the executor of his estate. She told them about the property Colm had apparently owned – it was down by the old pier and included a right of way and ten acres of land.

'Still,' Mary said thoughtfully, 'it's a nice property, but it's not exactly that big. Ian's taking an awfully big risk on something he could probably afford on his own anyway.' She unwrapped a boiled sweet in quiet contemplation. 'There must be something else,' she murmured. 'Something I'm not seeing.'

After she finished, they were all silent for some time, the only sound the distant ticking of a clock and Mary sucking determinedly at her boiled sweet.

'Wait, sorry,' Frances said finally. She turned to Emma. 'How exactly do you fit into all this again?'

Emma explained how she had run into Mary at the hospital and followed her to Mr Hollis's house. When she got to the point about the gun, Frances gasped.

'For feck's sake, Mary! What are you doing with a gun?'

Mary rolled her eyes. 'It's not a gun. Here, take a look yourself.' She pulled the gun out of her black bag and tossed it to Jimmy – Jimmy jumped to his feet, cursing and swearing.

'Jesus bloody Christ, Mary!' he cried. 'What are you doing throwing around ...' It was then that he looked at what he was holding. There was a moment's pause, then he started chuckling. 'Jesus, Mary – you're some woman, you are.'

Mary grinned. Frances looked between the two of them, dumbfounded. 'Will someone please, please explain what is happening in this house?' she pleaded. 'What is it?'

'It's a butcher's bolt,' Mary said, taking the gun back from Jimmy. 'It's like a high-powered hammer. The butcher holds it up to a cow's head and whack!' She showed how the steel bolt slammed forward in the barrel. 'Poor cattle never see it coming.'

'Oh, well, I'm glad you cleared that up, Mary,' Frances said sarcastically. 'Do you often need to kill cattle in your line of work?'

Mary raised her eyebrow. 'I've been a widow for more than thirty years. I live alone, and so I need protection.'

The simplicity of her statement took everyone's breath away. Mary looked at the bolt fondly, turning it over in her hands.

'My husband was a butcher, God rest him. At the funeral, everyone kept telling me how he was looking down on me from heaven – watching over me. He didn't leave much behind in the way of keepsakes or letters, or anything like that. Just this bolt here.' She considered the object in her hands. 'I don't know about heaven, but I know, right now, I have him here with me.'

Jimmy went over to her and patted her shoulder. 'I think we're going to get along just fine, Mary.' He smiled. 'Just fine, indeed.'

All of a sudden, Frances thought of something.

'We don't need to worry about the inheritance rules, anyway.' She quickly explained the news to Mary and Emma that Colm had woken up and was expected to make a full recovery – brushing past her own reaction. 'So, we just need to find that deed.'

As Frances, Jimmy and Mary all settled into their tea and small talk again, Emma felt she had to speak up.

'I don't think you were finished with your story, Mary,' she said patiently. 'Tell them the rest – what you told me on the way over.'

'Ah yes.' Mary put her teacup down. 'The reason I was at the Big House in the first place. And why I am here, drinking your tea and frightening your poor young friend.'

After Mary left Ian Flesk's office, she'd headed straight to the hospital. She hoped to talk to Colm; if he was awake, he might have another copy of the deed. But the guards turned her away, same as they did to Emma. So, she took matters into her own hands.

'I decided to go straight to the source,' she said. 'Ian might have the deed, but maybe Hollis made a copy or had the wire transfer, or something – anything. But then Emma here showed up. A step ahead of me,' she added, not unkindly. Emma swelled with pride.

But Frances and Jimmy were looking at each other, confused.

'Sorry – why would Mr Hollis have a copy of the deed?' Frances asked. 'What did he have to do with the property?'

Mary hesitated. She wasn't good at delivering bad news delicately. And this certainly seemed like bad news – pointing as it did to Colm's guilt. Or at least, to his definite involvement in the murder. Luckily, Emma saw her hesitation. 'How about I get us another cup of tea,' she said gently, 'and I'll explain everything.'

Emma made another pot of tea and poured it out among the cups. Then, she explained what Mary had found: that Colm had bought the property off Hollis just a few days before the murder in the Big House.

'But I don't understand,' Frances said weakly, 'Colm was broke. Poor, really. I saw the accounts myself – Ian wasn't lying about those.'

Mary nodded. 'The property was bought in Colm's name, but somebody else – a third party – paid for it. I wasn't able to see the full contract, just the deed itself.'

'So, you don't know who it was?' Jimmy asked. 'If it was someone local or from up North, or ...'

Mary shook her head. 'I'm sorry. I really am.'

Frances slumped back into the couch. 'So ... he's guilty,' she said flatly. 'My son ... a murderer.' Jimmy had the same look of shock across his face. Nobody moved, nobody spoke. From across the harbour, the first strokes of the Angelus lapped against the window. But then Emma spoke.

'Not necessarily.'

Everyone turned to look at her; she was smiling.

'Think about it,' she said excitedly. 'Mary, you said that the contract was already complete, right? Everything was finalised and the sale was complete?' She waited until Mary nodded. 'Don't you see? Why would Colm kill Mr Hollis? He'd already got the prize. There was nothing to fight over, no deal gone wrong – it was over. So, why would Colm kill him then?'

Mary mulled it over, adding a drop of milk to her tea. 'That's true,' she said slowly. 'There'd be no point – not for Colm, anyway.'

'Exactly!' Emma stood up and started pacing the floor. 'This whole time, that was the one thing I couldn't explain – if Colm was innocent, then what the hell was he doing there with Mr Hollis?' She reached the end of the room and spun on her heel. 'He was there on business. He was there about the property – celebrating the sale, maybe. Then, the third man bursts in.'

Frances and Jimmy were watching her curiously. A crack of light slowly spread across their faces – hope. Hope, at last.

Mary was watching her too.

'You know,' she said, with a wry amusement. 'You look like Sherlock Holmes, in one of his adventures, pacing up and down the floor. You only need a pipe.'

Emma blushed. 'And a bit of cocaine maybe.'

Mary laughed. But then she clapped her hands together and stood up too. She said eagerly, 'You know, I couldn't figure out why that piece of land was worth so much – but clearly Ian wants it badly.' She unwrapped another boiled sweet and popped it into her mouth. 'And if he does, then maybe somebody else does too. There must be something – gold or oil, or something about that specific property. Which means ...' She looked at Emma for confirmation. Emma nodded. 'Which means that if somebody wanted the property, they had to get rid of Hollis and Colm.'

Emma turned to Frances and Jimmy. 'And there, ladies and gentlemen, is our motive.'

*

Outside, the afternoon had turned into evening: the jackdaws and blackbirds were in their roosts, the cows had all returned to their sheds. Mary had insisted that they go back to the Big House right away, but Emma insisted right back.

'We need a plan. We can't go in half-cocked.' She looked at Frances and Jimmy, and they agreed. 'Okay then,' she said, relieved. 'We'll all meet at the library tomorrow morning, ten o'clock. And we'll make a plan.'

Mary sniffed. 'We could have the whole thing wrapped up by supper tonight.' But in the end, she agreed too.

After Emma said her goodbyes and left, Mary gathered up her black bag and her coat. Frances stopped her.

'Thank you, Mary,' she said. 'You were ...' Her voice caught in her throat. 'You were very good to come. I know I haven't always—'

Mary shushed her. 'Remember what I said about the boiled sweets – get that clockwork ticking right.'

She was halfway down the path to the gate when she heard a voice call out, 'Mary!' She turned; Jimmy and Frances were still standing in the doorway, Frances in Jimmy's arms.

'Why'd you do it?' he asked. 'Why'd you come here and help us?'

Mary hesitated. 'I knew your son,' she said slowly, like a patient taking their first steps without crutches. 'When he was a small lad, after my Mick passed – God rest him – people avoided me in the shop.' Mary's eyes narrowed. 'I guess they didn't know what to say at first. And then, after a while, they still didn't know what to say.' And now the tears came. 'I'd been holding a space before, and when I came back, there was no room for me. The more I tried to reach out, the more they thought I was mad. Or batty.'

Jimmy shifted uncomfortably, remembering all the times he had thought exactly that, but Mary didn't notice.

'But Colm never did. He was only thirteen or fourteen, but any time he was in the shop, he said hello and asked how I was doing – even though his friends teased him for it. He'd carry my shopping and ask me questions; and he'd listen to the answers.' She wiped her eyes with the back of her hand. 'Out of the whole village, it seemed like he was the only one who saw me.' She looked at Jimmy. And for the first time, Jimmy saw Mary for who she really was – a lonely, grieving woman. 'Colm was a good boy. And I'm sorry – I'm sorry that you lost him for so long.' And then she turned around, and she was gone.

*

Later, after they cleared away the last of the saucers and small spoons, Jimmy sat down wearily on the couch.

'Jesus,' Frances said, sitting down next to him. 'She's some piece of work, isn't she?'

'She's had a tough life,' Jimmy said fairly. Then he added, 'But yes, she's a real piece of work.'

'She's quick off the ball, though,' Frances said thoughtfully. 'You know, I always thought she was exaggerating about how important she was over there. But she clearly knew a lot more than she ever let on. And maybe she was right, about Colm.'

And then, all at once, all the weight she'd been carrying around with her suddenly broke, and she started to cry, her shoulders heaving against Jimmy's chest. 'I just want him to be good. Happy – like he was when he was little.'

Jimmy ran his hands through her hair, his fingers tracing the curve of her neck. 'I know,' he said quietly. 'That's what we'll do, so. We'll remember him like he was.'

And he held her as she cried. And later, when her breath evened out and slowed down, he stayed as still as possible until he was sure she was asleep. He eased himself off the couch, covered her with a blanket and quietly closed the back door behind him.

Frances and Jimmy had met when they were both eight years old. He'd arrived in from London; his father had taken a job as manager at the Lough Hyne quarry – a tough job, but it paid well. Very well, compared to the rest of the village; Jimmy's family took a taxi to mass, while Frances's family walked. 'And we lived much further out,' she'd always say. 'Much further.' Still, when they started going out, it was Frances's mother that was against it. 'You want a man who works in a shirt and tie,' she kept saying. 'A banker, not a builder.' They were twelve years old.

But it was too late; he'd already won her over. Jimmy did end up a carpenter, and he went to London for his apprenticeship. But as soon as he landed back, age twenty-one, they picked up right where they'd left off. And they stayed there, happy enough, for fifty-odd years. Through thick and thin, they always had each other.

Jimmy looked at his wife, almost five decades later, sleeping on the couch. Colm was awake – he was going to be okay.

And Jimmy thought, what a funny word 'okay' could be.

Chapter 26

The harbour was unsettled. The surface was choppy, grey, directionless – like hammered pewter in the early evening light. Otherwise, the air was still. The trees were full of corncrakes and starlings, like leaves ready to take flight. The sky was one continuous cloud.

Out in the country, in a small field beside the Big House, the darkness lay heavier and filled up the long valley. A small torch light swung left, then right, scything through the grass but leaving it uncut.

The stranger made two loops around the house, shining the light in the windows, until he was sure it was empty. He followed the driveway a little further. He could see two sets of tyres in the mud, with only one leaving. The other set belonged to the car that was still here.

Her car. The name the scared man had given to him. And told him to kill. He was close.

All at once, a thread of high beams cut through the darkening hedgerow. The stranger quickly threw himself behind the low wall and out of sight. When he heard the car slow down and then approach, he started to smile. She must've left in the other car, and now she was coming back to collect it. It was perfect. Once the driver pulled away, it would just be the two of them. His hand closed around the handle of the clawhammer in his pocket. He started to stealthily crabwalk along the length of the wall – but then stopped.

It was a man's voice.

'Jesus, lad, what the hell was she thinking – look at that engine!' There was the sound of a bonnet slamming closed.

'It's a joke,' agreed another man's voice. 'But let's just get it winched and get the feck out of here. This place gives me the creeps.'

The stranger cursed. He took his hand off the clawhammer and slunk backwards, away from the two men.

She'd got away this time. But he was close. Oh, he was close.

Chapter 27

Long ago, when Mary was eight years old, her father woke her up early one morning.

'C'mon, love,' he said. 'Get your wellies – we're going down to the pier.'

Mary rubbed her eyes. It was only half six – the sky was still dark. 'Now, Da?'

Her father nodded grimly. 'Now, love.'

Mary got dressed quickly and rushed downstairs, where she found her parents in a whispered argument.

'You can't take her, Kev – she's too young.'

'She needs to learn—'

'For God's sake, Kevin, she's only a child!'

'No, I'm not!' Mary piped up, startling her parents. 'I'm not a child, Mummy.'

Her mother smiled weakly. 'Of course, I know you're not. But I don't want—'

'That's enough now, Rosie,' her father said sternly. He turned to Mary. 'Ready to go?'

Mary nodded. Her mother came over and hugged her tightly.

'Be good for your da, you hear?' She looked her in the eye. 'Be brave.'

Mary nodded.

Then her mother went back into the kitchen, where her little brother bounced happily in his pram.

As they walked down from the village to the pier, Mary wondered what was going on. But she knew better than to ask. She followed her father, a hitch in her step to try and keep up with his long legs, doing her best not to skip.

'There's been an accident, love,' her father said finally. He explained that a ship had gone down in a heavy sea, just outside the harbour.

'Oh,' said Mary. 'Was it bad?'

'Yes, love. It was very bad.'

In a small voice, Mary asked, 'Did somebody die?'

Her father stopped; he knelt down next to her and looked her square in the eye. 'Yes,' he said. 'Somebody died. There were fifteen men on the boat, and we're going to be looking for them. Does that scare you?'

Mary started to tremble, and her eyes got wide and bright. There were sirens in the distance, down at the pier. A fire engine rushed by them, its spotlight tracing lines through the dark, high above. She remembered what her mother had said; she thrust her jaw out.

'No,' she said. 'I'm not scared.'

Her father looked at her, a mixture of pride and sorrow in his eyes. He took her hand, and they started walking towards the pier again.

'We're going to join the search party,' her father said firmly. 'You and me, we're going to help them search for those men.'

'We can save them?'

Her father shook his head sadly. 'I don't think so, love. It's been too long; the sea is cold and heavy.' He glanced over to see her reaction. 'If we find them, we'll be finding their bodies.'

Mary swallowed hard. 'Their dead bodies.'

Her father nodded, quiet.

'But ...' Mary struggled with the question. 'How does that help? If they're already ...' She hesitated. 'If they're already lost.'

Her father looked out across the harbour.

'Because it's the only thing we can do now.' He squeezed her hand. 'There are some people in this village today who have just lost everything. Lost a brother or a father or a son. And I wouldn't know what to say to them or the right way to greet them.' He shrugged. 'But we can do this. We can bring the bodies back. It's harder to do,' – he looked down at Mary – 'it's scarier too. But we can give them something better than a silly word or a cake; we can give them a chance to bury their dead. We can give them an answer, or closure maybe. A chance to say goodbye.'

*

Mary and her father spent all day down on the pier, walking the beach and peering out into the dark blue sea. There were dozens of boats out on the water, doing the same thing; the whole village turned out to walk along the beaches – Carrigillihy, Trá na Oileáin, Squince and all the small coves and inlets. Mary and her father didn't find anyone. But all the bodies were found, in the end.

After supper that night, when Mary went into the sitting room to say goodnight to her father, she paused in the doorway.

'What do you think happened to them?' She hesitated. 'Now they're dead?'

Her father looked at her closely, folding the paper onto his lap. 'I wish I could tell you, love, but I don't know. I really don't.' His eyes were bright. He patted the couch next to him, and she curled up into him. She only found out years later that one of his closest friends had been on the ship. 'I only know that what we did today, that's the hardest work – the best work. To bring the body back.' He pulled her close. 'Whatever you do, bring the body back.'

*

Years passed, and both of Mary's parents passed away – her father first, from a heart attack, and shortly after, her mother, from a stroke. Soon after that, her brother moved away – at first, she got a letter once a year, then once every two years, and then not at all.

Mary married young, to a nice man she met at the parish hall one evening. She had been alone for some time, and it was good to have someone to talk to. And he had kind eyes. That was good too.

It was a quick courtship and a small ceremony, but they were happy. They talked about children, but it didn't happen. It might have, eventually, but then one night after dinner, he went into the other room and lay down on the couch. He'd mentioned a headache and wanted to close his eyes for a minute. Mary cleaned up the dishes and boiled the kettle. For the rest of her life, she would wonder – if she hadn't cleaned the dishes, if she'd just gone to him instead, maybe she could've saved him. But she didn't; she cleaned the dishes and by the time she brought him his tea, he had followed a heart attack across the river and out of this world.

And just like that, she was alone again. She was eight years old.

Mary was the type of person who fell through the cracks – or was pushed through, maybe. The kind of person who didn't have the good graces or social skills a small village required – demanded, more like. And all too often, good graces were mistaken for a good heart. And vice versa. The village helped for a few weeks after the funeral, but when it became clear that Mary was not going to remarry – that she was going to continue to show up dressed in black, her head held up high – the village didn't know what to do with her. Women have been burned for less.

Kilcraven wasn't the type to burn anyone, but they needed a way to regard her, to classify her – a role to slot her into. At first, they tried pitying her. But she was still young and pretty, so that didn't last. Then they ignored her, but Mary just kept barging along, refusing to keep the noise down or her opinions to herself. In the end, they just decided she was a killjoy and a battleaxe and a hard sort of woman, and then they moved on.

At first, Mary didn't notice. Then, she discovered she couldn't change it. Finally, she decided she didn't care. Even though she did. She did care. Some nights before bed, after she said her prayers and kissed the pictures of her father, her mother and her husband – people who had loved her, now frozen in time behind glass, seeing nothing – she cared so much she thought her skin would peel off.

But now, she had a chance. A chance to help. A chance to show people she was more than a batty old woman. A chance to live again.

And a chance to bring the body back.

*

As the other man left the garda station after talking to Sergeant Noonan, he didn't feel so scared anymore. He had Noonan under his thumb; there was no backing out now – Colm Thornton would shut his mouth, one way or another. And that property – that fortune – would be his.

As he ran his hand through his greasy hair, Ian Flesk took a deep breath of the fresh country air. He wasn't so scared anymore, oh no. Not anymore. There was the question of who exactly had killed Hollis, but he didn't think it put him at any risk – the old man had plenty of enemies, plenty of scores to settle that didn't have to do with land.

And the stranger – well, he'd take care of his side of things soon enough. He had her name. She shouldn't have asked questions, shouldn't have stuck her nose where it didn't belong, shouldn't have threatened him. In his own damn office. The bitch.

Well, she'd get hers alright. The stranger would make sure of that. It was only a matter of time.

How hard could it be to track down an old biddy like Mary Bennett?

Chapter 28

The next morning, Mary burst into the library at precisely eight o'clock. 'Why didn't you push harder last night?' she demanded. 'We could've gone back to Hollis's house, got some answers—'

'Would you like some tea, Mary?' Emma interrupted, without looking up from the papers on her desk. 'I was just about to make some.'

Emma was alone in the library; Frances and Jimmy were running late, and Maeve wouldn't be in for another hour at least.

'Were you scared?' Mary asked, not unkindly. 'Was that it?'

Emma raised an eyebrow. 'If you remember, Mary, I'd started the day with a butcher's bolt pointed in my face. I think that just about covered my fear.'

She tried to hide her smile as Mary considered this – as if it were completely unrelated to her, like she hadn't been the one pointing the bolt in question.

'So, tea?' Emma asked again, already getting the kettle out.

Mary hesitated, then gave a formal nod and took off her coat and hat. Emma filled the kettle and dropped the tea bags into the mugs. Mary grunted quietly. 'You're a fierce one, alright.'

Emma grinned. 'Says the one going around like Dirty Harry.'

'Ah, well about that.' Mary hesitated again. 'I, ah ... well.'

Mary was not someone who hesitated often or apologised – it seemed like it was causing her genuine discomfort. But Emma understood.

'It's okay, Mary,' she said, handing her a cup of tea. She rested her hand on top of hers. 'Let's just keep your hands where I can see them from now on,' she added, grinning.

Mary looked down at Emma's hand on top of hers. Her breath stopped in her chest. And she realised, with some surprise, that she was suddenly on the verge of tears. It had been so long since someone had touched her; it caught her off guard. 'Well, my question still stands,' she said, coming back to herself and looking in her bag for a boiled sweet. 'Why didn't you push harder to go back to Hollis's house?'

Emma sighed.

'I'm a librarian, Mary. I can't go running around breaking into people's houses – into crime scenes – on some hunch.'

'You're more than that, Ms Daly,' Mary said, snapping her bag shut and popping a sweet in her mouth. 'You blushed the other day when I said you looked like Sherlock Holmes.' She frowned. 'Is it so hard to believe you might be something more than just a librarian?'

Emma didn't know what to say. It was slightly jarring to hear such kind words in such a stern tone. She decided to change the subject.

'Are you a fan of Sherlock Holmes?'

Mary sipped her tea quietly and smiled. 'My father used to read the adventures to me before bed every night.' Then, she hesitated. 'The other day, at the hospital, were you—'

Before she could say anything more, the bell above the front door chimed. Jimmy and Frances had arrived, and they had news.

*

Well, it was less news and more of a decision. They explained what had happened when Fintan offered to drive Frances and Jimmy to the hospital to visit Colm.

'She said no,' Jimmy said quietly, slumping over in one of the chairs in the pensioners' corner. 'She closed the door. And last night, we decided – for the moment anyway – that we want to keep that door shut.' He stared at his hands. 'We don't want to see him. Not yet, anyway.'

Frances looked at Mary and Emma helplessly. 'You must think we're heartless,' she started to say, but Emma cut her off by handing her a cup of tea.

'We understand, Frances,' she said gently. 'We really do.'

Mary wasn't sure that she did, but she let it pass. She added, 'Besides, it helps us.' The other three stared blankly at her, so she explained. 'We have even more reason to clear his name now. So, you two have long enough to change your minds.'

They were all quiet for a moment. Mary's stomach dropped – was she too harsh? Were they angry? Then, Jimmy leaned over and took her hand.

'Where have you been my whole life, Mary Bennett?'

The tension in the room then suddenly disappeared, and they all laughed and refilled their tea.

Chapter 29

A short while later, Frances and Mary were in town, parked in front of the office of Ian Flesk, Solicitor at Law.

'So,' Frances said, nervously cinching her jacket around her waist. 'Run me through the plan again.'

Mary turned and gave her a stern look. The kind of look that Mary was well known for, and that Frances recognised best on her. The kind of look that reminded Frances how strange it was that they were sitting next to each other now. Because Frances was discovering that once you warmed to her, once you gave her the benefit of the doubt – Mary's tough exterior was shot through with something close to humour.

Mary didn't answer; rather she slowly unpeeled a red boiled sweet, popped it into her mouth and looked back up at the sign.

Frances waited, then tried again. 'So what *is* the plan, exactly?'

Mary rolled the sweet over in her mouth deliberately, her thin lips stretched tight.

'Well,' she finally said, a soft clack as she slid the sweet to one side of her mouth. 'I don't think Ian will expect to see me today.

And I don't think he will expect that I went to you.' She rolled her eyes. 'He'd never give me that much credit. And he definitely won't expect that you actually listened.'

The sweet clacked audibly to the other side of her mouth. She looked up at the sign again.

'It's a small village; and someone like you, who everyone likes, he'd know there would be trouble if he was to be seen crossing you. So, it's possible that he'll give up the game straight away.' Mary shrugged. 'Admit he knew about the property – he was just trying to iron out the details before he got your hopes up.'

Frances felt a flutter of small wings unfolding in her stomach – something that felt a bit like hope. But Mary wasn't the type to beat around the bush; she was the type to machete right through.

'On the other hand,' Mary continued in the same impatient tone, 'I'm the only other person who's actually seen the deed. He's bound to have the original locked away, and if there isn't another copy, it might as well not exist. Without it, it'd be my word against his. And people don't like me.'

She raised a hand to stop the protest she knew was coming.

'It's okay, Frances. I don't care for most of them either, truth be told. They call me both an idiot and a know-it-all in the same breath.'

Frances couldn't help herself – she laughed. And for the first time that Frances had ever seen, Mary almost did too. Then she caught herself.

'Like I was saying,' Mary continued, frowning at Frances as if she'd been interrupted, 'as it stands, it's my word against his. And my word won't get you very far in the village.' She hesitated. 'I know you don't want to, and I'm sure you have your reasons, but you need to—'

'No.'

Mary made an impatient noise. 'You don't really have a choice here, Frances. You're going to need to talk to Colm eventually. Emma's a smart girl, but you and I both know that you're the one who will get the real answers from your son.'

Frances almost said 'no' again, in the same impassive tone, but she couldn't. Maybe she was wrong; maybe Emma could get some answers without her, but even then, it would only delay the inevitable. At some point, she would have to see Colm. To talk to him. To ask him *why*.

But then, just as she was resolving herself to face up to it and say 'yes, let's drive to the hospital', a memory swam in front of her and filled the car. Colm, age four, running up to her from the waves, laughing as he wrapped his cold, wet arms around her head, all baby fat and wild laughter. His small face pressed against her cheek, the way he grabbed her whole face to kiss her, the three words whispered over and over again.

It was all too much.

Mary pretended not to hear her crying. In truth, she was frozen. Nobody had cried in front of her for a very long time. She didn't know what to do; was it better to pretend it wasn't happening, or would that seem cold? Mary fiddled with her purse and considered.

After a minute, she reached over. 'Boiled sweet?' she asked, as kindly as she could.

And as Frances looked at the old woman next to her, clearly trying her best, her severe face pulled into her best approximation of sympathy but looking more like Winston Churchill, she couldn't help but laugh again. And this time, Mary joined her.

Then they got out of the car.

*

As Emma drove to the hospital, Jimmy was unnaturally quiet in the passenger seat. The few times he spoke, it was in a flat, lifeless tone.

Emma tried to keep his spirits up, distracting him with stories about the pensioners arguing in the library. All she could get was 'Oh, goodness' in return. She gave up.

But then a funny thing happened. As they neared the hospital and she saw the familiar building in the distance, suddenly the dynamic flipped. Suddenly, it was Jimmy telling funny stories and Emma responding in a flat tone.

'Did I ever tell you about the time me and Mossie Black tried distilling poitín?' he asked. 'Well, the end result was that we blew up half of Rabbit Island and had to disappear into the city for a few weeks. It all started ...'

As he talked, Emma glanced at him. This man was grieving, and dreading the hospital just as much as she was – more so, really – but he was stepping out of his own pain to try and help her through hers. She knew, again, that she was doing the right thing. She tried to join in.

'How's Charley?' she asked, as casually as she could. But it was clearly the wrong topic to try.

'Who knows?' he said, a slight bitterness in his voice. 'We haven't seen him yet.'

Emma frowned. 'That's not like Charley.'

'No, it's not.'

It struck Emma as odd that Charley had rushed home, only to then avoid his family. Was he here for a different reason? The Charley she remembered would've been more than able to support his grieving family. He'd done it before.

Charley's mum had died when he was ten. For some boys, it would've made them angry or bitter or closed off. But for Charley, it made him even more sensitive; more willing to share his emotions and help others with theirs. If Charley was indeed avoiding his family in their time of need, Emma wasn't sure she recognised this new version of him.

She was going to ask more, but she had to leave it there because they had arrived at the hospital.

Inside, on the ward, Jimmy only took a minute to get the guard's full attention, another minute to get his trust and then three minutes later, the way was clear. Emma slipped through the door alone, closing it quietly behind her.

Colm Thornton lay in the hospital bed in front of her.

Chapter 30

For the second time in a week, Frances sat in the chair in front of Ian Flesk's desk, staring with open dislike at the man. But this time, she wasn't alone. Mary was sat next to her. It seemed that the appearance of Mary had a transformative effect on Ian – when she walked in, it was like he had seen a ghost. He hastened out of his seat to greet them, but Mary stopped him.

'So,' she spat, 'are you going to do what's right?'

Frances watched Ian's face change. In the car, Mary warned that judging from the risk he was taking that there must be serious money on the table. And if there was enough money, Ian wouldn't care about making waves in the village.

From the guarded expression on Ian's face now, Frances knew Mary was right.

'Now, ladies,' he said amicably, 'I'm sure I have no idea what you're talking about.' He looked at Frances. 'Ms Bennett came in here the other day, complaining about some deed she'd seen that belonged to your son. I looked it up. I checked with Colm's parish and his bank in Belfast, and there were no records.'

He let that sink in. To an outsider, it might sound perfectly innocent; but his point was clear – there were no other records, nothing to corroborate their story. As long as he had the original, it was just like Mary said – his word against theirs.

'You bastard,' Mary spat again. But Frances could see she was rattled. And Ian could see it too. He ignored her and leaned over to Frances, a smile resting easily on his oily face.

'Please don't tell me you've let this woman convince you of her delusion. Women of her age, of her temperament, they find it hard to adjust to change. She's nothing but a disgruntled employee – a disgruntled *former* employee now, I should imagine – seizing on a vulnerable woman's grief—'

'That's not true!' Mary shouted. Her whole body slumped, like she was trying to disappear into the handbag on her lap. 'It's not true,' she said again, her voice small and weak.

And in that moment, Frances truly saw Mary. She leaned over and took her hand. Mary looked at her gratefully, and Frances smiled at her. Then, she turned to Ian.

'This morning, I called a solicitor of my own,' she said coldly.

Ian frowned. 'But why would you ... I've been your solicitor for years, and there's nobody—'

Frances held up her hand. 'A solicitor in Belfast,' she said. 'And I've been speaking to the guards as well.' And she watched as the colour drained from Ian's face. She nodded. 'Oh yes. Because if you remember, there's still a murder that needs to be answered for. They're looking for a motive. Looking for a smoking gun, as it were. And a property like that, that's an awful big motive, wouldn't you say?' She paused for effect. 'So, I don't think we'll be needing any advice from yourself, whether or not you do the right thing.'

For a moment, Frances thought she had won. That it was over, that she could bluff it out and he'd simply hand over the deed. For a moment, he looked defeated. He ran his hands through his hair, and he looked wildly around the desk, as if to find something to steady himself. But Ian was made of stronger stuff; Frances could see the gears turning as he pulled himself back together.

'Well then,' he said, smiling with just a slight hint of indecision. 'I'll get in touch with your contact at the garda station, then. What was his name?'

Frances could feel him searching her face for a reaction, to see if she was indeed bluffing. She held steady.

'He'll be in touch, Ian,' she said, standing up decisively and cinching her jacket tightly around her waist. 'I can promise you that. And don't think for a second I don't already know you have Sergeant Noonan in your pocket.'

She saw that blow land – but then his expression darkened and became hard to read. He jerked his head to the door.

'Out,' he said hoarsely.

Frances turned on her heel and strode out of the office, Mary close behind.

'What do you think?' Frances asked as they stepped back out into the fresh air. 'Do you think he believed me?'

Mary considered. 'Well, it'd be an awful big risk for him not to,' she said. Then she added darkly, 'But he might not see us as much of a risk.'

Either way anyway, they both knew it didn't matter whether he believed them or not.

The cards were all on the table now.

Chapter 31

Colm's hospital room was dark; the blinds were pulled shut, and all the lamps were off. After the brightness of the corridor, Emma had to squint. She could just make out the shape of a man in the bed.

'Colm?' she said quietly. The dark shape shifted slightly. 'Colm?' she said again.

The shape shifted again, this time to an upright sitting position. Emma's eyes had adjusted – she could see him clearly now.

Colm's hair was unkempt; his eyes were red-rimmed and dark, but he looked alert. His face was handsome, even in its current state – pale and unshaven. The resemblance to Charley struck her again.

'Sorry, Mr Thornton. I'm Emma—'

'You're not a nurse,' he said, frowning at her. 'You're not a guard either.'

'That's correct. My name is Emma—'

Colm's expression darkened. 'You're a journalist, aren't you?'

Emma quickly sat down next to the bed. She pulled the chair closer to him.

'I'm a librarian, Colm.' She waited for him to laugh, but he didn't, so she took a deep breath. 'Your parents sent me.'

Colm stared at her. One of the monitors beeped softly. Emma looked anxiously towards the door, but no one came in.

'Colm?'

He rolled over onto his side, turning his back to her. 'Go away.'

'But Colm, if I could just explain—'

'Do you know what happened this morning?' The pillow muffled his voice, but his words were hard and bitter. 'A garda sergeant came in and charged me with murder. Never asked me a single question. Just read me the charges and then handcuffed me to the bed.' He raised his right hand angrily to show the manacle. 'I don't want—'

Then he stopped. He lowered his hand and exhaled heavily. His shoulders slumped. 'Just please,' he said quietly, 'go away.'

But Emma wasn't going to give up so easily.

'I know it's going to be hard to see your parents,' she said. 'But Colm – they believe you're innocent.' He rolled over and looked at her; she nodded. 'That's why I'm here. But I need you to trust me. I need you to trust your parents.'

Colm's face clouded again.

'I left a long time ago. Even before all of this – I don't know what I'd even say.'

Emma shook her head. 'Then don't say anything, Colm. They're your parents, they love you.'

'Then where are they now?' he asked suddenly, as if trying to convince himself. 'Why are you here instead of them?'

Emma pointed at the door. 'Your dad is out there right now, distracting the guard, so I can sit here talking to you.'

Colm glanced at the door, as if expecting to see Jimmy's face peering around it. He was silent for a moment. When he finally spoke, his voice was low and careful.

And scared. Very scared.

'These are bad people, Emma. I don't want my parents getting caught up in the middle of it.'

'They already are,' Emma said gently. 'They're your parents, Colm. No matter what, they're going to be involved.' She leaned in. 'You need to tell me the name of the other man in the house that night. Who shot Mr Hollis?'

But Colm had his eyes shut tight.

'Tell them to leave it alone,' he pleaded. 'Leave me alone. It's my shit to clean up.'

Another monitor started beeping; Colm's chest heaved. His knuckles were white; he twisted the bed sheet in pain. Emma knew she only had seconds.

'Colm! Who was the third man, Colm?'

The door burst open and the guard from the hall shouted, 'Hey!'

She could hear the sound of a struggle as Jimmy tried to hold him back. Emma sprang to her feet and took Colm by the shoulders. His gown was damp, and his hair was matted with sweat, but she leaned in close anyway.

'My mam ran off when I was six years old.' His eyes flicked to hers, and she nodded. 'I know what it's like to lose someone you love. So, trust me when I tell you – no matter what happened, no matter what you did, they're not going to stay out of it.'

A hand grabbed her shoulder roughly and pulled her backwards, off the bed and towards the door.

'For feck's sake, lady, you're not allowed—'

She heard Jimmy bellow.

'Hey! C'mere out of that – keep your hands off her!'

In the midst of the scuffling, shouting and swearing came a tiny voice.

'Dad?'

Jimmy froze, one arm wrapped around the guard's chest, the other shielding his face.

'Colm? Oh my God – Colm!'

The hand on Emma's shoulder disappeared. She could hear a hard scuffle behind her as Jimmy struggled to get past the guard into the room.

Emma took advantage of the distraction. 'Colm,' she said, snapping her fingers to get his attention. 'Colm!'

He looked at her, still bewildered. A whole range of emotions played out across his face, but Emma didn't have time to try for interpretation.

'Who was the third man, Colm?' A thought occurred to her. 'Was it Flesk? Ian Flesk?' There was no flicker of recognition in Colm's eyes, just confusion.

'Ian Flesk?' he repeated.

'The solicitor?' Emma tried. 'Big man, greasy hair. Ian Flesk.'

But Colm shook his head. 'No, I've never heard of Ian Flesk.'

'Then who was it?' she cried.

But before he could answer, a large arm folded around Emma's neck, and she was dragged backwards again, this time for good, out of the room.

*

After he got Emma and Jimmy back into the corridor, the guard didn't mince words.

'For feck's sake, Jimmy,' he said angrily. 'I could have you arrested right here.'

Jimmy rubbed his jaw tenderly. 'Yes, and how would that look?' he asked bitterly. 'I can see the headlines: "Pensioner visits critically wounded son in hospital – is violently removed and then charged".'

Emma had never seen Jimmy so upset. She had also never realised quite how large he was. The guard was clearly having the same epiphany.

'Look, I don't want any trouble,' he said, raising his hands in surrender. 'I'm just doing my job. And nobody's allowed in. That's all. Just my job.'

Jimmy snorted angrily. 'Some fecking job. You on the same take as Noonan?'

The guard's eyes flared, and Emma quickly steered Jimmy towards the door.

'Go out to the car, I'll be with you in a second.'

She turned and came back to the guard, whose eyes were still blazing.

'On the take – how dare he, how—'

Emma cut him off. 'He's upset. That was the first time he's seen his son in thirty years, and you manhandled him out the door.'

The guard grudgingly conceded the point. Emma leaned in.

'But what's with the handcuffs? He's clearly the victim here, and even if he wasn't – he's only just a few hours out of a coma. He's not exactly flight-risk material.'

The guard shrugged. 'Boss's orders,' he said. Then he hesitated. 'Look, I agree with you. But I have to do what I'm told. I can't lose my job.'

Emma looked at him – judging from the tight fold of his collar, he was only a few weeks on the job. The starch only lasted five or six washes. She nodded.

'I understand. I'm just trying to get to the bottom of it all, that's it. Like, why is the sergeant rushing this through? Colm said he didn't ask him a single question, just charged him. That's strange, isn't it?'

'It is,' the guard agreed. 'They're trying to rush him out of here as well.'

Emma stared at the guard.

'What? But he's barely healed – they want to move him to jail?' The guard nodded.

'Orders came down last night. Sergeant's insisting. He'll be behind bars in a day, maybe two.'

Chapter 32

The day slid down into the sea and pulled the evening further up into the sky. The shadows grew longer, the fields erupted in murmurations of black birds and golden sun. Emma made her way through the village to the library. It had just gone past closing, but she wanted to think. She also wanted to avoid her dad. He didn't know she was investigating, and she'd like to keep that true as long as possible. As she got closer, she could see someone standing at the door to the library. It was Charley.

'Looking to renew your membership?' she asked.

'Something like that,' he said. 'But I'll settle for a cup of tea.'

Emma was about to smile, but then she remembered the crestfallen look on Jimmy's face on the car ride home. 'Why haven't you seen your grandparents yet?'

Charley's face fell. 'Ah, well.' He shifted uncomfortably. 'I've not been by the house yet ...'

'Jesus, Charley.' She tried to keep the exasperation out of her voice but didn't quite manage it.

'I know. I know. I keep meaning to, I just ... I wouldn't know what to say.'

'You don't need to say anything. Just be there.'

Charley nodded. 'I'll go tonight.'

'Go now.'

Charley straightened up and then he looked at her keenly. Not up and down, just straight at her. Like he used to.

'Emma Daly,' he said quietly, 'you haven't changed a bit.'

After he left, Emma stood there in the doorway for a moment. She mulled over his last statement. Was she the same? Maybe. Maybe he was right. And sure, maybe that was a good thing. But maybe – maybe that was a problem. *The* problem.

But what the hell was going on with him?

As she walked back into the library, she said, 'You can come out now, Maeve.'

But to her surprise, it wasn't Maeve hiding in the darkened library.

It was Mary. And she had a plan.

'I want to break into Ian Flesk's office,' Mary said simply. 'Tonight, after dark.'

Emma frowned.

'You want to find the original deed?'

'Yes.'

'Then why not try Mr Hollis's house again?'

Mary shook her head. 'There's something else going on here, Emma. You should've seen Ian this afternoon.' She shuddered. 'I've seen greed, and I've seen him pursuing money, but this is something else. He was frightened.'

'Well, that's to be expected. He'll go to jail if anybody finds out he tried to steal—'

'He doesn't care about that,' Mary said impatiently. 'Frances threatened to call the guards, then and there, and he didn't budge.' She leaned in, her voice low, even though they were alone in the library. 'I think there's something big happening in the village,

Emma, and Colm's deed is just the tip of the iceberg. I think even Ian is scared of something.'

Emma remembered Colm's words: *These are bad people, Emma.*

'And you think Ian's got the answers in his office?'

Mary nodded. 'I only saw Colm's deed because he wasn't expecting it. He had no idea that Hollis had sold the property to Colm until that deed landed on my desk. I bet he's got the rest of the paperwork, the paper trail to the whole thing, hidden away somewhere in his office – off the books.'

Emma thought for a minute. Only this morning, she'd dismissed breaking into Mr Hollis's house as too crazy, too risky. And that was an empty house in the middle of the country. Ian Flesk's office was in the middle of Main Street in town. He was sure to have security or locks, at least. It was madness.

Then she remembered Jimmy's face in the car again. And Colm's fear and shame.

She took a deep breath.

'Okay,' she said. 'How do you propose we do it?'

Mary took a boiled sweet out of her purse and popped it into her mouth. 'I thought you'd never ask.'

Chapter 33

The air was strangely quiet, as if all the birds had been startled into silence – the gentle rustle of the wind rocked back and forth across the grass-heavy field that surrounded Frances and Jimmy's house. Connie should've cut the field weeks ago – it was nearly November, and he wasn't a lazy man. It was possible that he knew something, some disturbance of the natural cycle of things – that some hidden pendulum hung suspended in the air somewhere, waiting to crash back down into its orbit.

Maybe Connie knew the end was coming. Or maybe he'd forgotten. You could never tell, and Connie wouldn't tell you one way or another.

You just had to wait.

*

Town was damp with rain; the road was slick and cracked. The night felt heavy, like a towel flung down to hang on the streetlamps. It wasn't late – just gone eight o'clock.

'Shouldn't we wait until later?' Emma asked uneasily. 'Isn't this a middle-of-the-night sort of thing?'

But Mary shook her head.

'We'll be going in through the front door. Hiding in plain sight. I've still got my key, and if anyone sees us they'll just think I'm doing some last-minute filing – or retrieving a Danish, or something like that.'

Emma took a deep breath. But it wasn't fear she felt – it was excitement.

'Do you remember that one adventure where Sherlock breaks into a house?'

Mary smiled. 'Charles Augustus Milverton.'

Milverton was a notorious blackmailer and had backed one of Sherlock's clients into a corner. So, Sherlock and Watson broke into the house and stole the evidence.

'He said he'd always imagined he'd make a first-rate burglar, and he was right,' Emma said, grinning. 'I don't know why, but I always loved that story.'

'Same reason as everyone else,' Mary said, 'You want to know if you've got the stomach for it.' She took a quick look around the corner of the building. There was no one in sight – the road was clear. Satisfied, Mary clutched her bag to her chest and nodded at Emma. 'Now let's go and find out.' They hurried across the street, stepping around the hazy yellow edges of the streetlamps. Mary had the key ready in her hand; they barely paused in the doorway and then they were gone.

*

From across the road, a man watched them disappear into the office. Then, he too looked up and down the street.

A car passed. Then another. In the faint distance, a dog barked. A woman stepped outside her flat and lit a cigarette.

No matter, thought the stranger. *I've got time.*

He reached into his coat pocket; the handle of the claw-hammer was cold.

The street would clear soon. He had time.

*

Frances didn't know what to make of Charley when she opened the door and found him standing there, shame-faced.

'Well,' she said, after a long pause. 'About time.'

Then she pulled him into a hug, laughing and kissing him.

Charley had been young when he left for London. He'd always been different from his father. Adam was solid and dependable, the kind of man everyone looked to in an emergency. And as a kid, Charley had shown flashes of the same – just flashes, though. Mainly, he was wild.

But as Frances reminded herself now – who wasn't wild as a young one? It took a bit of wild to break free from a village like Kilcraven – it was a matter of self-preservation.

Looking at Charley now, as he hugged Jimmy and made himself at home in the sitting room, Frances found herself surprised by the changes she saw in him. He was thoughtful, like his father, but where his father thought calmly, Charley was restless. He had a steady stream of questions, for everything from their letterbox to the type of hob they had, all the way to their herb patch; nothing escaped the leaps of his attention. Charley was halfway through explaining a new way of composting when she finally interrupted.

'Well, that all sounds lovely, Charley.' She patted his cheek fondly. 'But as much as I love to hear about counterclockwise mulching and nitrogen mixtures, I assume you're here to join us for dinner?'

She raised her eyebrow.

'And at least one round of cards?'

Chapter 34

Mary flicked on the light in the office reception area. Emma started to protest, but Mary shook her head.

'Hiding in plain sight, remember?' She strode across the room to Ian's office and quickly unlocked it. She looked at Emma, who was still standing in the doorway. 'Well, come on!'

Ian Flesk clearly had a lot of trust in a locked door. Or at least a lot of trust in his own invincibility.

'Jesus Christ,' Mary said, as she opened another cabinet drawer and pulled out a file. 'He doesn't lock any of this up? This is the Porter case – just sitting here.' She whistled. 'I can't imagine Ger would be too happy to know all the sordid details were here, in my hand.' Mary considered it for a moment.

Emma snapped her fingers.

'Mary!' she said urgently, bringing her back to the task at hand. 'Clock's ticking, remember?' Emma looked helplessly at the drawer she had pulled open. 'I don't know what I'm looking for here.'

Mary put the file back and closed the drawer. She crossed the room to a small cabinet.

'This one was open, that day I came in about the deed.'

Emma examined it. It was locked. Maybe Ian wasn't as stupid as they thought. 'One minute,' Emma said, as she pulled a bobby pin from her hair.

Mary looked at her incredulously. 'No way you can pick a lock with a bloody bobby pin.'

Less than a minute later, Emma slid the drawer open. She tossed the bobby pin to a speechless Mary and grinned. 'You'd be amazed – the books we get in the library.'

Mary turned to the drawers and started rifling through the files. 'She'll be robbing banks with a stocking next,' she muttered. But she was grinning too. Then, she held up a file. 'Bingo!'

She opened it, and her face fell.

'Is it the deed?' Emma asked excitedly.

'No,' Mary said slowly. 'He must have that hidden away. This ... it's the receipt. The person who paid for the property.'

'And?' Emma waited. 'Who was it?'

Mary didn't answer; she was reading quickly through the paperwork.

'Mary?'

But Mary shook her head. 'Nobody bought it,' she said, like she didn't believe the words herself.

'What are you talking about?' Emma frowned. 'Colm bought it.'

Mary nodded. 'Yes, sorry, you're right,' she said hastily. 'Colm bought it. Or at least, the ownership was transferred to him.'

Emma wasn't following. 'Right ...' she said slowly. 'Is there a difference?'

Mary handed her the file. 'See for yourself.'

Emma skimmed the file. 'This says that nobody paid for it.' She frowned. '*Nobody*.'

Mary nodded. 'Hollis gave it to Colm for free. He made it look like it was sold – the paper I saw made it clear that it was a normal sale. But he wrote it off. *He gave it to Colm for free.*'

'But he'd never met Colm before,' Emma said. 'Why would he do that?'

Mary gestured at the file cabinet. 'My guess? The answer is in here somewhere.'

Emma looked at the clock. They'd been there for four minutes; they'd agreed to stay no longer than ten. She nodded. 'Then let's get reading.'

Mary handed her a file. 'Spoken like a true librarian.'

*

Neither of them heard the soft click as the front door of the building opened then closed. Neither of them heard the soft tread of footsteps on the reception carpet.

Neither of them heard the stranger creep closer to the office door.

And then he reached for the handle.

Chapter 35

Sunday roast was a serious affair at Frances and Jimmy's house, especially on Saturdays. Potatoes and greens and carrots and lamb chops with honey, all heavy enough to make the table buckle, drenched in butter and salt. They had beer and wine and sherry and whiskey and a trifle for afters.

'This isn't anything special for you,' Frances told Charley, seeming to read his mind as he looked at the table. 'It's always like this. Since we retired, Jimmy and I don't move a muscle the whole day – we just sit here eating and drinking.'

'Don't move a muscle the next day either,' laughed Jimmy, already piling carrots onto his plate. 'Can barely lift our head off the pillow. But hell, where would we be going anyway?'

Charley knew they were lying for his benefit – he knew these were all the meals that neighbours had brought them after the news about Colm, and they'd laid on extra for him. He had seen the final notices on the fridge too, before Frances whipped them off and disappeared them into a cupboard somewhere. But he knew better than to say anything.

As they ate, they talked about anything and everything, within reason. They talked about the big storm and the way the fields were looking and what they thought might happen to the fishermen, as well as the stretch in the evening. They talked about Charley's work in London and how busy Adam was. They did not talk about Colm. Eventually the talk made its way to what Charley was planning to do next.

'And would you not take your chances in London?' Jimmy asked. 'Whatever you want to do, there's more of it there.' He inspected his whiskey glass, trying to keep his voice casual as he asked the question everyone wanted to know. 'Something drive you off?' He waited, but Charley didn't answer; he kept his eyes down and busied himself pushing potatoes around his plate. So, Jimmy tried a different tack. 'Or something keeping you here?'

Frances shrugged. 'Or some*one*, maybe?'

Charley blushed and started inspecting his own whiskey glass. Frances winked at Jimmy. 'You know, Emma Daly is looking very well these days, isn't she, Jimmy?'

Charley turned brighter red and didn't look up.

'Ah yes,' Jimmy said, winking back at Frances and pretending to think hard. 'And now that I think about it – you and Emma courted for a while, didn't you?' He waited. 'Long ago?'

Charley now looked like he was trying to crawl into his glass of whiskey. He mumbled something. Jimmy put his hand behind his ear. 'Sorry, didn't catch that.'

Frances took pity and shushed him. 'C'mere, leave the poor boy alone.' She stood up and took down the bottle of sherry. Then she added, 'She's single too, if you were asking.'

Charley didn't answer.

'You know,' Frances said after a while, 'we might be old, but Jimmy and I ... we can give advice on more than just your career – if you understand me?'

Charley started to mumble, to change the subject, but stopped himself. He'd been tossing and turning over it all. Wondering if Emma had felt the same as him – wondering what it is exactly that he had felt.

'I like her,' he said simply. Frances and Jimmy both beamed at him. 'I don't know what to do about it, but I like her. And I think she likes me.' Quickly running out of confidence as he heard how silly he sounded, like a child plucking flower petals, he continued, 'It's just a bad time, I think.'

Frances and Jimmy nodded quietly, and the three of them sat in the comfortable silence that followed Charley's revelation. Unexpectedly, it was Jimmy who broke the silence.

'Isn't it always?'

There was a pause, then they all burst into laughter. And just like that, Charley felt a heavy weight lift off of his shoulders. Jimmy stood up. 'Who's up for a game of Graveyard?' he asked, crossing to the kitchen. 'But first, one for the road?' He held up the bottle, and Charley nodded.

*

The evening turned to night; the chill settled into the clover and crept up along the edges of the window. They moved from the kitchen to the sitting room, and they were all still heavy with dinner. As they sat, comfortably reclining, Charley finally brought up the subject he'd been avoiding.

'Granddad – when I talked to Emma at Nolan's ...' He hesitated. 'She said you had asked her to look into Colm. Into what happened, like. Is that true?'

Jimmy sighed. 'You both must think I'm barmy – getting my hopes up. I know your dad does.'

Charley shook his head. 'God, no, Granddad. I just wanted to make sure you were okay. With ... with everything.'

Jimmy reached over and took Frances's hand. Then he turned to Charley.

'We've been having a bit of a rough go of it lately.'

Charley nodded grimly. 'I know. What you had to go through, with Uncle Colm, I'm so—'

Frances shook her head. 'No, it wasn't just with Colm.' She looked sadly over at Jimmy. 'I'm afraid we've been having a bit of trouble. Financially, I mean.' Seeing Charley start to say something, she spoke sternly. 'And I'm only telling you this because you're in no position to help us at all. Do you understand? Not a word to your father – he's in no position to help either.'

Charley started to protest, but he saw Jimmy's expression: *Don't bother*. Charley reluctantly agreed.

Frances took a deep breath. Then, with Jimmy holding her hand tightly, she told Charley the whole story. Jimmy getting laid off, and his pension – their life savings – disappearing. They had a bit from the state pension, and Frances had earned a few stamps herself, but it wasn't nearly enough.

'We've applied to every job that's come up,' Jimmy said, forcing a smile. 'Your grandmother here was nearly a night watchman.'

'Jesus,' Charley said.

Frances nodded. 'That was what the hotel said too.'

Jimmy cleared the small table, piling all the cups and saucers onto the tray, and nodded at Frances. 'Go on, tell him the rest – about Colm's property.'

After she finished, Charley was so mad that he was practically hopping around the room. 'But that's bullshit, Granny, that's bullshit!' he cried. 'You know as well as I do that Ian's trying to pull a fast one. Dad's always hated him – he's a prick.'

Frances and Jimmy both nodded wearily.

'We agree, son,' Jimmy said, patting the seat next to him on the couch. He waited until Charley reluctantly sat down. 'But there's a big difference between knowing and proving.'

Frances, seeing that Charley wasn't going to be dissuaded so easily, took a different tack. 'Do you believe in signs, Charley?' she asked. 'Do you believe that God can send us signs?'

He shrugged. 'What do you mean?'

'Well, before Colm reappeared, we never had so much as a mouse in our back garden. And then, out of nowhere, just as I'm coming down the road, thinking about Colm, a baby fox comes crashing in.' She smiled weakly. 'When I first saw her, I thought she looked like Colm. Lost. And scared ...' She paused. 'Then, she came back. Jimmy heard her running around the back garden the other day, when Mary visited us. And I knew it wasn't a coincidence. It was a sign from Colm.' A tear ran down her cheek. 'From my baby.'

*

After Adam, Frances and Jimmy had three miscarriages in four years. The doctors couldn't explain why; each time, they just assured Frances it was just something that happened sometimes. And then, she got pregnant one last time. At first, things went well. She carried her baby for seven months. Long enough that they named him. Colm. And then, one night, the world fell apart in a disarray of boiled water and ripped-up sheets. When the priest came in, she thought he was there for her confession.

'I just couldn't understand what he was talking about. Last rites.' She looked up at Charley, her voice cracking. 'Last rites for who?' She tried to hold back a sob. 'Not Colm. Not my Colm.'

Jimmy held her as she cried, tears in his eyes too. For a long time, they stayed there, holding onto one another. After so many years, it was all they could do.

'And of course, they were wrong. Colm made it ...' Frances shook her head, wiping her eyes with the backs of her hands. 'But he was so sick – for nearly two years. And after a scare like that, and how it brought back all the memories of the other times, I wasn't right. I wasn't right for a long time. And I keep thinking – that I wasn't there for Colm. Because I was grieving. He was only a little boy himself; a sick little boy. I should've been there for him.' She covered her mouth with her hand, her eyes shut in pain. 'Maybe he ran away because he thought I abandoned him. And maybe that fox coming here was a reminder that I don't deserve—'

'C'mere out of that,' Jimmy said firmly. 'You were there for him, you always were.'

Frances shrugged helplessly. 'I hope so,' she whispered. 'I hope so.' Charley took her hand and squeezed it. 'He'll tell you that himself,' he said. 'Because if there's anyone that can get him out of this, it's Emma. She'll make it right.'

Chapter 36

'Jesus,' Mary kept saying. She'd flipped through four or five of the files, and her disbelief seemed to grow with each one. 'Jesus Christ.'

'What is it?'

Emma was reading a file too, but she couldn't make heads or tails of it. Or at least, what she could understand didn't seem out of the ordinary. It was just a load of real estate transactions, the same as the other two files she had read. None of them seemed to be big transactions either – if anything, they seemed smaller than Colm's property.

'Mary?'

Mary didn't answer; she kept flipping through the pages, muttering to herself. 'They can't seriously … oh my God, they did. The bastards. The absolute bastards …'

Emma eyed the clock anxiously. They were three minutes over. Any second now, someone could come bursting in here, demanding to know what they were doing, breaking into a solicitor's office after hours. In fact, was that a noise she heard in the hallway? Yes, that was definitely a noise.

'Mary!' she hissed urgently. 'Time to go!'

Mary looked at her in confusion. Then she snapped back into focus. 'Right, so,' she said. 'Let's go.' She started shoving files into her black bag.

'What are you doing?' Emma demanded. 'We can't take anything with us – he'll know he's been robbed. That we were here.'

Mary shook her head. 'I told you – there's something big going on here. And whatever it is, the answer's in here.' She held up the files and shook them. 'I can see the outline of it, but only just. If I could just dig through them a bit more ...'

But Emma wasn't moved.

'Any trouble will blow back on Frances and Jimmy.' She reached for the files. 'I'm sorry – you have to leave them here.'

Right at that second, there was a muffled thud from behind the office door. Emma spun towards the noise. Mary took advantage of her distraction to stuff the papers from the file she was reading into her waistband under her blouse, and pulled her coat tight. When Emma turned back around, Mary was prim and proper – smoothing down the front of her coat.

'Come on,' Emma whispered.

The reception area was empty – all shadows and silence – but Emma and Mary didn't waste any time looking around. They raced to the front door and out into the street, Mary remembering at the last second to lock the door behind her. Just before they got into the car, though, Emma thought of something.

'Hold on,' she said. 'Let me see your bag.'

Mary huffed impatiently. 'Here,' she said, and thrust the bag towards Emma. After Emma saw that there were no files in it – gingerly avoiding the bolt – she handed it back sheepishly.

'Sorry,' she said, as she started the car. 'Just had to be sure. I don't want to get Frances and Jimmy in trouble.'

Mary nodded. 'I know.'

And as discreetly as she could, she touched the papers tucked roughly into her waistband, to make sure they were still there.

*

After the excitement of the night, Mary and Emma went their separate ways without saying much. They thought they could go through it all in the daylight, and besides, the adrenaline had worn off and left them exhausted. Mary needed her bed, and Emma needed a drink. So, after Emma dropped Mary off at her house, she went to Nolan's.

Frances, Jimmy and Charley were also heading to Nolan's in search of a drink.

Nobody had noticed the man standing in the shadows across the street from Mary's house. A cigarette burned in his mouth; the rest of the pack lay scattered around his feet. He stood for a long time, watching.

Waiting.

He'd been all set to catch them in the solicitor's office – he was reaching for the door handle when a commotion outside on the street spooked him. He nearly dropped his clawhammer, and then he heard Emma ask about the sound. So, he'd bolted.

But now he was in position. He had her. He'd been watching the house for nearly an hour – Mary clearly lived alone. He broke in through an open window near the back of the house.

And then he waited.

And then, as the stranger sat in the dark and empty home, the front door swung open.

Mary Bennett was home.

Chapter 37

Before they built the causeway, the harbour ran right up to Kilcraven's main road. If the tide was heavy – from a full moon or a winter rain, for example – the ocean found its way into back gardens. And if a heavy tide ever met a southeasterly wind, the ocean rose and rose and rose until it seeped through the floorboards in the village.

The summer of 1967 there was a flood so bad the water came up to the fourth step in the old post office, where Clare and John Hurley lived. It was so bad, it carried Clare's piano out the front door. They found it the next day, washed up beside Nolan's pub.

It was an odd thing. Pianos, generally, don't get washed away in a few feet of water. The flood had, of course, carried lots of odds and ends away; lots of small odds and ends, though – lamps and shoes and things like that. But then, there was the piano. How the feck did a piano make its way out the door and up the street?

Clare and John's house shared a back garden wall with the old Casey's pub. If there was ever a raid on Casey's for a lock-in or a noise violation, everyone would pile out the back of the pub and into Clare and John's house, where they'd all exit through the front door. It was hard to know what the guards made of fifty-odd people streaming out of a small house at three in the morning, but they always found Casey's empty, so they couldn't prove anything.

Clare didn't mind that too much – the noise and the commotion sometimes woke her up, but John was usually somewhere in the crowd and told them to keep it down. Besides, she didn't want anyone getting in trouble.

But Clare had her limits – the times when the crowd didn't leave straight out the front door. They'd pile over the wall from the pub and set up shop in her sitting room, to play the piano and sing rebel songs until the morning. Clare was sympathetic; she was a republican herself – but she preferred to be one during business hours.

Then, one night, a crowd piled over the wall and started banging on their back door. John wasn't with them. He wasn't even home. There was no raid or anything; they just wanted a sing-song. Clare, to put it mildly, was not subtle in expressing her displeasure, and the crowd departed. But Clare had had enough.

She was sure the problem was the piano. But she couldn't throw it away – it had been her mother's pride and joy. No, she couldn't just throw it away.

But Clare. Had. Had. Enough.

And then, a few nights later, the storm came.

To this day, there are those in the village who claim they saw the piano floating down the street all by itself, caught up in the swirling currents. And there are those who swear they saw Clare wading out into the middle of the flood, pushing that damn piano and whistling cheerfully as the rain lashed down all around her.

Clare, for her part, swore she never knew a thing about it. Like most mysteries, it was a bit of both, and neither.

Either way anyway, that was how Nolan's got its piano, and why, if you want to play it, you have to shift the notes up half a step – water damage.

*

That night, when word went around that Frances and Jimmy were finally out again, back in the pub and ready to be cheered up, nobody arranged anything. There was no mention of a party, or any call to action to rally round. It just sort of happened, the way these things do.

A sudden gust swept from across the harbour, pulling a fine grey mist over the village – like a mother drawing the blanket up over an anxious child.

*

Emma sat for a minute on the bench outside the pub. It was late enough – behind her, Nolan's buckled outwards. It was like all the people inside were pressing their hands against the walls, pushing with all their might. She could hear the wild laughter and friendly shouting, muffled by the heavy brown door. The blinds were already drawn; the door was locked. The door opened; Emma's heart skipped a beat. But it wasn't Charley, it was a middle-aged man named Graham who sat down on the bench beside her. Graham, a bachelor, never left the house without fixing his hair in the mirror and practising a wide range of facial expressions – but now, he looked troubled.

He asked her for a cigarette, and as he lit it, he nodded up the road and picked up the conversation he seemed to think they were already having.

'I just don't know what happened.' Graham looked mournful. 'The damn thing's still over there.' He pointed down the street: a car sat in the gutter, its hazard lights dazed, muffled in the grey mist. The car was on its side.

Emma gave a low whistle.

'I must've just missed it,' she said. She'd only just sat down outside the front for a minute – or at least ... actually, was it a minute? It was hard to tell. She could've been driving the car herself, for all she knew. Emma turned to ask Graham, but he'd slumped through the door again and into the pub.

'I must've just missed it,' she said again.

Emma stood up, flicked her cigarette and went back into the pub.

*

Mary opened her front door.

She paused. Something wasn't right. The house was dark, with just the shuffle of the streetlamps in the doorway, and her eyes hadn't adjusted. She couldn't see anyone. But she knew. She couldn't even put her finger on what it was – but she knew there was something wrong.

She hung her handbag up on its hook and slowly walked upstairs to her bedroom, frowning. What was it? It was only after she had taken off her coat and sat down on the bed to take her shoes off that she suddenly realised.

When you lose one sense, the others become heightened to adjust for it, that's what they say. That was happening in the darkness of her hallway, but it had also been happening for the last thirty years. She had always opened the door and been alone.

And never once, in thirty years of opening her front door, had she smelled aftershave.

And now, as she sat on the bed upstairs, frozen, she heard a faint noise from downstairs. Her whole body tensed. A creak, then another.

For the first time in thirty years, she was not alone in her house.

*

Late or not, the party was roaring. In the Jazz Age, people called it going *on* a party, rather than going *to* a party, like riding on a wave – and this wave hadn't broken yet. It might've been six at night, it might've been two in the morning, it might've been two weeks from now for all anyone knew or cared.

The room was tight with people; the air was warm and close. Emma had to gently push her way through, mouthing apologies and saying hello. Half of the village greeted her like they hadn't seen her in months, the other half like they'd been talking two minutes ago. The whole village was here: *the Marlows, hello, the Fitzgeralds, hello, no I don't think he's coming down, hello Christopher – no, I'd say he's gone to bed; yes; yes; oh, will do, of course; the Melvilles here, I know, wasn't that funny?* Everyone moved like they were tied to a string and occasionally jerked from side to side. More beer was spilled than drunk. *If I could just squeeze by – Jesus, Stephen, you're looking well, no stay here bai – no, herself – oh; oh; I'm sorry there – I'm sorry – sorry, could I? Cheers.*

Emma found Frances and Jimmy by the bar; she tried to keep her eyes from roving across the pub, trying to catch a glimpse of broad shoulders and tanned arms and—

'Emma!' Frances cried. 'Darling, I'm so sorry for bursting in earlier.' Emma laughed and waved it off. It was easy; she had no idea what Frances was talking about. Jimmy hopped up and offered her his bar stool, which she accepted gratefully.

'How's the form, love?' Jimmy was busy rummaging in Frances's handbag for change. 'What happened – oh! Is Frances telling you about the fox cub?' His entire arm disappeared into the handbag, feeling back and forth. 'Fecking thing. Scared me half to death, then disappeared. But today, the bugger ate one of the apples I left out for it. And that's the main thing, isn't it? Ha, here we go!' He produced a pound with a flourish, gave Frances a kiss and then wandered away in the direction of the pool table, still clutching the handbag.

Frances watched him, then raised an eyebrow to Emma and burst out laughing. 'I'd apologise for him,' she said, 'but I love him too much.'

Emma grinned. 'How's he liking *The Sea Wolf*?'

Frances rolled her eyes. 'You couldn't have given him something else, like? He's going around asking to have raw meat for tea, like he's Jack London or something.' She snorted. 'Poor thing couldn't be further from it. Could you get him back on the Binchy?'

Emma laughed. 'I'll try my best. The man seems to like his ships, though.' Then, staring at her pint and trying to keep her tone casual, she asked, 'So, is Charley here?'

Frances waved her hand distractedly.

'He is. And I'd say he won't be leaving anytime soon now.'

Emma frowned. 'What about his girlfriend?'

Frances turned in her seat to face Emma and smiled. 'He doesn't have a girlfriend, Emma.' She raised an eyebrow. 'In case you weren't just asking about his schedule.'

Emma turned red and kept her eyes on her pint.

Then Frances sobered up. In tone, at least. 'C'mere to me. Thanks for that ... helping us out. I mean it.'

Emma flushed and approached the topic of Colm and how Frances was getting on, but Frances just nodded and patted her hand, so Emma quickly moved on.

'Did Jimmy say you found a fox?'

There was a wonderfully convoluted story that Emma couldn't quite hear – the pub was very loud, and Frances was gesturing to the point of speaking sign language – but as far as she could make out, Jimmy had been chasing a fox cub around the garden. And he wouldn't leave. Or wouldn't come back. It was hard to tell. But Frances looked happy.

'That bastard Ian,' Frances started, 'I'm sure you'll give him hell, though ...'

But Emma was distracted and already drifting politely – across the pub, she saw who was standing next to Jimmy at the pool table.

Charley.

'My round,' Emma said.

*

Graham was telling the men in the corner about the car.

'I just don't know what happened,' he said mournfully. 'Blink of an eye and all that.'

'Jesus,' Charley said. 'Terrible news. We'll need a drink for that.'

'You're not getting one for that,' an elderly friend of the family named Hannah argued. 'Your father said—'

'My father? How can we talk about my father with poor Graham here in such a bad way?' He caught her in a hug and waggled his eyebrows mischievously until she laughed. 'And himself already at home, tucked away in bed.'

Adam had come down to say hello to Frances and Jimmy. After two pints, and feeling that they both looked much improved, he made his excuses. (He'd spotted Billy making his way over to him, a grim look on his face and a well-read pamphlet in his hand.)

'It was looking pretty grim, alright,' Graham said. 'And Jesus, the thought of telling my dad what happened.'

Graham said that when he told his dad, he expected a fierce argument. Maybe the belt. But his dad never said a word, he just took a deep breath and ran his thumb over Graham's forehead, like he was wiping away the cuts.

'He didn't even ask to go out and see the car after,' Graham said, in a tone of wonder. 'He just patted me on the back and bought me a pint.'

'Of course he did,' Hannah said firmly. 'At the end of the day, a car is a car, and a son is a son.' She looked pointedly at Charley. 'Even when the son makes an ass of himself.'

And nobody mentioned the fact that Graham's father, a quiet man who'd never raised a hand to anyone in his life, had been dead for six years now.

Instead, Charley said, 'My round.'

*

'My round,' Emma said.

*

Mary had to think quickly. The movement from downstairs was careful, slow and deliberate. She had an advantage for the moment – the intruder didn't know that she knew he was there. But that wouldn't last long.

She considered the window – she could fling it open and start screaming? No; the whole village was at Nolan's – she could hear the chaos from here. No one would hear her.

She could jump? No; no, she couldn't. *Think, Mary, think.*

Her handbag, with the butcher's bolt inside, was downstairs. It was on the hook, just at the foot of the stairs – she could rush for it. Maybe, if she caught him off guard. And the papers—

Her heart began to thump in her chest.

Of course. They were after the papers. They must've seen Emma and her break into Ian's office. They must have known that Mary took something somehow.

Mary picked the papers up from the floor and skimmed through them quickly again. There was something there, she was sure of it. Clearly, there must be, if it had brought danger to her front doorstep. And not just her doorstep.

Oh God.

Emma. Emma was in danger too.

Mary took a deep breath. She looked down at the papers. And she made a decision.

*

'My round,' Graham said.

*

Somehow, even in a small pub like Nolan's, it took some time for Charley to find Frances and Jimmy again in the crowd.

It was good in a way, to have a lot of alcohol immediately after reuniting after all these years – it meant they could skip a lot of the formalities. A lot of the words too.

Jimmy slapped Charley affectionately on the back. 'Good to have you back, lad, good to have you back.'

Charley laughed and said something they couldn't hear.

'Well said,' Frances said, smiling at him. 'Well said.'

They stood there awhile, grinning and shouting and occasionally bumping into each other as the crowd pushed past them.

It was good to be home, Charley thought. Or said. Or cried.

*

Graham had recovered most of his senses just in time to quickly start losing them again.

'And I swear,' he said, laughing, 'I thought I was nearly after a stroke. I really did. Christ, I was sweating.'

Mrs Porter, who was as old as she was short, snorted.

'Sure, you hit a ditch – what's a ditch?' she asked loudly. 'I've hit a ditch; that's what they're there for.' She hiccupped. 'Sure, I once hit an owl ...'

Emma and Jimmy gave each other a look. Graham started to ask how, but Mrs Porter had only just got started.

'I've hit a rabbit,' she continued, brightening at the thought. 'I've hit so many rabbits I stopped keeping count. And then, Jesus, when I hit the donkey ...' With each animal, the old woman punched the air with her glass of Beamish for emphasis. 'I've hit four cats and two turtles. Made an absolute wreck of my undercarriage, they did.'

'Was that all at once?' Emma whispered to Jimmy, who snorted into his pint.

Mrs Porter was still going; if anything, she'd picked up momentum. 'I've never hit a dog ...'

'What restraint.'

'... but I've hit a rake of goats.'

'Jesus Christ.'

'An absolute rake of goats. And sheep? Of course I've hit a sheep. When you're up in the mountains, bai, you better get ready to hit a sheep or two.' She thought for a moment. 'I've hit six.' And then, clearly feeling that she had made her point, Mrs Porter shot Graham a dark, unimpressed look and then disappeared to the bar for another glass of Beamish.

Nobody knew what to say after that.

'My God,' Jimmy said, in a tone of wonder. 'I mean ... did she hit a zoo? How the feck do you hit an owl with a car?'

'It's not as bad as all that,' Graham said fairly. 'She's, what, eighty-two? She's driving a long time.'

Jimmy shook his head. 'She only got her provisional last year.'

But Graham had already disappeared, following Mrs Porter in the direction of the bar.

Jimmy was still shaking his head. 'Sure, she's never driven further than the shop and back. What fecking mountains is she talking about?'

Emma didn't know what to say to that either so she ordered another round.

*

Emma and Charley finally crossed paths while standing at the bar.

She touched his arm. 'You look good, Charley.'

He shifted. He looked uncomfortable. Or nervous.

Emma put her hand to her mouth. Of course, she'd almost forgotten – the dead body. The murder victim. His uncle was a suspect. His father was a doctor. Was that – that was something, wasn't it, the doctor bit? Jesus, she was tilting.

'I'm sorry for your doctor,' she managed.

There was a long pause.

'I'm not sure I understand—' Charley began, but Emma cut him off.

'So, are you seeing anyone?'

Shit. She hadn't meant to say that. Bad idea. *(Good idea?) No, bad idea. Definitely a bad idea.*

'I'm sorry for the dead body,' she said, getting it right this time.

Or did she?

Charley didn't answer; he changed the subject. Or he cheated on the subject. Or was very French and modern with the subject. (*Jesus fucking Christ,* Emma thought again, *what's wrong with me?*)

'My round,' Charley said.

*

Mary closed the bedroom door behind her. She prayed that Emma was half as clever as she hoped she was. She wished she'd time for more than a half-scribbled scrawl. But it was done now. She'd just have to trust.

Slowly, as quietly as she could, she moved one step at a time. The stairs were shaped like an L, with a small landing at the turn.

Her hands trembled. A bead of sweat traced its way down her forehead and got caught in the hollow of her eye. She blinked hard.

She just needed to make it to the landing. It was only a few stairs to the bottom, then a metre or two to the coat hook. To her handbag and the bolt. To her Mick.

Just a few more steps. Just a few more – from the sitting room, a dull thud. A shout.

And then it happened, all at once and for forever.

*

The pub was blistering. Everybody was either shouting or laughing or singing or crying. Some people were doing all four.

The older crowd, in the back corner of the room on the barrels, had figured out the problem of the younger crowd, what with all that nonsense a couple of years back – wanting the divorce. I mean, Jesus, like. No, the older crowd got right to the heart of the matter. Solved it. They were pretty sure they'd solved it. They hadn't written it down, or maybe they had – Michael? Michael, did you write it down? No? Okay, no, maybe they hadn't written it down, but they had got close. Right? They had it down pat. Somewhere. Pat?

'Was it matchmaking?'

'Sure, sure, sure – all those music videos and shite.'

'Dead right. The TV licences, that's the solution.'

'No, that's the problem.'

'Is it?'

'Is what?'

They argued loudly and agreed quietly – then they agreed loudly and argued quietly – and then they argued loudly again, for a change.

One woman named Aoife was swept up with the excitement. She stood up on a barrel. 'Don't you remember the old matchmaking festivals?' she cried, to a loud disagreement. It seemed a promising start, only nobody in the room was old enough to actually remember the old matchmaking festivals, so Aoife staggered around a few different ideas ('And the farmers ... it was good for the farmers! Or ... yeah, no it was. Wasn't it?') before finishing on a recent story in *The Cork Examiner* about a farmer who called Interpol when he lost his jacket.

'And then, well, I don't know really, I suppose he ... well, I don't know really, but it really made me think.'

She got a rousing cheer from the group, who disagreed strongly.

*

Emma was outside, on the street. Smoking. Minding her own business – a bit of fresh air. Then wham! Out of nowhere, the pub fell over on its side. Just like that – wham! It probably happens all the time. It's probably under-reported. But still, you don't ever expect it to happen to you. One second, you're standing there doing whatever it is you're doing, and the next, the stars swing wildly around, and the pub falls over and the road comes up and smacks you in the face.

'Jesus, Emma,' Graham said as he ran over. A second later, he hauled her up to her feet. The pub was right side up again; he brushed the dirt off her. They sat on the bench, and he told her about crashing his dad's car, and they both looked at the perpendicular car sticking out of the ditch. Emma knew Graham's dad; there was going to be a scene. She followed him back inside.

'My round,' Emma said.

*

'Your round,' Jimmy said.

*

The pub was a collection of sudden and startled reactions. Laughter crawled up the walls. Glasses were raised and the glasses came together and shattered, and a great laugh was cried.

*

'My round,' Jimmy said.

*

'My round,' Charley said.

'What's that?' Emma asked Charley. He stared blankly back at her.

'Huh?'

'What'd you say?' she repeated louder.

'Did I say something?'

'You were saying something about ... well, you said something anyway.'

'Did I?'

'Yeah.'

'Well, I must have.'

'You were really on to something.'

'Yeah?'

'Yeah.'

Emma burst into tears. She pushed her way through the crowd; she pressed her hand against shirts soaked with sweat and perfume, through the rose and golden light. Somehow, the crowd made room for her, like they were stepping upwards on their laughter, balancing on their pint glasses, until they reached the ceiling. She could smell the warmth – the burning of a thousand eyes at once. And everyone was joyous.

Everyone but her.

*

'My round,' Frances said, as she finally fell off her barstool.

'C'mere love,' Jimmy said gently, helping her up to her feet and into a hug. 'Let's go home.'

*

Outside the back of the pub, Emma could hear the warm thump of the party inside. The wall felt cool through the back of her damp blouse.

Charley was concerned. 'You okay?'

Emma frowned. 'Yeah, why?'

'I ... you ... ?' Charley tried to remember. He shrugged. 'I don't know.'

Emma lit a cigarette while Charley threw up into a bush.

Emma looked around for Graham's car but couldn't see it now. The mist had turned thick and heavy.

Charley looked at her. 'Want one?' He pointed at her cigarette.

'Thanks.' She nodded solemnly. Then she added, 'You're welcome.'

'Okay.'

She looked at him. He looked back. Emma knew they were going to kiss. She was going to take him to that bush over there. It looked wet, but that was okay. They'd have each other again. Just like old times.

Just like old times.

'Wait,' Emma said.

Charley waited.

She imagined what it would be like – to untie his fingers, to drink his mouth, to hold his body between her lips. God, she wanted to.

'We can't. Not here.'

Or maybe she said, 'Not tonight.' Or had she just trailed off after ... we can't? It was like trying to grab a fish underwater – the way the light bent so you had to aim slightly off the mark to hit it—

'Are you okay?' Charley asked, sitting down. Frances stayed standing.

No – not Frances. Emma. *Emma* was standing. No, Emma was sitting, everybody else was standing. Why was Frances here? And when had Emma sat down?

'Everything alright, Charley?'

'I think Emma is going to get sick.' Then he threw up into the bush again.

'We'll give her a hand, love. Won't we, Jimmy?'

'Sure, it's on the way. Maybe give me a hand there with him too ...'

*

Mary could see out the window – it was snowing. It was nothing much, it'd barely cover the ground, but it was beautiful – it danced and swirled against the glass, lit up by the last golden light of evening.

Incredible, she thought. *Just ... incredible.*

As the stranger's hands closed even tighter around her neck, as she gasped for her last breath, as she felt the weight of death and terror pressing down on her shuddering chest, she kept her eyes fixed on the snow outside the window.

And then all she could hear was the rustling of snow, like the world was shuffling past her.

Chapter 38

The morning light broke weakly through Emma's bedroom window. She tried to stay still. She had a hazy recollection of getting home last night – maybe writing something down. Her skin was clammy and uncomfortable. Her whole body felt like old cardboard left out in the rain.

Jesus, she was still drunk. No, it wasn't possible to be drunk if her head hurt this much. But her body felt unsteady, like she had to concentrate on each movement. So far, she'd only moved her fingers, but still. Even that was too much.

Songbirds dived past the window, trilling and singing and, although nobody ever noticed, sighing.

*

Two hours later, Emma had recovered enough to go downstairs, her duvet wrapped around her shoulders like the Queen's best cloak. She managed to make a cup of tea and sat down at the kitchen table.

Her dad came in, a bag of shopping under his arm.

'Jesus,' he said, laughing. 'The state of you.'

Emma groaned. He laughed again as he started unpacking the bag, pulling out rashers and sausages and eggs.

'In fairness, I'd imagine the whole village has the same hangover you do.' He glanced at her. 'Well, maybe not that bad, but still.'

He left her to her tea, and he flew around the kitchen, worrying up a small fried feast. When it was ready, he considered between the two teapots; looking over at Emma again, he took down Betty – the large one.

And, because these were desperate times indeed, the sugar.

Sam was shy to the point of vanishing but he had a quiet charm that made you lean in to hear what he was saying. Emma loved him with all her heart; she particularly loved him at that moment, as he slid a plate across the table to her: fried eggs, rashers and sausages, a slice of warm brown bread with lashings of butter and strawberry jam. And tea. Wonderful tea.

'A job for Betty?' she asked, her mouth full already.

'Seemed so. And sugar, too.'

'Oh, Da.'

'You look like you need it.' He waited for her to take a few more bites and get her tea laid out and ready. (She ignored the sugar.) Then he sat down next to her. 'So tell me. What happened?'

She hadn't seen him before she went to the pub last night, or much at all the last couple of days, so she had a lot to tell him.

'Look, I know you told me not to, but Jimmy asked me to help them out and you won't believe it ...'

As she explained, at some point he got back up, but he listened attentively as he cleaned the kitchen, keeping the tap down low so he could hear as he rinsed off the pots and pans. When she finished, he turned off the tap and faced her.

'Okay, right. I wasn't asking about the Thorntons; I heard all that from Mrs Deasy at the shop this morning. I mean what happened last night?'

Emma frowned. She didn't know what he meant – she obviously hadn't told him everything, particularly the part about breaking into a solicitor's office.

'I told you – Colm might be innocent—'

He cut her off. 'I don't mean that. I mean, what happened to make you write this?'

He took out a sheet of paper and passed it across the table to her. At first glance, it looked harmless. Like a monkey had tried to write Shakespeare with his foot. Or a seismograph. It looked like a music sheet written from a small rowboat in a drunken storm. In other words, it looked like gibberish.

But on second glance, Emma's wince turned into a shudder, as words started to form in the scribbled waves. Words like *desperate* and *going nowhere*. *Bored*, *miserable* and somewhat alarmingly – as she'd realised, of course, that it was her letter, written in a drunken storm of her own – a word that was either *Sisyphus* or *Syphilis*.

She pointed.

'That says "Sisyphus",' she said. 'Just so we're clear. Not "Syphilis".'

Sam nodded as he sat down next to her, wiping his hands on a dish towel. 'Yeah, I guessed. That's not great either, though, is it?'

Emma didn't answer.

'Still. I was more asking about this line.' He pointed at the phrase: *burying my head in the sand.*

'Ah.'

'Yes. Ah.'

'I'm not burying my head in the sand, not at all,' Emma said, ignoring the memory that suddenly flashed in her brain – her, after Cordelia, staring longingly at the ships. 'I was just drunk; it was just a bit of ... frustration.' And at the word 'frustration', she remembered Charley and went red. Her dad pretended not to notice.

He got up and took a slipper down from the top of the bookshelf. As he sat back down, Emma poured out a cup of tea. Sam's dad had smoked, so he rarely did. But when he did, he smoked a pipe. He kept a pouch and his pipe in a slipper – *same as Sherlock Holmes*, he always said.

'Oh dear. A three-pipe problem?' she asked.

He smiled as the match flared, smoke spilling out the sides of his mouth.

'No – a three-pipe story.'

Emma groaned but made no effort to move.

Sam loved stories. Ever since she was a kid, he was telling her stories. She'd ask him a yes or no question and she'd get a story in return. She'd come home from school crying; she'd get a story. Laughing – the same. The man was a living Aesop.

'You couldn't grow up where I did and not hear a million shipwreck stories,' he said, leaning back in his chair. 'There were a lot of bad ones. Crews going crazy in the middle of the Atlantic, breaking down or cracking up. And plenty of stories about shipwreck victims turning on each other, resorting to cannibalism—'

'Jesus Christ, Da,' Emma interrupted. 'I'm eating breakfast here, like.'

He laughed.

'I just mean there were a lot of stories about things going wrong. Irishmen have been fishing the Atlantic for centuries, and the Atlantic was a difficult place to fish.' Sam took a long drag of his pipe, lost in the memory and the docks of childhood long ago. 'But there was one story in particular, one story they told over and over. Howard Blackburn.' Another drag of the pipe. 'Blackburn was a fisherman, way back when, who found himself a thousand miles from shore, in a rowing boat, with his only companion dying. In the middle of winter.'

'Prime conditions, those,' Emma said, her mouth full of egg.

Sam nodded. 'But even after his companion died, Blackburn didn't go cannibal. He knew he might change his mind later, when he started getting desperate, so he made it so he couldn't. He froze his hands to the oars.'

'What a good friend.'

Sam grinned. 'And then he rowed. Day and night, for five days. And he actually made it back. Lost all his fingers, of course, and his toes, but he died a hero fifty years later.' He tapped his pipe into his now-empty mug and looked at her. 'Well, what do you think?'

Emma tilted her head and pointed her fork at him. 'I think you're trying to tell me not to eat my friends.'

He laughed. 'Try again.'

Emma thought about it, seriously this time.

'You're telling me to put my head down and work hard. Freeze my hands to the oars, don't give up, like.'

Sam shook his head. 'No, Emma,' he said softly. 'That's not what I'm saying.'

Emma frowned. 'I don't get it so.'

Sam stood up and carried their mugs over to the sink. Emma watched his broad back moving as he delicately scrubbed them. She knew he was giving her time to think, but she was genuinely at a loss.

'I really don't know, Da.'

With a sigh, he closed the tap, wiped his hands on his shirt and turned around. 'I think you've frozen yourself to the wrong oars, love.'

Emma stared at him. Her heart sank. It was like pulling the plug on a cold bath; and she knew right away that was exactly what she'd been worried he'd say.

'What? What does that even mean – the wrong oars?'

Sam started to answer, but she cut him off.

'There's not exactly another pair of oars handy at the moment,' she said, her voice rising. 'And so what if there was? What difference would that make?'

'Emma—'

'A slightly different grip, is it, Da? Is that what you're telling me? To get a different grip?'

'Because it's a stupid thing to do,' he snapped.

Emma was startled. Sam never raised his voice. But he raised it now.

'Sure, it sounds great – and it makes for one hell of a story. But how many hundreds of people did it *not* work for? How many men drowned when their boat flipped over because they were frozen to the oars? How many starved, surrounded by fish, because they couldn't use their hands?' He took a deep breath. 'And most importantly, Emma, life is not a rowing boat. I know you, love – I know that as much as you're enjoying the investigation, it's killing you too. Because you think that road is closed.' He shook his head emphatically. 'But Emma, it's not. Blackburn had no choice, but you're not stuck in the middle of the bloody Atlantic – you're twenty-six years old. Maybe you can't be a detective here, but there are other places, other countries, other opportunities. It's not closed.'

'What do you mean, other opportunities?' Emma shouted, the legs of her chair scraping the floor as she stood up. 'Are you trying to say I should be happy that I got fired?' Her eyes filled up with tears. 'I should be happy that, oh, I can just leave everything behind? Oh, right, it's not closed, Emma! You can run away and start over—'

'Emma, for God's sake!' Sam shouted. 'Will you stop?'

She stopped. Her breath was shaky and ragged. She sat back down. She hadn't even realised she'd been standing. Or that her fists were clenched. But Emma couldn't stop there, not quite yet.

'I've built the library from scratch,' she said, her voice quiet but breaking. 'I've built something that's important to people—'

'But is it important to *you*?' He asked it quietly, gently. But it was a cannonball through her stomach.

'What do you mean?' She shook her head fiercely, a tear working itself loose from her eyes. 'Da, how can you even ask that?'

He came over to her and put his arms on her shoulders. She shrugged them off.

'I'm sorry, acushla. But you have to understand. Just because something is a good thing, just because it's the right thing to do – doesn't mean it's right for *you*.' He put his forehead against hers; a rabbit kiss, like they always used to do. But suddenly, she shoved him back.

'I'm not a little kid anymore, Da—'

Her voice was raised, so he had to raise his again. 'I *know* that, Emma; what I'm trying to say is—'

'And I can't believe you don't believe in me, or what I'm trying to do, what I've been doing—'

'But that's the point, Emma, I *do* believe in you—'

'... and I know everybody thinks I'm a failure, that I'm a joke, that I couldn't do anything right, so I just moved back in with you, but I never thought *you* thought that—'

'I never thought that,' he begged. 'Please, Emma.'

'I'm going to prove Colm innocent. Then you'll see. Everyone will see.'

Sam held out his hand to her again, but before he could reach her, she'd turned and stormed out the door. She slammed the gate so hard the whole fence rattled, her feet kicking into the path. For a moment, he considered chasing after her. But he slowly turned back to the dishes in the sink.

He'd wanted to say: *Emma, I am so, so proud of you. I love you, and what you've done for the Thorntons, for the library, for the village – it's an incredible achievement. And you're right, they do need you.*

Tears fell down his face, mixing with the suds. She couldn't hear him, but he said it out loud anyway:

'But there's a whole world out there that needs you too.' He wiped his eyes. 'Don't freeze your hands to the oars just yet. Not these oars. Not Kilcraven.'

But she was gone.

*

Emma was strong, but there had always been something missing. Like no matter how much she talked, or how crowded the room, nobody heard her. And as she got older, she had found some people who had, like Charley – but they had all left her in the end. And then the empty echo came back louder and louder.

And she knew that was a weakness, and she knew that she wasn't weak. But right now, now that someone had kicked over the table she'd worked so hard to set, she knew she didn't really care.

Right now, she wanted two things: a quiet corner and Charley Thornton. And she knew where she'd find them both.

*

It was only when she came over the hill that she heard the sirens from the village.

Chapter 39

The hospital room was quiet. Every so often, a screen murmured, telling Colm that he was still alive. *There, there, you're still alive, that's all.* If he kept his eyes closed, he could be anywhere. So, he kept his eyes closed.

Colm didn't want to see the same sterile walls, the same sterile bed, the same sterile window that looked out over the same concrete carpark and abandoned scaffolding every day. And that was only when someone bothered to pull back the curtain for him – otherwise, it was just the same sterile curtain.

And they rarely bothered to open the curtain. Patients accused of murdering defenceless old men didn't rank very high on the list for nurses. Colm didn't blame them. He'd have been the same, and that was coming from a priest.

Well, a former priest, anyway. The letter had arrived last night.

'In light of recent circumstances, His Holiness the Archbishop of Belfast hereby revokes you of your vestments, your position in the Church ...' and on and on.

He'd expected it, but he thought they might've waited until the trial, at least. But clearly the guards had told the bishop that the trial would be more of a formality than anything.

And that was if he even made it to trial. He was getting transferred tomorrow – one of the nurses said it earlier, when they thought he was asleep. He still couldn't sit upright without help, but whoever Sergeant Noonan was, he was apparently insisting.

'He must have his reasons,' one nurse said. The other nurse laughed.

'Yes, and he accepts those reasons by cash or cheque.'

No, it was best for Colm to keep his eyes closed just a little bit longer. Just a little bit—

'Colm?'

It was just one word. It had been thirty years since he'd heard her voice. But before he even opened his eyes, he knew.

'Mum?'

*

She kept rearranging herself on her chair – crossing and uncrossing her legs, smoothing down the lap of her dress, tugging on her neckline. She was trying to look unruffled, uncurious, but she was failing – she couldn't help stealing furtive glances.

God, he had changed. He was thirty years older. He wasn't just a man – he was a middle-aged man. Of course he had changed.

But there was something else, something she could sense just in his bearing, just from the way he lay there. The way he stared at her.

'I don't know what to say,' he finally said.

'I know.'

His voice was a hoarse croak. 'You're ... you believe I'm innocent,' he said. 'You're trying to prove me innocent.'

But Frances shook her head.

'I was,' she said quietly. 'That's all I wanted to do – I wanted to believe that you were innocent and prove you innocent. But things have changed.' Colm could barely look at her. It felt like he had a magnet buried in his chest, drawing all the iron filings out of the air. But Frances leaned over and took his hand.

'I still want to prove you innocent, love,' she said. 'But I can't do that. A brave woman,' – she paused, her voice caught in her throat – 'a friend, died last night, trying to do just that.'

Mary's body had been discovered early that morning by the postman. When she hadn't come to the door, he'd looked through the window and seen her body lying on the floor. As he told the guards, and then the rest of the village, her neck was all black, and her tongue too. But the worst part was her eyes – they were still wide open, staring back at him.

Colm struggled to sit up. 'It wasn't Emma, was it?'

Frances shook her head. 'No, it was an older woman – Mary Bennett.' She waited to see if he remembered her, but he just frowned.

'I'm sorry,' he said. 'I'm sorry that your friend—'

Frances took her hand off of his to stop him.

'That's not going to help her,' she said. 'And that's not what she would've wanted. But listen to me, Colm.' She pulled her chair forward until he had no choice but to meet her eyes. 'You need to tell me the name of the third man in the house that night.'

He started to protest, but she shouted, 'No, Colm. No!' She stood up, waving her hands in front of her face. 'I don't care if you're trying to protect us, or whatever it is you're trying to do – I don't even care if you're not as innocent as you're making out. But it stops now. Hey – look at me.' She waited until he met her eyes again. It took a few moments, but he did. 'Mary Bennett was a good woman. And she believed in you. And someone killed her for that belief.'

Frances picked up her coat and straightened her hat, getting ready to leave. 'So, whether or not you help us now, Jimmy and I are involved. And you can either help us, or you can bury us too.'

And as she waited for his answer, the room filled with the silence of the monitors and the shadows across the ceiling.

And then, for the first time in thirty years, Colm told his mother the truth.

Chapter 40

It had only been a few hours since Mary's body had been discovered, and Emma found herself in the Skibbereen Garda Station for the second time in less than two weeks. This time, it was only Sergeant Noonan. Liam was still at the crime scene.

'Look,' Noonan began, 'before we start, I just want to say that I'm sorry about your friend.'

Emma stared at him.

'My condolences, like,' he explained. 'On the passing of your friend.' He leaned back in his chair and ran a hand through his hair. 'Although ... I have to admit, I didn't know that you and Mary Bennett were friends.'

Emma just continued to stare at him. The whole way running down to the house, talking to the guards there and then driving over here now – she had only felt numb. Shock, she understood, but now – now, her numbness had given way into anger. Fury. At one man.

'You stupid. Fucking. Prick.' she said, spitting each word onto the table between them. 'Let me guess – you have a suspect, right? The third man from the Hollis murder?'

Noonan's mouth hung slightly open – the two front legs of his chair clicked as they landed back on the slate floor.

'Well, we, erm ...' he stammered. 'We're certainly looking into all possibilities.'

'Oh, I'm sure you are.' Emma shoved her hands into her coat pocket and squeezed until she felt her nails draw blood from her palm. 'Except, the third man doesn't exist, right? It was only the moonlight. And it must've been the moonlight that killed Mary – just another trick of my imagination.'

Noonan started to speak, but Emma suddenly slammed her hands on the table.

'For fuck's sake, sergeant!' she shouted. 'Just shut the fuck up!'

Noonan was staring, horror-struck, at the slight smear of blood on the table under her hands.

'We were doing the best we could,' he said, in a distracted tone. 'There was no evidence – no trace of footprints or anything that backed up your claim—'

'Oh, cut the shit, Noonan.' It felt good to give into the anger. To give into it fully. To dig it out of her chest and hurl it at this man. He deserved it. 'There were footprints there, we both know it.'

Noonan's eyes narrowed. 'Now, listen here, girl.'

'And you know damn well why you covered them up. And you're going to cover it up now.'

Noonan's chair slammed backwards – before she knew what was happening, he was halfway across the table to her, a single finger from his fist pointing directly at her face. His own face was bright red and thunderous.

Emma just laughed. A dark, cold laugh.

'You think I'm wrong?' She leaned in, until his finger was nearly on her forehead. 'Where exactly was your boss, Ian Flesk, last night?'

And in the stunned look he gave her, she knew three things.

One: yes, he was in bed with Ian. But the whole village knew that already.

Two: that he wasn't involved in Mary's murder.

But three: that he believed her when she said that Ian was. He believed that his friend could kill.

Emma walked out of the garda station deep in thought. Noonan was definitely mixed up in Hollis's death, she could feel it, but she believed him when he said he wasn't involved in Mary's. Did that mean there were two separate conspiracies? Or two separate murderers?

Or, even worse, was the one murderer starting to panic – to lash out, to spiral out of control, beyond the reach of even Noonan?

She wasn't sure Ian had the stomach to kill. But the one thing she knew for sure was that he was behind the killer.

So how was she going to stop him?

Chapter 41

Hurley's Car Garage and Funeral Home, on the outskirts of Kilcraven, never struck the villagers as odd. The garage was downstairs, and the funeral home was upstairs, and that's just the way it was.

On the rare occasions that it registered (for example, when an out-of-town motorist stumbled into a wake while looking for an oil change) the villagers briefly wondered if it was an odd business model – mechanics and undertakers sharing office space. But people die and cars break down, even in a small village. And Kilcraven was too small to support a garage or a funeral home on their own. So, no, come to think of it – it wasn't that odd a business model. And sometimes a funeral needed an extra two or three mourners; and other times, cars broke down on the way to the graveyard.

People die and cars break down, that's just the way it was. And when that happened, the village came to Hurley's. And they were there this morning, for Mary Bennett's wake.

*

In fact, Mary's funeral could've used a few lost motorists. The village always turned up for a funeral for one of their own, but the funeral of a murder victim could go either way – depending on the circumstances and the quality of the person involved, sometimes it was best to just pretend that nothing had happened. Hollis's funeral, for example, had been attended by just the priest and an altar boy. The village, without ever saying anything, had just agreed to let it disappear. Let the moss grow over the castle, and soon it will just be moss and rocks.

And Mary's funeral was suffering from her friendships, funnily enough. Frances was at the hospital, ensuring that her death wasn't wasted. Jimmy was in the funeral home, but he was barely there at all – he was convinced that it was his fault, for starting the investigation in the first place.

But Jimmy's guilt couldn't compare to that of Emma's. Which is why, as the bells of St Brigid chimed for the start of the funeral mass, Emma was still standing outside the funeral home.

'It's okay, love,' Sam said, for the third time. 'Nobody expects you to go in – and if anyone did, they'd understand.'

And for the third time, Emma didn't hear her father. Things were still awkward from the day before, from their argument, but in fairness, Sam had been right by her side the whole way through.

But maybe if she had listened to him, if Emma had kept out of it, Mary would still be alive. It was her fault that Mary was dead. It was her fault, her fault ...

'It's not your fault, love,' Sam said. He pulled her into a hug. 'It's not your fault.'

But it was too late. Emma had made up her mind. She wasn't going to go into the funeral home, or to the church, or the graveyard. She had fucked up enough in this poor woman's life; she wasn't going to disturb her peace now to beg for forgiveness. Especially since, well, Mary was dead; if Emma asked Mary to forgive her, she was really just asking herself.

It was too late for all that now.

'I'll see you at home,' she said to her father. And before he could answer, she took off down the road.

Sam watched her go. Then he sighed and went inside the funeral home.

*

Maybe it was because he was worried about Emma, maybe it was because of the stress of the past two weeks, or maybe it was because Sam was just a trusting person.

But when a man approached him later, at the cemetery, and asked about his daughter – he didn't think much of it.

Sam didn't even notice his accent. Or the fact that he was a stranger.

*

Emma didn't know where she was headed. She wasn't running away from Sam or even from the funeral, she was just running. Picking a direction and hoping that she'd meet a reason for it. And sure enough, she found one – Charley Thornton, walking to the funeral.

Or maybe, it would be more accurate to say that he found her.

Charley saw Emma up in front of him, halfway down the road.

'Hey!' he shouted. But she didn't stop.

When he finally caught up to her, he touched her shoulder and she spun around, catching him off guard.

'Hey, Emma,' he stammered, 'I'm really sorry – I was coming to the funeral to ... I don't know ... I thought you might need some company.'

Emma's eyes were filled with tears and she was looking anywhere but at Charley. 'No, no, I—' she began.

But then suddenly, she hugged him tightly. Her shoulders started to heave. 'I'm sorry,' she whispered, the hair getting caught in her mouth. 'I'm sorry.'

Charley hugged her back.

'It's okay,' he said, understanding that there was something else happening but not knowing what it was. 'It's okay.'

Emma took a deep breath and pushed her hair out of her face. 'Would you like to ... could you keep me company for a bit? If you're not busy?'

The morning air was heavy with salt and fog. There was nobody on the road as they walked out past the shop, up and around the Blackfield, all the way up to the church. As they walked, Emma turned to Charley.

'It's not you,' she said. 'I wasn't running away – it was just ...'

'I know.'

Emma frowned. 'You know?'

Charley struggled for a minute, then gave up. 'No, I'm sorry,' he admitted. 'It just seemed like the right thing to say.'

Emma smiled and nodded. 'Well, thank you for that. You always seem to know what to say.' She glanced at him. 'Although, it seems like there's been something you *haven't* been saying recently, that's weighing you down.'

Charley knew that he was supposed to be strong for her – that she was the one who was upset, and he was supposed to be helping her feel better, not the other way around, but he could feel himself collapsing under the pressure of trying to hold himself together. And he knew – he hoped – that she could understand.

'I think it's my fault,' Charley said quietly. He wasn't looking at her; his hands were shaking. 'When I met Henry—' He stopped suddenly and looked at Emma. He struggled to find the words, but they were hard to find. 'I met Henry. And he told me why Colm was in trouble. That he was alive.' He was crying now, speaking through sobs. 'I think I could've helped Colm, if I'd told my dad or Frances. But instead, I didn't say anything. I kept silent. I told myself it was the right thing to do – that I didn't even know if this guy was telling the truth – but now Colm has killed someone, and my dad is *so* angry, and Mary is *dead*, and it's all my fault.' His whole body trembled now. 'I could've helped. But I didn't. I ran away.' He folded his arms around himself. 'It's my fault you and Mary got mixed up in all this. It's all my fault.'

Then, just as he was about to collapse onto the footpath, Emma stopped and caught him. She pulled him into her chest until he was able to stand himself. And she held him for a moment. Then, when Charley caught his breath, she kissed him.

'You're a smart lad, Charley,' she said. 'You know much better than that.'

And even though he didn't know better than that – the fact that she had stayed, she hadn't got annoyed with him, that she had kissed him, that she had ... oh my God, she had kissed him ...

He looked at her in surprise and despite herself, she laughed. And then she pulled him in for another, much longer kiss. So, he told her how he had met a very drunk man named Henry Farrell in a pub in London, and what Henry had told him.

'So,' Emma said slowly, after Charley had finished. 'Your Uncle Colm – he was in a relationship with this man. In Belfast, like.'

Charley nodded.

'He was a priest at the time. Apparently, they were going to run away together, but Colm got cold feet at the last minute. Broke Henry's heart.'

Emma whistled.

'Well, if Colm is gay, that could explain why he ran away as a kid. Small village and all that – maybe he was getting bullied. But that's not the big question. The big question is why he came back.'

Charley agreed but couldn't think of anything else to say. So they kept walking. And Charley waited.

*

Later, they walked in silence, holding hands – two birds, with wings made of feathers and wax, melting in the evening sun. And then Emma told him. She explained what had happened four years ago and what she was still doing in Kilcraven.

She had done well in university – she had done exceptionally well, really. She graduated at the top of her class and could've had her pick of careers. But Emma Daly had only ever dreamt of one thing – becoming the first female garda inspector and then, after a long career, Garda Commissioner. She had never been sure what came first, her love of books or her desire to join the guards, but the two fed off each other. Just like Sherlock Holmes, she built a file of crimes and their solutions. But unlike Sherlock, she didn't limit herself to true crime. She saw novels as a type of research – learning detection from crime plots, psychology from character development and dramatic flair from Poirot.

But, in her first year at Templemore, she fell in love.

'His name was John Byrne,' she said quietly. 'He was married.'

He was seventeen years older than she was, and he was well respected in the force. He told Emma that he loved her, that he would leave his wife for her, that she was special.

Six months later, she was two weeks late. Then three, then four. 'He said it was okay, that we could go to London. But I didn't want to go to London. Not that I ... it's not a sin. It's not wrong. But I loved him.'

To John, it wasn't love. It was the end. He had his career to think of, he told her. He had his family too. Everything he had said he would throw away for her suddenly became the centrepieces of his life. A life that didn't have any room for her anymore.

'I'm sorry,' he told her. 'It's just too complicated. Maybe if you were older ...'

'If I was older,' Emma said now, laughing darkly, 'he never would have looked at me in the first place.'

The same day John apologised, Emma was pulled into the Garda Commissioner's office – the very office she had dreamt of one day stepping into – and was fired. In disgrace, they said. For the disgrace she had brought to the guards, to her family, to the country of Ireland.

In forty-five minutes, Emma was called every name under the sun.

John's name was never mentioned once.

'In the end, it didn't matter. No laundry for me. A few days after I told my father, I wasn't pregnant anymore. Just didn't work, I guess.' She tried to shrug, but her eyes were bright, and her voice was shaking.

Charley squeezed her hand but stayed quiet.

She struggled, afterwards. 'They didn't know what was wrong,' Emma said, 'other than that I wasn't coping.' She was unfit to be a guard, to be a mother, to be a woman, to be alive at all. But Sam fought for her. She moved back home. A week later, she was rushed to the hospital.

'They called it a breakdown,' she said in a flat tone. 'They brought me in and put me on round-the-clock watch. Of course, they didn't actually have enough nurses to cover the ward fully around the clock.'

The third night Emma was there, a little boy crawled into her hospital bed. He was in the room across from her – long-term care. He was only six years old.

'I miss my mammy,' he said. 'My mammy didn't come today.'

Emma didn't know what to do. But she remembered what it felt like to be six years old and scared and all alone. She knew how it felt to miss your mammy. Emma cuddled into him and sang him a song and they fell asleep.

'The alarms started going off around midnight,' she said. There was no emotion in her voice. Or rather, there was so much that it didn't allow any in. 'He had a seizure. Out of nowhere, apparently. And I still can't forget the look on his face when the doctors pulled him out of my arms. Like he knew already ... he was going to die. And he wished he'd seen his mammy.'

Emma stopped walking. Charley pulled her into a hug.

'And I don't even know if I get to grieve him,' she said. 'He wasn't my kid. I didn't know him for more than a few hours. I just ... I just—'

'Of course you do,' Charley murmured, 'of course you do.'

'Frances and Jimmy,' Emma said into his shoulder, 'they were there every day, stopping by the hospital, bringing me books from the house, whatever I needed. Other than my dad, they were the ones who got me through it. And got me home. Four weeks later.' She smiled weakly at him. 'And your dad, Adam, checked on me too – he pretended it was aftercare. But I knew it wasn't.' Emma looked at Charley. 'I owe your family my life. And I wanted to help them. But I'm not sure I did.' Her voice caught. 'I think I just made it all worse.'

And it was Charley's turn to stop her; to hold her and to kiss her. And they stood there and held each other as long as they could. There was nothing he could say, and he knew that, but he could hold her, and he could kiss her.

And sometimes, that was all you could do. And sometimes, that was enough. Or if it wasn't enough – it was close enough.

*

Eventually they fell silent and started walking again.

They walked out of the village, towards Ballincolla, past the Blackfield pitch and the old fairy rings. Out by Carrigillihy beach they stopped. A cliff flared over and around the beach like a horseshoe – they walked along the edge of the sand, then slowly picked their way across a ledge of rocks to their old spot, a tiny cove in the side of the cliff.

The small cove was barely bigger than a sitting room, but it had a small landing site of smooth, rounded stones. Unless you were on the water or standing directly above it, it was hidden from the rest of the world.

'Will you go in?' Charley asked her, staring out at the water.

Emma looked at him. 'Only if you will.'

'Sure, it'll be freezing this time of year. I'll need someone to hold me.' They laughed, and then they were quiet. They stared at each other; they both slowly started to undress. Emma pulled her dress down off her shoulder. Charley unbuckled his belt. Slowly, very slowly; they watched each other stepping out of each piece of clothing.

And then they were naked.

Emma hugged herself, partly from the cold. Her pale skin was covered in goosebumps, across her chest and down the length of her arms and legs.

'Ready?'

Charley couldn't decide what to do with his hands. But Emma wasn't looking between his legs.

'Ready.'

She turned and ran into the water, and he followed close behind her. They dived under and came up gasping and sputtering and laughing. When they wiped the water out of their eyes, they looked at each other. Then Charley moved closer, and she moved closer to him. They kissed. He tasted the salt water in her mouth; she folded into his familiar, forgotten arms. As they pulled each other closer under the water, he bent down to kiss her chest – her swollen nipples hard against his tongue; her hands ran through his hair and down his back. And then the sky fell down into the sea in bursts of blue and gold and white.

A little while later, their bodies were numb, and they came out of the water again, stumbling and laughing and grabbing at each other. They made love right there on the rocks, surrounded by the sea and the cliffs and the lonely, holy sky.

'Jesus,' she said. She wiped her mouth with the back of her hand. 'Well, I suppose that was making up for lost time.'

He laughed. 'Lost time, indeed.'

Eventually, they would go down to the sea again to rinse and to fall into each other again. But for now, for a moment, they lay next to each other and quietly watched the clouds disappear into dusk.

And they both wondered, as the tide rose all around them, what would happen now.

Chapter 42

The grey sky above Kilcraven grew darker and darker; the smoke from the village chimneys moved through the air like ink drops in water. The harbour was still. Across the water, the watch bell on a fishing ship bound for Portugal quietly murmured. A seal's head appeared briefly in a wave, like a black shadow, then disappeared.

The bats in their belfry stirred, shook their wings and let go. Their wings beat against the sky, flying up above the village – far above the beach where Emma and Charley lay tangled up in each other's arms, far above the house where Frances and Jimmy sat, wondering about the world, far above the causeway where Sam stood alone, crying – flying towards the Blackfield. Owls shuddered across the sky, the mice and the rabbits twitched in their sleep. And a small fox cub trembled in a hedge, jumping at every sound, its stomach growling in the dark.

Everywhere, the waves mixed with the mist and the shore and the darkness spread out against the sky, then fell; it was night, and the world folded up into a dream.

Chapter 43

The stranger had made his way out of the funeral home, blending into the crowd. It'd been risky, talking to Emma's dad like that, but he had guessed that Sam Daly would be distracted. And he had also guessed that Emma hadn't told her dad just how much danger she was in.

And she was in a lot of danger.

The stranger had his orders: Mary Bennett. That's who he was paid to kill, and the stranger wasn't someone to work for free. But he was also a professional. He didn't leave loose ends.

It was clear that Mary and this girl were in league together, snooping around and breaking into Ian's office. Which meant that Emma was a loose end. A nosy little loose end, too. The stranger knew that if she kept turning stones over, the path could lead back to him. He'd been careful, but you never knew. So, it was in his best interest to cut off this loose end. Permanently.

He might not even charge Ian.

The stranger got into his car. He had a pretty good idea of where Emma would go, if she was still investigating.

And he was going to meet her there.

Chapter 44

For a long time, neither Emma nor Charley said a word. Then the night air turned cool and told them it was time to leave. The sand fell down their backs as they quickly dressed and retraced their steps out of the cove. When they got to the edge of the village, Emma stopped Charley. 'Thank you,' she said quietly. And then, after looking to make sure no one was around, she kissed him.

Charley kissed her back. Then he smiled. 'So, I take it we're keeping this a secret?'

Emma raised her eyebrow. 'We're taking whatever *this* is ... slowly.'

Charley took her by the shoulders and leaned in until their noses were touching. 'I know, Emma,' he said gently. He kissed her again. 'I know.'

They kept walking and soon they were in front of the Thorntons' house. Charley had just turned the key in the door when he stopped.

'Will you be okay?' he asked. 'You know, tonight, with everything that's happened?'

Emma's stomach did a somersault. She knew he meant emotionally; dealing with Mary's death. But her first thought was about the third man – that she herself was in danger too.

'I'll be fine,' she said, trying to keep her voice light. 'I'll have my dad with me anyway.'

Charley looked at her doubtfully.

'Honestly,' Emma said. 'I mean it. I'll be fine.'

'Okay,' Charley said slowly. 'But if you need anything – anything at all – I'll be here all night.'

Emma nodded.

'I know, Charley. I know.'

The street was empty as Emma walked the long way around the causeway. A few seagulls hung in the air above her, caught in the space where two currents met, pushed up into the sky and held there like a kite. The only sound was the waves lapping against the far side of the causeway.

And then she was standing in front of Mary's house.

How many times had she walked past this house on her way to work? Had she ever stopped to look at it, to wonder about the woman who lived inside? She had known Mary, of course, but she knew the rumours and the whispers, not the woman herself. Not then, anyway.

Now, as she looked up at the lace curtains in the dark windows, a lump slowly twisted in her stomach. There was still crime-scene tape on the front door, but there was nobody inside. Before she knew what she was doing – like an internal autopilot had suddenly taken control of her feet – Emma had slid open an unlocked sash window and hopped inside.

It was a small sitting room, but it looked like a library. There were three large bookshelves, including where the TV would normally go, with books crammed into every corner. For the first time, Emma wondered why Mary never came into the library. She looked through the shelves, noting that all the spines were worn in and well-loved, which partly answered her question. But she wished she could've asked. And she couldn't find the book she was looking for. So, she went upstairs.

Mary's bedroom was full of books as well. They were stacked up on the floor around the bed – someone, the guards most likely, had knocked a few piles over – with two smaller stacks on the nightstand.

Emma sat down on the bed. She didn't know what she had been expecting, but it wasn't this. She had the strangest feeling – the same one she'd been having all day. Like Mary had just vanished around the corner ahead of her. Like she had just stepped out of the room.

Like she had known Mary a hundred years, instead of a few days. Like Emma had been here a hundred times before, instead of just once.

It was all very strange.

What was Mary's life like? Emma wondered. It seemed, just judging from the room and the choice of books, that they were pretty similar.

Is this what Emma would look like in thirty years? If she let herself be buried by her past – if she stayed in Kilcraven for the rest of her life? Mary had lost her husband, the love of her life – Emma had lost a job. Maybe there was a way out, maybe she could change. Mary had – at sixty years old, she broke into a solicitor's office. And she had made new friends.

Two pictures sat on the nightstand – one of them was Mary and Mick's wedding day. The other was her family: Mary, her father, her mother and her little brother. They stared out of the past at Emma.

And then, she remembered. The reason she had come in. She was looking for Mary's Sherlock Holmes anthology. A keepsake, to remember her.

It took her a few minutes to find it – it was shoved under the bed, underneath a jumper. For a second, Emma wondered if Mary had hidden it – the rest of the house, even where the guards had rummaged, was so ordered and precise. This small bit of mess didn't quite fit in.

And as she picked up the book, she realised why.

A thick fold of papers was tucked into the binding. right in the middle of the book, halfway through 'The Adventure of the Musgrave Ritual'.

As Emma sunk down on the bed again, she saw a hastily written note. It started: *Dear Emma ...*

Chapter 45

When Charley walked into his house, he nearly tripped over Adam standing right behind the door.

'Dad, Jesus,' Charley said, laughing. 'Are you spying through the keyhole?'

Then he noticed Adam's expression, as well as the coat he was pulling on.

'Is something wrong? Is it Granny?'

Adam shook his head and put his head down as he buttoned his coat. 'No – well, yes, sort of. She just called from the hospital.' He quickly explained that he'd been at Nolan's when Frances rang. She'd spoken to Colm and had asked Adam to call over to her and Jimmy's house. They had a lot to discuss.

'She asked me to invite you too,' Adam said, unbuttoning and rebuttoning his coat. 'Only if you wanted to, like.'

Charley hesitated. 'Dad—'

'Ah, sure look, I knew you wouldn't want to—'

'It's not that. Of course I want to come.' Charley took a deep breath. 'It's just I think I know what she's going to say.'

Charley started to sob, but just then, Adam caught him. He held him close for a moment, then when Charley caught his breath, Adam told him to get his coat on.

'You can tell me on the walk,' he said gently. 'Whatever it is, we'll figure it out.' He opened the door. 'Together.'

Charley, overwhelmed and light-headed with a combination of relief, nerves and shame, nodded and did what he was told.

The night air hung down all around them. It sat on the hedges in great folds and lay across the fields like melted candle wax. They walked up the lane, past the old post office and the pub, out towards Ballincolla. And as they walked, Charley told Adam the story about Henry Farrell and Colm.

After he finished, the two men kept walking in silence. Charley glanced over at Adam – his dad was blinking hard.

'I messed up,' Charley said, ready to rip the whole plaster off at once. 'I thought I was doing the right thing. I thought that if he wanted to be found, he would've come home himself. And I couldn't get a straight answer out of Henry anyway.' He was blinking hard now too. 'And I know that doesn't make it right – I was wrong. I just didn't know ...'

He trailed off, so Adam finished the thought for him. 'How we'd react?' he guessed.

Charley nodded.

'Charley, what happened wasn't your fault.' Charley started to protest, but Adam didn't stop. 'It wasn't your fault, Charley.'

And then Adam told Charley a story, about two boys sitting on a pier in the moonlight, daring each other to jump off.

*

After that night on the pier, Adam and Colm did jump together. And Abby was there to see it. But when she caught Colm staring at her male cousin while the older boy changed into his togs, she called him a name. A bad name, the worst name – the only name that carried a jail sentence with it.

And all the other kids pointed and laughed.

Colm, starting to cry, looked at his older brother. His protector. But Adam looked around at the other kids, and for one brief second, he faltered – and he laughed with them.

As Colm ran off the beach and up the pier, his arms and legs flailing wildly, he heard his brother calling, 'Colm! Wait, come back – I'm sorry, Colm!' But Colm didn't stop, he ran all the way home until he collapsed into his mum, sobbing and not able to stop shaking. She begged him to tell her what was wrong – but he couldn't say. He just ran and ran, further down into himself.

*

'I apologised over and over,' Adam said now, his voice choking. They reached the top of the lane and looked out across the valley spread out beneath them. 'He forgave me eventually, but the damage was done. After that, he didn't trust me anymore. And if he couldn't tell me what was happening, I couldn't protect him. He ran away a few years later.'

Charley shook his head. 'It wasn't your fault, Dad. You were just a kid. You were brothers, like – that's what brothers do.'

But Adam just walked on ahead.

Chapter 46

Maeve was enjoying a lovely evening in the pub. She often did. When Fintan said that she was the main reason he kept buying diet tonic water, he was only half kidding.

'You know your man Ray Kroc?' he'd say. 'He discovered the McDonald's brothers when he noticed they were buying twenty times more milkshake equipment than anyone else. Well, if the Ray Kroc of Cork Dry Gin ever came sniffing around, he'd only find our Maeve here.'

Maeve frowned. 'Have you been dipping into my supply there, love?'

And Fintan laughed and gave her the next one on the house.

But now it was time to head home. Maeve wearily picked her head up off the bar. Back to the barber and his gout and the shadows on the wall. But as she walked up the street, she saw something strange.

The light in the library was on.

Maeve blinked a few times in the general direction of her watch. It was ... it was too dark to see what time it was, so it must've been late. Well, if Emma was in there she'd need backup.

A few minutes later, Maeve opened the library door.

'Emma?' she called. 'For God's sake, Emma, you haven't gone and fallen asleep again, have you?'

'I'm back here!' Emma called from the back corner of the library. She was sitting in one of the pensioners' chairs, a whole pile of official-looking documents spread out on the table in front of her. 'Will you get us a cup of tea?' As Maeve leaned over her shoulder to look at the documents, Emma grimaced.

'Steady there, Maeve – you smell like the British Navy.'

Maeve grinned, swaying slightly. 'Well, when I saw the light on, I thought you might want something a bit stronger than tea.' Then she grew sombre and put her hand on Emma's shoulder. 'I was sorry to hear about Mary, love. I know you two were getting close.'

Emma nodded, not trusting herself to speak.

'I thought we could give a toast to her,' Maeve said quietly. She sat down next to Emma and rifled through her handbag. 'I've got it in here.'

Emma frowned. 'You've got ... Jesus Christ, Maeve, what the feck is that?'

She was staring at what Maeve had pulled out of her handbag. It was a little half-pint milk bottle, holding a clear liquid.

'Is that water?' Emma asked.

Maeve looked at her incredulously.

'That's gin, love.' She said it like it would've been strange to have been carrying anything else in a milk bottle in her handbag. 'And just a drop of tonic. For the quinine,' she added, reasonably.

Emma shook her head, smiling. 'You're the tonic, Maeve,' she said, and took her hand. 'Thank you.'

Maeve blushed and waved her off. 'Anyway – what's this you're working on?' She looked at the papers and frowned. 'These don't look like anything for the library.'

As Emma explained about the investigation, the break-in to Ian Flesk's office and finding the papers in the Sherlock

Holmes book, they passed the milk bottle back and forth. Which might have explained why Maeve took it all so in her stride – even the break-in.

'Oh, that was clever,' was all she said, during the story of Emma picking the lock. 'Very handy.'

But after they'd covered the past and were caught up to the present moment, Emma sighed.

'I just don't know what any of this means,' she said, gesturing at the documents. 'Mary left me a note, saying that she was sure the answer was somewhere in here.' Her voice caught. 'And that she knew I'd figure it out. But I don't – I failed her. I'm not Sherlock. I'm not even close.' She hung her head, a tear rolling slowly down the bridge of her nose.

Maeve didn't say anything for a while. She put her arm around Emma and leaned her body against hers.

'Can I tell you something, Emma?' Emma sniffled, which Maeve took as a yes. 'Sherlock Holmes is bullshit.'

Emma snorted. She looked at Maeve incredulously.

'It's true, love.' Maeve raised her hands. 'I mean, I love the books, and I know you do too, but they're not mysteries.'

'Maeve, they're literally the most famous mysteries of all time—' It was Maeve's turn to snort.

'Seriously, Emma, aren't you supposed to be the smart one?' She waved her hands. 'Look at *The Sign of the Four*. The first half is Sherlock bragging about how he could totally use the clues to solve the mystery, but instead he just runs around wearing a wig. He doesn't even solve it! A bloodhound does! Because the villain just so happened to step in creosote. And then the second half is just the criminal explaining the entire story, as well as the Indian Rebellion of 1857. It's absolutely mad.'

Emma wanted to respond. She really did. She just had absolutely no idea how to.

'But …' she spluttered finally, 'but what does that have to do with me?'

Maeve exhaled. 'Because you're running around pretending that you're following in Sherlock's footsteps. But you're not.' Maeve leaned over and took Emma's hand. 'You've been doing it all yourself. And look how far you've come,' she added, gesturing at the documents on the table. 'Look what you've got here.'

Emma looked at Maeve hopelessly. 'And what exactly do I have here?'

'If Mary said the answer is in here, then it's in here.' She took a sip of the milk bottle. 'And we're going to find it.'

And without waiting for an answer, Maeve picked up a document and started to read. A minute later, Emma did too.

And a few minutes later, Maeve gave up. 'I just don't understand it,' she said.

'Which part?' Emma asked.

'Any of it,' Maeve replied.

Emma was still flipping through. 'Most of these are deeds of sale … and they're all in the last eighteen months.'

'So?' Maeve still had her head in her hands.

'So,' Emma explained, 'these are four villagers who have suddenly sold their houses … that's … I mean, how many houses in the village are there to start with?' She looked at Maeve. 'How have we not heard about any of this. How have *you* not heard about any of this?'

Maeve picked up one of the documents that Emma was looking at. 'No, this isn't right,' she murmured, squinting through her reading glasses. 'Breda Deasy didn't sell her house – she remortgaged it. Just last year.'

Emma shook her head. 'No, she sold it. That's the deed of sale right there.'

'Breda didn't sell anything,' Maeve insisted. 'She'd never sell that house. Her brother would have her committed, for one thing. But she remortgaged last year when Finn lost his job.' She looked at Emma. 'Although you didn't hear it from me, girl.'

Emma stared at Maeve. 'You're sure about that?'

'Positive.'

They both looked down at the document again. The silence filled the room. Finally, Maeve spoke up.

'Okay, well, if you're not going to point out the obvious – then I guess I will.' She looked at Emma. 'If Breda says she never sold her house, then how the feck does Ian have the deed to her house, showing that she did sell it and she sold it to the council?'

Emma nodded.

'That's the million-dollar question.'

*

Later, after they had cleared up the papers from the table, Maeve looked at Emma, her eyes bright with drink and with love.

'We make a good team,' Maeve said. And Emma smiled.

'So, will you come to the Big House with me?' she asked, grinning. 'To try and find ... well, I'm not entirely sure what we're looking for, to be honest. To find out if Ian put his threats into letters, for example.'

Maeve stared at her for a moment.

'You can feck right off with that,' she said indignantly. 'We make a good team alright, but you'll be wanting someone else for that sort of work – not an old biddy like myself.' Maeve practically shoved Emma out the door then, saying, 'Call to me the next time you need some brain power – but now, you go and get that strapping young Thornton lad.'

*

Mike Keohane never went to Nolan's pub. If he ever wanted a drink, he went into town. But that night, Mike went to Nolan's. And five hours later, he was still sitting in a dark corner of the pub.

If he had been in his right frame of mind, Mike never would've talked to the man next to him. He knew enough not to talk to men in dark corners of bars. But he'd been there for five hours – he was talking to anyone who would listen. When Maeve left, then came back and ordered a milk bottle of gin – he even weighed in on the argument over whether she should get a bulk discount.

When Maeve explained that the gin was for a friend who was investigating a murder, the man next to him seemed to lean forward. But Maeve didn't notice; she paid quickly and hurried out the door. And Mike didn't really notice either – only in a half-hearted sort of way.

If he'd been in his right frame of mind, Mike certainly never would've answered any questions. Not from the odd-looking man sitting next to him.

After half an hour, the man paid his bill.

'Where you off to?' Mike asked, more for conversation than for anything else. 'Back home?'

And the man gave a strange grin and leaned in close.

'I think I'm going to head up to where that murder happened. The Big House.' He patted Mike on the shoulder. 'I'm meeting a friend up there.'

Mike didn't know what to say to that – the man's tone left his blood cold. But when the stranger got up to leave, and Mike saw the pistol tucked into his waistband, he didn't think much of it. Well, he did think about it, but only in the deflected manner of the drunken barfly.

And after all, a man's got to protect himself. It's a dangerous world out there.

Chapter 47

Ian ... You can't do this.'

'And why is that?'

'Because, because – Jesus, you'll get caught, man.'

'That's where you're wrong.'

Ian had a low, deep voice and drainpipe eyes, dark and full of rotting leaves and run-off. His resting facial expression told the businessman two things: Ian was thinking dirty thoughts, and it was the businessman's fault.

And he had just told the businessman that he had him over a barrel.

Well, actually, it was worse than that – Ian had told him that he would make him quite rich.

Eoin Fielding had lived in town his whole life. His family had been one of the richest families in the area going back almost a hundred years – Eoin's businesses included a home-appliance shop, an electrical repair shop, a garage and various rental properties around West Cork. He had, of course, been approached with his share of unscrupulous dealings before, and had even considered a few of them – but nothing quite like this.

'So,' Eoin said slowly, 'you've got all this property – half the village it seems like.' He quickly added, 'And before you start to say anything – I don't want to know anything about how you pulled that off. But now you're going after ... what, the whole council planning board?' He shook his head in disbelief. 'Even if you could do it – which, Ian, you can't – these guys are your colleagues ... they're your friends.'

Ian's eyes narrowed.

'This is business. That's all. You of all people should understand that.'

There was a threat somewhere in there, but Eoin couldn't pin it down exactly. And it chilled him to the bone. He couldn't understand it; he'd cut a few corners here and there, sure, but nothing illegal. Not even close. So why was he so nervous?

Now that he'd made his point, Ian leaned back in his chair. He gave a friendly sort of smile, like they were just pals again, an indulgent parent patting a child on the head after a tantrum.

'You don't need to worry about how I got the property,' Ian said, his voice practically a coo. 'And you don't need to worry about how I'm going to get rid of the board. Although,' he said, thinking it over, 'it might help you to know. Seeing as you'll be taking over as chief executive ...'

Eoin pointed his finger at Ian angrily. 'Now, listen here,' he interrupted. 'I've said no such thing—'

But Ian ignored him.

'... it'd be good for you to know the reasons the last council planning board had to be tossed out,' he continued. 'The thing is – and I know I can count on your full discretion here – the board haven't exactly been ... above board for a while now.' He chuckled. 'Above board, that's a good one.'

Eoin paused, his finger still hanging in the air. 'How do you mean?'

Ian gestured at the chair. 'Well, if you'd be so good as to sit back down, I'll tell you.'

Eoin hesitated. Then, despite himself, he lowered his hand and sat back onto his chair.

Ian came around to the front of the desk and leaned against it. He lowered his voice. It was all very practised, very coordinated, but Eoin still felt the performance working on him.

'For a few years now, I've sat back, and I've watched as the board have lined their pockets with their constituents' hard-earned money. Every single one of them has taken a bribe here, a cut there. Nothing in this parish gets built without greasing their already greasy hands.' Ian looked at Eoin keenly. 'You know it's true. Remember the trouble with Casey's liquor licence? That was a great pub, and now it's gone. All because poor Casey didn't have enough to pay those bastards.'

Eoin could recognise all the signs of a sales pitch. He knew that this was just a rehearsal for what Ian would say to the village in the wake of whatever he was going to do. And even as he understood that, he knew just how effective it would be. The village had been up in arms when Casey's had to close. Eoin even felt himself getting angry all over again. He just nodded dumbly and listened to Ian explain how it'd come down to a bribe that wouldn't be paid.

'But I've got them now,' Ian crowed. 'Oh, I've got them now. They used me on a few of the contracts – as a sort of consultant, to help them figure out the legal side of things.' Ian looked at Eoin, with his face the picture of wide-eyed innocence. 'They forced my hand, you understand. They made me hide their dirty money – I had no choice. But I kept records of everything. And now, I can't turn a blind eye anymore. This village deserves better.'

Yes, thought Eoin, *now that you've got the last piece of whatever you needed, it's time to turn the guns around.*

As if he could read his mind, Ian nodded.

'Of course, I expect that once the scandal breaks and a new council planning board is elected, they'll need someone to oversee the accounts. And ...' He paused for effect. 'I imagine they'd be grateful to the man who brought them the deal of a lifetime.'

'And of course,' Eoin said bitterly, 'they'll have to be grateful to the man who got them elected in the first place.' A thought occurred to him. 'I assume you have some sort of dirt on them, too. Just to make sure.'

Ian raised his eyebrow. 'You tell me.'

All Eoin could do was shudder. Ian patted him on the shoulder, then crossed the room and pulled a book off the shelf. He folded out the pages onto the desk; it was a map of the village and the surrounding townlands.

'Look at this here,' he said, pointing to the harbour. 'We have one of the most picturesque harbours anywhere in Ireland – and the bottom is all silt and sand. What does that tell you?'

Eoin shook his head. 'I don't know anything about harbours, Ian—'

'Well, you're going to have to learn,' Ian said impatiently. 'It means that it'd be easy to dredge – to build one of the finest piers in Europe for leisure boats. Look at the location.' He tapped the map again. 'We're the easiest port for England, for the Continent and America. Think of the potential.' He leaned in. 'Think of the money. If we were able to transform Kilcraven from a puny, backwater little village into a – no, into *the* premier tourist destination in Europe.'

Eoin could see that. But he could also see the major problem. 'The commercial boats would never allow it,' he pointed out. 'And nobody would want to holiday next to a pile of dead fish, no matter how pretty or convenient it is.'

Ian grinned. 'Well, it just so happens that the leases on the port are all coming up for renewal soon. In a few months' time, in fact. And, well, maybe a couple of years ago the village might have been upset about losing the fishing boats. But now?'

Ian let the question hang in the air. And Eoin knew he was right. In the past few years, as the fishing boats worked to compete against the Norwegians and the Americans and the French, they'd been increasingly turning to foreign labour. Or rather, exploiting foreign labour. Eoin had heard one of the boat owners brag about how he preferred to hire a crew from all different parts of the world, so they couldn't talk to each other. Kilcraven wouldn't go to war for the fishing boats. He could also read the writing on the wall.

'And I suppose that's where all that property comes in?' he said. 'That's all in your name too, is it?'

'No, of course not,' Ian said, in mock indignation. 'I just told you that was the planning board's work.' His voice turned solemn. 'No, I only have a small piece of land. Just a small piece.'

And when Ian showed him where it was on the map, Eoin understood. He understood two things, in fact. He understood why that piece of land was so valuable. And, when he recognised the land as formerly belonging to Mr Hollis, he understood that resistance would not only be futile, but fatal.

He sank back into his chair, utterly exhausted. Ian didn't turn around, he kept his hands on the desk, poring over the map.

'Why me?' Eoin asked in resignation. 'You could've picked any number of men in this parish; men who would've done anything for a quick buck. Why me?'

Ian didn't bother to turn around.

'Because I knew that you were a good man,' he said simply. 'And good men, once they put that goodness down, have much more to lose than men who never had any to begin with.' Ian turned around, his eyes hard and cold as they raked over Eoin's slumped body. 'And I knew as soon as you agreed to this meeting with me, that you would put that goodness down. You know who I am and what I do, and you came anyway.'

And Eoin didn't know what to say.

He crossed the line. It was as easy as falling asleep. And every bit as welcome.

Chapter 48

Charley and Adam walked through the door and up the stairs to the sitting room. Frances and Jimmy were on the sofa, waiting for them. Never in their lives had Charley and Adam seen the pair like this. A handful of lamps were turned on, seemingly at random, lending the room an unbalanced lighting – like the darkness was crawling up out of the floorboards and folding over Frances and Jimmy from the ceiling. The two pensioners had never looked so old.

'We have a story to tell you,' Frances said quietly. 'About Colm.'

Charley and Adam looked at each other. Then, without saying a word, they sat down on the sofa facing the couple.

'Some of it, I remembered.' Frances's voice cracked. 'Of course, I didn't know what any of it meant at the time.' Jimmy took her hand and squeezed it. She looked at him gratefully. 'It only makes sense now, looking backwards.'

And then Frances told them what Colm had told her in the hospital. Why he had run away, and why he had come back, and what had happened when he did.

*

Colm was a good boy. He was short for his age and underweight, but he had a quick and curious mind. He was quiet, and after the incident on the beach with the cruel girl and Adam's betrayal, he became even quieter.

Suddenly, he was an outsider. Not just because of that girl or what she had said, but because he knew it was true. He had been looking at that other boy. He had wanted that other boy. And he knew what the priest said – that was wrong.

Colm was on the outside looking in. He watched the others, their easy way with each other, sure of at least that one big thing. The only thing that mattered. And Adam had laughed.

For his part, Adam apologised over and over. *I was stupid, I'm sorry*. He asked for forgiveness; but he didn't know just how far down the hurt had gone in Colm. And Colm didn't have the language to explain it. He forgave Adam, but he withdrew.

Before, Colm had always been good at being alone. He raided any bookshelf he found for books on any range of subjects – and their house had plenty. The pile next to his bed included Plato, a collection of medical journals, an astronomy textbook, *Ivanhoe*, a Sherlock Holmes anthology and notebooks filled with drawings and poetry. He read them all; the second he finished, he was bored again. And a new stack grew.

But then, Adam laughed.

Frances noticed a change – her frightened rabbit wasn't so frightened anymore. But not in a good way. The stack of books were put aside and collected dust. His eyes didn't go wide anymore, they didn't tremble at the edges. But they didn't get excited either.

She thought it was just puberty. She bought him new notebooks and the charcoal pencils she knew he loved. He opened them, thanked her politely and then never touched them again. Frances told herself it was just a phase – that teenage boys were like wells; you can toss a penny in, but it was up to the well to make the splash. It was clear he was in turmoil, but all she could do was wait and keep tossing pennies.

And that summer, a spot as an altar boy opened up. Colm didn't want to be an altar boy.

'Do I have to, Mammy?' he kept asking.

Frances looked at him – her frightened rabbit, trying to be brave. She considered giving in and briefly weakened. But she knew he needed to get out of the house, with kids his own age. And the Church would help – it helped vulnerable kids like Colm, that's what it was there for. She reached over and took his small hand. 'It'll be okay, love. It'll be okay.'

He had his first day. And then his first week, and then his first month. The priest seemed nice; he took an interest.

Little by little, and all at once, Colm stopped laughing. It was like a light had gone out. A match thrown into the ocean and gone forever.

*

In every village, there was a certain spot. The place where all the things that couldn't be thrown out – or that needed to be thrown out in secret – got dumped. Bottles maybe, bloody sheets or empty crates, sometimes. In Kilcraven, everybody knew the spot, where you disposed of things discreetly. On the small stretch of road between the main village and the old pier, where the sea to the left falls away from the road down a steep cliff. Where you just tipped the black bags over the wall into the dark throat of the shadows below.

Everybody knew the spot, especially the watchmen – the nosy neighbours along the road peering out their windows, the curtains twitching. They saw everyone who went to the spot. They saw everything: who was disposing of what, and how much, and how often. And they decided whether it was everybody's business or nobody's.

The watchmen saw everything. And when the streetlamps were put in along the road, they made sure to put one just above the dumping spot, so nobody could go in under cover of darkness. No matter what, when somebody needed to bury something, the watchmen saw. And, discreetly, they passed it on.

In various ways, what anyone did, everybody knew. The drunk, the wife-beater, the child-hater, the drugged-out and the fenced-in – eventually, someone would see them under the streetlamp tipping the black bags over. The watchmen did their job and the village decided how to handle it. They looked out for each other. They protected each other.

Most of the time.

But sometimes, something went wrong. The watchmen saw something they'd wish they'd never seen. Maybe it was too horrible, or maybe it was a friend, or maybe it was just easier to look away. And suddenly, the responsibility was too much.

So, every so often, they did something they should never do. They went down to the dumping area, they climbed the street lamp and they broke the bulb. So they wouldn't have to see. So they wouldn't have to say.

And one day in Kilcraven, the summer that Colm became an altar boy, a watchman did exactly that.

*

Two months after becoming an altar boy, Colm walked out past the old courtyard and down to the old pier, down to the village dumping spot with the broken streetlamp above it.

When a fisherman heading down to the pier for his overnight shift found him half an hour later, Colm was nearly hysterical, throwing stone after stone after stone at the dark lamp, tears pouring down his pinched little face. The fisherman caught him and folded the small boy into his arms. He didn't say anything, he just held him as Colm gasped and heaved.

'Why won't it turn on?' Colm cried, over and over, into his shoulder. 'Why won't it turn on?'

The fisherman never told a soul – Colm had begged him not to. And then a week later, after the fisherman was far away at sea, Colm was gone too.

*

The light that Henry Farrell found that day in the cove in Belfast lasted a long time. He found a partner in London and ran a successful property management business.

But unlike Henry's light, Colm's light didn't last. And when this light went out, the only light for so many years, he fell into the darkness. He thought of coming home to Kilcraven so many times, just like he had nearly every night since he left, but he knew he couldn't.

Every day that he was gone, every day he stayed away, it got harder and harder to come back. What if he had been wrong; what if his parents didn't blame him or hate him? What if they accepted him? What if, in fact, they were every bit as angry as he was? Would that be better – or much, much worse?

So, he stayed away. And every day – every wasted day – was added to the total. And every day, it got harder and harder to come back.

Until one day, Henry Farrell came looking for him. Not in person – just a letter. It turned out that Henry had never forgotten Colm or stopped loving or worrying about him. He'd even sent an anonymous letter to Frances and Jimmy, letting them know Colm was alive and in Belfast. But Colm didn't seem able to be saved.

Henry's property business was large, one of the largest in London. And one day, a document purporting to be the property portfolio of Colm Thornton, from Kilcraven, County Cork, came across his desk. The same Colm Thornton who Henry knew was living in virtual poverty in Belfast.

Henry did some digging and confirmed the real Colm Thornton was still in Belfast and had no property holdings to speak of.

And so he sent a letter to Colm.

*

'Wait, hang on,' Adam interrupted. 'I don't get it – somebody was pretending to be Colm in London? Why?' He gestured helplessly. 'Who would do that?'

Frances grimaced. 'Someone who had heard the story of Colm Thornton – the runaway boy who everyone assumed was long dead.'

'But crucially,' Jimmy chipped in, 'had never actually been declared dead. Legally, like.'

Adam shook his head. 'That doesn't answer either of my questions.'

Frances sighed. 'Mr Hollis.'

Adam and Charley started, and Frances nodded wearily. 'Apparently, he was under some sort of pressure from a local thug to sell the property for cheap. Only Hollis didn't want to sell.'

An idea suddenly clicked for Charley – something Emma had said earlier.

'So, he pretended to sell it,' he said excitedly. Then he caught the look on Adam's face and sobered up. 'He set up an account for himself in Colm Thornton's name – at a London bank – making it look like Colm bought it and was living in London.' Charley frowned. 'And then, what, he'd tell the thug that the property was gone – nothing he could do?'

Frances shrugged. 'It seems like that was the plan. He had an old business manager set up the account in London – he had plenty of contacts there. But we'll never know for sure. Because before it could get any further, Colm burst onto the scene.'

*

Colm had been confused by Henry's letter at first – if someone wanted to steal his identity, they were more than welcome to it. But then he realised that there was a chance that Frances and Jimmy might catch wind of it somehow. They might think he really was out there – and buying property in his old village, without even contacting them, throwing salt in the wound from afar. He knew his parents were elderly, and he knew they'd never given up looking for him. Something like this could kill them.

And all at once, Colm was furious. He was going to kill this man, this Hollis. He was going to strangle him with his own two hands. He booked a ticket for Kilcraven that night.

By the time he arrived in Kilcraven, in the middle of Storm Cordelia, Colm had calmed down. Now, he just wanted to talk; to understand what Hollis was playing at. But he still went straight to the Big House.

He knocked on the door and was let in by a burly, shifty-looking man. He showed Colm into the front room where an old man, clearly Hollis, was pacing back and forth. The old man was agitated. He was also holding a hunting rifle.

Colm made his case: he just wanted to understand what was going on. He just wanted to protect his parents. Surely a man like Hollis could understand that? But Hollis was having none of it. He didn't listen to a word Colm said – instead, his pacing got even more frenzied. He ranted and raved at Colm.

'Lies!' he kept barking. 'Lies! Lies! Lies!'

The burly man tried to intervene, but just as Colm was about to give up, it all happened. It happened just like these things always did.

Hollis brought the rifle down off his shoulder and into his front hand. And he pulled the trigger.

The shot caught Colm in the shoulder. Time slowed to a crawl, and as his body spun around in space and the ground rushed up to meet him, Colm wondered if he really ever believed in God. He didn't remember hitting the floor, or hearing the second shot, but they must have happened.

It could've been twenty seconds or twenty hours later when he felt himself being slapped awake. He was dimly aware of a face close to his. The burly man. He smelled of sweat. He sounded like John Lennon.

'Don't you fucking dare say a word of this,' the face said angrily. 'I know who you are and where your family lives. You understand?' He pressed his gun into Colm's hand, then put his finger in his face. 'Not a fecking word or I'll kill your ma.'

And then it was dark again.

*

When Frances finished her story, the room felt heavy and unbalanced. A small radio murmured in the corner. The timber sheeting in the walls stretched and rustled in the warmth.

And then, suddenly, the silence broke. 'I'm so sorry,' Adam sobbed. 'I'm so sorry.'

Jimmy came over and took his face in his hands. 'You were just a kid, Adam. You were just a kid.'

Adam put his forehead on Jimmy's and nodded. 'You couldn't have known. He said so himself.'

It was Jimmy's turn to cry now.

Charley still had his head down. 'I'm sorry I didn't tell you, Dad – that I didn't give you the chance to—'

Adam cut him off and pulled him into the hug. 'It wouldn't have made any difference. He could've told us himself – he could've come back. He just didn't want to be found.'

The three men held each other as they cried.

Frances watched them, then she slowly walked over to the mantelpiece. She picked up the framed picture of Colm.

'I took this when he was eight years old,' she said, her voice shaking. 'He had just come home from school, with a letter from his teacher. She had read his poem out loud at the school assembly.' She looked at Jimmy. 'Remember? He was so proud.'

Jimmy nodded, wiping his eyes. '"The Frightened Rabbit",' he said. 'I remember.'

Frances was looking down at the picture again, her fingers tracing the outline of Colm's face, smiling up at the camera. Up at her. All those years ago. 'My frightened rabbit,' she said softly. 'That's what I always called him. My poor little frightened—'

And then she collapsed onto the ground, her sobs gasping from deep within her chest.

Chapter 49

Far away, in a hospital on the other side of town, Colm sat in his bed. He felt ... well, he expected to feel sad. But instead, he felt giddy. Weightless nearly. He knew it wouldn't last – he was standing in front of a long and painful road ahead. Every step would be agony.

But Colm knew it would be worth it.

For so long, he had told himself, he couldn't rise above it. He couldn't move forward. He told himself: some of us are broken, some flowers can't bloom.

But that was never true, was it?

All of us can bloom, out of all the places we've been broken.

*

Colm fell asleep. He didn't hear the door open. He didn't see Sergeant Noonan standing over him, a grim look on his face.

Chapter 50

From the kitchen, Charley looked into the sitting room. Adam had his arms around Frances and Jimmy had them both wrapped in a hug. Charley had been part of the hug too, but he'd understood that they needed some time together, just the three of them.

He put himself in charge of arranging the kettle and the mugs and the tea. There was a knock on the front door. It didn't seem like anyone else had heard, so he went and opened it.

Standing in the doorway, looking slightly frantic but mostly triumphant, stood Emma. Before he could say anything, she said, 'We did it. Maeve and I – we did it!'

She waited – clearly expecting him to start jumping for joy. And Charley might have, if he had any idea what she was talking about.

'Do you want to come in?' he asked tentatively. 'Everyone's here, you can tell us what happened—'

But Emma shook her head. 'I'm sorry,' she said. 'There's just not enough time. Can you come with me – right now?'

Charley frowned. 'Where are we going?'

'We're going to break into the Big House.'

Charley hesitated. But only for a second. 'I'll grab some torches.'

A few minutes later they were walking up past the Blackfield towards Hollis's house, their torches lighting the way.

'Maeve and I know what happened,' Emma said, as they crossed the road onto the country lane that would take them into the townland and up the hill to the Big House. She briefly explained the documents that Mary had taken. 'Ian's clearly been forcing the village into selling their houses to the council,' she said excitedly. 'Nobody will admit it, or speak up, so he must've been blackmailing them somehow. Or getting Noonan to frighten them.' She took a deep breath. 'We think Ian wanted Hollis to sell his property, but Hollis refused. Then he sold the property to Colm.' She looked at Charley expectantly. 'Don't you see? Ian had Hollis murdered and set Colm up to take the fall. In one swoop, they're both gone and he can weasel his way into the property, claim it as a fee or something.'

'That – well, that all makes sense.'

Emma beamed. But Charley wasn't finished.

'But only part of it.' He explained what Colm had told Frances.

'So ...' Emma tried to fit the two pieces together. 'Ian was forcing the village to sell the properties. And he was pressuring Hollis to sell too. But Hollis beat him to it and transferred the property to ... a fake Colm?'

Charley nodded.

'Exactly. So, Ian couldn't have been the one to kill Hollis. According to Colm, Hollis shot him. And the only other person in the room was the burly man.'

Emma stepped around a large branch that stretched halfway across the road – a remnant of Cordelia, maybe.

'So, it must've been him – the burly man – who killed Hollis. After Colm passed out.' She frowned. 'But why was he there? If anything, it sounds like he was working for Hollis – that business manager who set up the fake account in London, maybe. But why would he shoot Hollis?'

Charley didn't have an answer, so he stayed focused on trudging up the hill. But he still nearly knocked Emma over when she suddenly stopped.

'Jesus, sorry, sorry—'

But Emma cut him off. 'You said Colm said he sounded like John Lennon?' she asked.

'Yes.' He paused. 'Why?'

Emma stared at him.

'I know who killed Hollis.'

Chapter 51

The Big House, despite its name, wasn't actually that big anymore. Time, neglect and Mr Hollis's hoarding had rendered most of the house off-limits. There were stairs that led to a second floor, but the wood was so rotten, they seemed unlikely to hold weight. In all the time he'd been here, the stranger had only ever been in the front room and the kitchen.

He was in the kitchen now – the smell of damp and mildew pressing in against him, the cold seeping through his socks and into his bones.

The stranger hated this place. He always had. He was sitting on the floor, his back against the cabinets. Hollis had been a necessary evil, but the money was gone now. There was no reason to stay. It was time to move on; the stranger wondered if the Continent was still big enough to hide a man like him.

But first – the last loose end.

Like the shutter of an old film reel, a torch beam cut through the darkened room, sweeping left and right, through the window and along the wall in front of him. Then, another torch beam twisted into it.

The stranger pressed further back into the cabinets underneath the window, blending into the dark and empty boxes. He could hear the murmur of voices – two people. He sighed.

He never should have taken this job. He never should have come to Kilcraven all those years ago. He never should have left his daughter.

The stranger shook his head. *Don't think about her*, he told himself. *Not now. You need to focus. So focus.*

But it was impossible. Caitlin was his entire world – the reason he was here, crouched in the dark in a decrepit house, getting ready to do something unspeakable. Something his daughter would never forgive him for.

But his daughter hadn't seen him in ten years. Ten years and two months and twenty-seven days. She'd made it clear: she'd take whatever he gave her – it would never be enough – but she never wanted to see him again. And he knew it was more than he deserved. Far more.

And now, the stranger was a grandfather. If you could call it that. And a father, a grandfather, a decent human being – they all provide, don't they? They provide.

As the stranger wondered about all this, he heard the front door slowly swing open.

Chapter 52

Emma's torch followed the front door into the dark hallway of the Big House. Dust floated through the light beam and seemed to be sucked through the bulb.

Emma looked at Charley. 'You ready?'

He gave a tight nod. Then, just as she started to step forward, he grabbed her arm.

'Look,' he whispered.

Emma followed his gaze down to where his torch pointed on the floor. She gasped.

There, on the floor, like an animal track in snow, was a footprint in the dust. Emma followed the trail as far as she could see – it disappeared behind the furniture but seemed to lead towards the back of the house.

'What should we do?' Charley whispered again. 'Those look fresh.' He was right. Emma couldn't write a monograph on 150 different types of footprints in dust, like Sherlock Holmes probably could. But she didn't need to.

Emma took a deep breath. She switched her handbag to the other shoulder, so she could have her strong hand free. Then, she stepped into the house.

'Why'd you bring that bag anyway?' Charley murmured, as he closed the door quietly behind them. 'I don't think I've ever seen you with a handbag before – and now, at a break-in, of all places – you've gone and lugged this big one along.'

Charley was clearly a nervous talker. And, while Emma was sympathetic – this was uncharted territory, after all – she also needed to concentrate.

'Charley,' she whispered.

'Yes?'

'Shut the feck up.'

'Understood.'

As they got further into the house, it became clear that the crime-scene team hadn't exactly put their top crew on the clean-up. The dark outline of Mr Hollis's blood was still visible – and covered in a swarm of black flies. And there was a dark streak across the floor where Colm had been lifted onto the stretcher.

To be fair, the team must've known the Big House would never be lived in again – the only complaints to demolition would be from the armies of rats and flies that had taken over. (Or, given Hollis's hoarding, had simply just come out of hiding.) Judging from the squeaks and the shuffled patter of feet that fled the white touches of the torches, there were enough rodents to make a point, if not a movement.

'Emma?' Charley whispered.

'Hmm.'

'What's the plan here?'

'Oy!' Emma suddenly shouted. The last few rats scuttled back into the walls. 'We know you're here, ya gobshite!'

As far as she knew, Sherlock had never done that. Which was something that Emma could feel proud about. And she did – for a moment.

*

And then, the stranger stepped out of the shadows.

Both Emma and Charley shone their torches in his eyes and he instinctively threw his hands up to cover them. For a second, they couldn't see his face.

But Emma knew who it was; she'd known ever since Colm said he sounded like John Lennon. There was only one person in the village with a Liverpool accent.

'Hello, Tito,' she said.

Chapter 53

Tito still had his left hand in front of his face, shielding his eyes from the brightness.

'Could you lower the torch, love?' he asked, his voice as pleasant as could be. Like they were just friends meeting behind the Blackfield after secondary school. Like he hadn't murdered Mary.

Like he wasn't holding a gun in his right hand.

'I don't think so, Tito,' Emma said. 'Not until you tell us why you did it.'

Tito sighed theatrically.

'For the record,' he said. 'I didn't kill Mary. She had a heart attack. I was only planning on scaring her a bit. I grabbed her and then she just went down like a tonne of bricks—'

'You're a liar,' Emma spat, her hands trembling with rage. 'The guards said she'd been strangled. You strangled her.'

Tito shook his head. 'I'd been hired to kill her. But she was already dead when I got a hold of her. Ian wouldn't pay me for a heart attack, so I ... well, I needed the money. You can fill in the rest.' A faint scuttling came from the room next to them; the torches shuddered in the dark. 'My employer was dead, and Ian knew it. I've got a daughter back in England. Actually …' He shielded his eyes so he could see Emma. 'You remind me of her a bit.'

If Emma had a gun, she would have shot him right there. Instead, she spat on the ground in disgust. Charley moved closer to her.

'Then why'd you kill Hollis?' he asked. 'If you were working for him – you were the one that set up that fake account in London – why'd you kill him?'

Tito looked at Charley appreciatively. 'He was going to kill that man. Your Uncle Colm. It was clear that the kid just wanted some answers, but Hollis was like an animal. I couldn't stand by and let it happen.' Tito shrugged. 'So when Hollis shot him, I shot Hollis.'

Emma laughed, a high and nervous laugh. 'You're trying to tell us … what?' She shook her head in disbelief. 'That you're the good guy in this story somehow? Because you didn't kill Colm? Instead, you just threatened to kill his family if he told anyone.'

Tito held up his hands.

'I'm not the good guy here, I know that,' he said. 'I'm just explaining what happened. And you can believe me or not about Mary. That's up to you.'

Emma's eyes narrowed. 'And I suppose that's it, is it? You came here just to have a talk and explain your side of things and now we can all go our separate, merry little ways?'

'Ah, well. No.' Tito sighed. 'No, we can't do that. And I think you know that.'

Emma gave a tight nod. 'I do.'

Charley was looking back and forth between the two of them. He didn't have a plan. He realised all at once – and about twenty minutes too late – that they should've discussed a plan. He wondered what Emma was thinking. He saw her slowly reach into her handbag.

And suddenly, Charley realised where he had seen that bag before.

It was Mary's black bag.

It happened in the time it took for Charley to blink. Emma leapt forward. Tito brought his gun down. Emma's torch beam went dark.

CRACK.

The muzzle flashed orange for a split second. Charley could just see Tito's face, illuminated and furious. And then it was darkness.

There was a loud crash as two bodies collided and fell to the floor.

CRACK.

A second shot – but different from the first. It wasn't quite the crack of a gunshot, more of a sharp thud. Like a hammer hitting bone.

In the confusion, Charley had dropped his torch. He picked it up now and turned it on. He sucked in a quick breath. Then, he shone the torch into the corner.

Emma stood there. There was a body at her feet – Tito. He wasn't moving.

Charley rushed over to Emma. 'Are you okay?' he asked, feeling her shoulders and chest all over for blood. 'Are you hit?' He took her by the shoulders. 'Are you okay?'

Emma just nodded dumbly, still staring down at Tito. Then she looked at Charley.

'I knocked his arm,' she said simply. 'The shot went wide.'

Charley nodded, relieved. 'That's good. That's great.' Then he looked down at Tito. 'How did you …' He trailed off.

Emma held up her hand. She was holding what looked at first like a gun. Then Charley noticed the strange barrel.

'It's a butcher's bolt,' Emma explained. 'I took Mary's bag from her house after she died.' She paused. 'When I went to her house after *he* killed her.' She looked down at Tito again. 'I didn't mean to kill him. I got him in the heart. I don't even know how.' She looked at Charley now, tears streaming down her face. 'I didn't mean to kill him.'

Charley hugged her tightly.

The two of them held each other for a long time, then walked slowly out of the house.

Chapter 54

Ian Flesk's office was quiet. He had his feet up on the desk as usual and a glass of whiskey to hand. As he stared at the ceiling, Ian wondered how he would spend his money.

This was a game he liked to play. His purchases varied, depending on his mood and how promising his various schemes looked. Some days he wanted a big mansion with plenty of servants and a wine cellar in which he could survive Armageddon. Other days he wanted a yacht – he'd sail the world and find a few brides along the way. And on some days, like today, he just wanted to sit and count the notes.

There was a knock on the door.

'Come in,' he called, his eyes closed. 'Although if you're here about the entitlement documents, Michael, I hate to tell you that—'

'I'm not here about that,' a quiet voice said. Ian's eyes snapped open.

It was Frances Thornton. And her eyes were hard.

'Look, listen …' Ian stammered, hastily taking his feet off the table and nearly dropping his glass. 'I'm not sure how I can help you, but maybe if you made an appointment … shit!' He wiped at the spilled whiskey on his shirt. 'Now just isn't a very good time.'

Frances smiled coldly. 'Oh, it has to be now, I'm afraid.'

Ian stopped blotting his shirt and frowned at her. 'Is there an emergency?'

Frances shook her head. 'There almost was,' she said. 'My son, Colm, as you know has been in hospital. And last night, something dreadful happened. Well – almost happened.'

Ian's blood went cold. That moron Noonan – he'd fecked it up, somehow. He tried to keep his voice neutral as he asked, 'And what was that, Mrs Thornton?'

But it was Frances's turn to frown at him. 'You can drop the act, Ian. The game's up.'

And behind her, the door opened again. When Ian saw who it was, he leapt to his feet – both his chair and his glass fell on the carpet. 'Y— you?' he spluttered. Then his face grew furious. 'You!'

Sergeant Noonan nodded. 'Me.'

Noonan had stood over Colm in the hospital for almost ten minutes, trying to get up the nerve to suffocate him. He kept telling himself he didn't have any other option, that he had to do it. But every time he stretched out his hand, he saw his mother.

He had blackmailed, threatened and even committed violence for Ian Flesk. But he couldn't do this. It had taken years, but Sergeant Noonan had finally found his line.

Frances patted him on the hand, then turned to Ian. 'Last night, Sergeant Noonan here went to the hospital – on your orders.' Her eyes narrowed. 'To kill my son.'

Ian had recovered. He forced a laugh. 'Well, that's just outrageous,' he said. He pointed a finger at Noonan. 'This man has been blackmailing and strong-arming half the village, you know. And a week ago, he came to me and he—'

Frances cut him off.

'You can stop all that now, Ian,' she said briskly. 'You're making a fool of yourself. The sergeant here has already made a confession and is cooperating with the guards.'

Ian looked like he had been slapped.

Noonan stepped forward. 'Of course, I'll be resigning immediately,' he said, his head held high and his shoulders square. 'And I'll be facing punishment of my own. But they let me be here for this. To put the handcuffs on you myself.'

'You see,' Frances explained to the stunned Ian, 'Noonan realised he couldn't kill someone for you. He'd done enough. So before you could come after him, he decided to take you down instead. Of course, his wasn't the only confession the guards have.'

Ian stared at her. She nodded.

'Tito is dead, Ian. But before he died, he confessed that he killed Mary Bennett, on your orders.' Her smile was tight-lipped. 'It's over, Ian. It's all over.'

And as Ian slumped against the wall, he knew she was right. 'Look, you have to understand,' he said, with a voice as weak as water. 'I was only trying to help the village. Nobody was supposed to get hurt.'

Frances snorted. 'I've known you your whole life, Ian. You've never so much as sneezed to help someone else.' She nodded at Noonan, who quietly crossed the room, taking his handcuffs out.

Ian looked wildly around the room. Frances recognised the look – like a fox caught in a snare. She knew what was about to happen just moments before it actually happened.

'Wait—' she began. But it was too late.

The whole interview, Ian had been sitting still in his chair. But as Noonan reached down to take one of Ian's hands, Ian suddenly came alive. He grabbed a pen off the desk and, holding it like a knife, stabbed at Noonan's exposed neck.

It was a cliché that Frances hated, but time really did stand still. For that moment, Frances was certain that Noonan was dead. Or would die. The pen stuck out of his neck at a strange angle and quivered slightly. Even Ian stared at it, horrified.

But as Noonan straightened up and pulled the pen out of his neck, Frances's brain finally caught up to what her eyes had seen. The pen had gone less than a centimetre into his neck. It certainly hurt – Noonan's groan as he pulled it out was genuine – but it was only slightly worse than a bad scrape. As long as he didn't die of ink poisoning, Noonan would survive with a plaster.

But it did give Noonan permission to hit Ian back – and this, he did with relish.

'That's enough of that now,' Frances said sternly. But it was mostly for form's sake. After one last slap, for good measure, Noonan had Ian handcuffed and on his feet. Never had a man looked so defeated as Ian did now.

'Attempted murder of a guard,' Noonan growled in his ear as he marched him to the door. 'Assault with a deadly weapon. Even if we didn't have anything else, you'd be going away for good.'

And as Frances enjoyed both the sight of Ian's defeated face and the idea of a pen as a deadly weapon, she couldn't help one last parting shot. 'And just think, Ian, when you're in your prison cell – it was Mary Bennett, an old biddy, who put you there.'

Ian groaned, his normally ruddy face completely white and speckled with blood. For the first time in his life, he didn't have a comeback.

And then Sergeant Noonan led him through the door.

Chapter 55

'So, what happened?'

Sam placed a mug of tea next to his daughter on the kitchen table. She'd only just got in from the garda station; Charley had driven her home. But already, any of the exhilaration she'd felt, any of the anger towards Tito, had receded, to be replaced by the heavy weight of grief.

'What happened?' he repeated.

Emma took a deep breath. Sam waited. Then she told him everything – helping with the investigation, breaking into Ian's office and the showdown in the Big House.

'And now, I just feel empty,' she said, her voice starting to break. 'It's done. It's over. Mary is dead, and it's all my fault. I don't know what to do anymore.'

Sam didn't say anything at first. He just reached over and hugged her, and she cried into his shoulder.

Then he stood up and started fishing around in the cupboard. 'First of all, Emma, you're not responsible for Mary's death. Whatever makes you feel that – you need to let it go. From the sound of it, you gave her the happiest days of her life.'

He waited for her to agree or argue, or say anything at all. But she didn't. She was staring straight ahead. With a sigh, he left the biscuits and sat back down.

'Emma, you know—'

'I'm not in the mood for another lecture, Da, or another story about how I'm a lost little sailor,' she snapped. 'I already know—'

He held up his hand. 'It's about your mam.'

That caught her off guard, enough for her to fall silent. After a beat, two beats, three – she nodded her head. 'Okay, so.'

'When your mam left,' he said, 'I didn't know what to do. I didn't know why she'd left, or where she'd gone, or anything like that. And there you were – four years old and crying for your mammy.' His voice shook. 'I didn't know what to tell you – I didn't have any answers, just questions. Endless, horrible questions. We were lost, acushla.' His voice broke now, he put his head in his hands. 'We were so, so lost.'

Emma reached out and took his hand and rubbed her thumb across his knuckles. After a minute he nodded and raised his head, still holding onto her hand. He cleared his throat.

'But I'm thinking, hell, maybe she'll come back. Maybe I won't have to explain this, because she'll write a letter or visit – something. She was always much better at explaining things to you than I was back then. I just wanted her to ... I don't know.' He sighed heavily. 'I just didn't know what to do.'

The old ship's clock in the corner of the room chimed. A shadow fluttered across the table; two butterflies hung in the air outside the window.

'And I couldn't explain that to you either,' Sam continued. 'But then, there was a whole new question you had – not right away, of course, but when you got older. I could see you puzzling it out: how do we mourn her, exactly? Can we even mourn her at all?' Sam shook his head. 'The whole village knew she'd left us. And they were angry. But their anger at her got misplaced somehow; they didn't treat you like a little girl who'd lost her mam – they refused to even acknowledge your mam. They wouldn't talk about it; she was dead to them.' His voice shook. 'So they pretended nothing had happened. You were a little girl who had lost her mam, and they wouldn't even let you grieve. And you couldn't understand it.' The tears were rolling down his cheeks, getting lost in the tangles of his short beard. Emma had never seen him cry. Or at least, not that she could remember. 'Some days, you thought she was dead. Other days, you weren't sure.' His breathing was ragged now, gasping nearly through the tears. 'And I didn't know either, but you were looking to me for answers. And for so long, I didn't have any. I just cried with you and held on as tight as I could.'

Emma's cheeks were covered in tears now, too.

Sam wiped his eyes. He took a deep, rattly breath, then he asked her if she remembered a specific night. A night when he thought things changed. She said no. So, he told her.

*

Twenty years ago, Sam walked into his daughter's room. It was late, she'd been crying again – but when she heard him, she turned to the wall and pretended to be asleep. She didn't want to worry him. He sat down on the edge of the bed.

'You okay?'

Emma was quiet, but her whole body was shaking. He waited.

Then, quietly, she spoke. 'These kids at school – they were saying …'

She didn't finish. But she didn't need to; Sam understood. He leaned back on the pillows beside her. He stroked her hair as she buried her head in his chest and sobbed.

'Shh,' he said. 'It's okay. It's okay.'

After she'd cried everything out, her snot and tears soaking through his shirt, he spoke quietly, like he was telling her a bedtime story:

'You know, for hundreds of years, people were trying to fly. They looked around; they saw the birds flying, and they thought that must be the way to fly – the only way. And so, for hundreds of years, they copied the birds – they strapped on great feathery wings, then jumped off the nearest ledge and flapped like hell.'

Emma giggled at both the image and the swear word.

'They thought wings and feathers would make them fly,' Sam continued, 'because wings and feathers made the birds fly. Of course – what actually makes birds fly?'

'The Bernoulli effect,' she answered quickly.

'Good woman yourself.' He smiled at her proudly. 'Now, do you know what I'm trying to say?'

'Yes,' she thought for a moment. 'You're saying – just because I don't have feathers, doesn't mean I can't fly?'

'No.' Sam shook his head. 'I'm saying that people are idiots.'

Emma giggled again. He looked down at her and waited until she looked up.

'Especially those kids at school.' He grimaced. 'And the world is a confusing place. Nobody's going to have all the answers. Not even me. Especially not me. It took hundreds of years for Bernoulli to notice the curve in the wing, the little detail that actually makes birds fly. But you, acushla, are smart.' He put his hand on her cheek. 'Sometimes, you need to look past all the feathers and the wings and find the way the wing curves underneath it all.'

Emma's eyes were sleepy, half-closed. 'Will you stay until I fall asleep?'

Sam nodded quietly. She closed her eyes and fell asleep easily, falling forward into dreams.

*

Sam looked at his daughter, twenty years older now. 'Now, do you know what I'm trying to say?'

She tried to laugh, the tears welling up in her eyes. 'What – look for the curve in the wing?'

'Ah ... no. That was maybe a bit of whiskey talking there.' They both laughed. 'No, what I'm saying is that I don't know how I made it through.' He shook his head again. 'Facing my own grief, while helping you through yours; not to mention, working and trying to give you a normal, happy childhood. But I can tell you, before that night I was falling apart, trying to figure it all out.' He took a deep breath. 'But I realised that I didn't need to know. I didn't need to have all the answers; I just needed to do the best that I could, with what I had, with each moment in front of me.' He took her hand. 'I couldn't put your world back together – but I could tell you a story. I could make you laugh and get you through that night. I took it bit by bit, story by story; I muddled through.' Sam held Emma's hand to his cheek. 'You're smart, acushla. And tough and clever. But what you're struggling with, nobody could tackle it all at once. So, yes – look for the way the wing curves underneath. And then, put the kettle on and muddle your way through.'

Emma nodded happily, the tears pouring down her face.

They sat there awhile, listening to music and drinking tea and laughing. Two damaged people, muddling their way through to happiness.

Chapter 56

'What'd you do?'

'What could I do? I ran over here.'

'You could've tried to stop them, like.'

'It was too late. By the time I found them, there was shit everywhere.'

'I thought you said they were stuck behind the fire screen?'

'They were. Everywhere – all over the grate and everything, like.'

'Well, they were panicked—'

'Jesus, *they* were panicked? What about me?'

'So, they've probably made absolute shit out of the place. You just left them in there; what if they knock over the fire screen? What if they get out? Did you open a window or anything?'

'Jesus, Frances. We'll see how smart *you* are the next time you're sitting there, having a scone, when a bunch of bats—'

'A cauldron.'

Everybody around the table stopped talking and looked at Charley.

'*What?*' Frances demanded.

'A bunch of bats is called a cauldron,' Charley explained sheepishly. 'Unless they're in a cave, then that'd be a colony. But since these ones were in your fireplace—'

'How'd you know that – that they're called a cauldron?' This was from Colm, who seemed to be trying to steer the conversation into something else. Colm had just got home a few hours ago – this was his homecoming. Well, it was his homecoming, and it was Sunday tea. So, it was mainly Sunday tea.

Charley shrugged. 'I've always liked bats. I've actually—'

'A cauldron, right,' Adam interrupted. 'Whatever you want to call it, when those fecking things burst in – well, Ma, I don't think you'd be minding the windows when a cauldron of bats is after falling down the chimney on you.'

Jimmy, with a noise like a disgruntled farm animal, slapped the table and stood up. 'Right,' he said. 'If nobody else is going to do it, then I will. I'll go sort those bats out myself.' He gave the table a withering look. 'Cowards, the lot of you.'

If this was bravery, Charley was quite alright to concede the point. Apparently, everybody else around the table was too. They watched with a great deal of interest as Jimmy began rifling through the cupboards, producing a tea cosy, an oven mitt, a baking tray and a tin-opener in quick succession. With each discovery, he gave a noise of grim satisfaction.

'And just what do you think you're doing with all that?' Frances asked warily as he added a meat thermometer to his bundle and started out the door.

'I told you – I'm going to sort those fecking bats,' he said over his shoulder, in the manner of a man going over the trench.

Most of the family followed him out the door, clearly eager to see what, exactly, he was going to do to the poor creatures. Frances, still sitting, just rolled her eyes at Charley, then they burst out laughing. Colm laughed too.

'They're fecking mental, these ones,' she said, as she stood up and started to clean up. 'But you have to admit – they keep things interesting.'

'They do that, alright,' Charley agreed, as he stood up to help her.

They made short work of the place, Frances scrubbing the dishes in the sink, as Charley cleared and then dried. Colm disappeared into his old room for a nap. After a few minutes of quiet work, Charley reached into the sink and stopped Frances scrubbing.

'How are you, Granny?' he asked gently. 'Been holding up?'

Frances looked at him. She wiped her hands dry on her dress and gave him a hug. 'I'm good, love,' she said. 'I really am.' She gestured in the direction Colm had disappeared. 'It's all a bit raw, of course, but it's like a dream come true. Jimmy can barely sit down he's so excited. Did you hear Colm is staying?'

Charley had heard that his uncle was moving into Frances and Jimmy's house – at least temporarily. It would take a little while for an unemployed priest and recent murder suspect/gunshot victim to get up on his feet.

Frances made an impatient noise, which meant he was slacking in the dish-drying department. He threw a dish towel at her, and she laughed.

'And c'mere to me you,' she said. 'Why are we sitting here talking about bats, when it's you we should be talking about!' She gave a low whistle. 'What's the decision? Are you staying or are you heading out on your next great adventure?'

Charley laughed.

'Besides, I remember how much you like bats,' she added. 'Those are probably the last three in West Cork, so if you want to see one, I'd hurry. Jimmy looked fairly determined with that tin-opener.'

Charley frowned. 'What do you mean – the last ones?'

'There was a story in the papers a few weeks back,' she said, turning back to the dishes. 'Some construction or something knocking down their trees and leaving them with nowhere to live. There's been a few in people's chimneys, like your dad's there. But the rest are dying out like mad.'

Charley wanted to ask more questions, but Frances quickly moved on to other topics. Mainly, how lovely that Emma Daly was looking these days.

*

When Charley left Frances's house, it was already dusk. He met Emma coming around the causeway.

'Hello there, stranger,' she said.

'Hello, indeed.'

They fell into each other's arms. 'How's your dad?' asked Charley.

'Oh, you know Sam.' She laughed. 'He's been telling me stories about demented inventors and frozen rowers – he's tired himself out now.'

Charley laughed too.

As they talked, they walked aimlessly through the village. Without either of them realising it, they soon ended up at the Protestant church.

The long sweetgrass had been cut – the old parson had moved away to a new parish, and his replacement had no patience for either the bees or the birds and the bees. But it still smelled the same. And right on cue, the bells chimed.

Charley looked up at the bell tower, but only a few jackdaws came flying out.

'So, it's true,' he said quietly.

Emma frowned. 'What's true?'

He pointed. 'There used to be a whole colony of bats that lived there, in that bell tower. Don't you remember?' His voice was worried. He remembered what he read, long ago, about how bats notice tiny changes, tiny disruptions long before anything else. And now they were disappearing. 'I used to watch them fly over us, when we'd lie here. I think—'

Emma turned and stood in front of him, then pulled his face down to hers. She stared at him until he finally met her eyes.

'Hey,' she said.

His eyes softened. 'Hey.'

They sat down together on the stone bench by the path. From here, with the grass cut, you could see the whole of Kilcraven harbour and most of the village. The lights were coming on in the houses, the shades being drawn. Inside, they could imagine the stoves being lit and the families around their tables. Children would be born here, grow up here – call this place their home.

Emma turned to Charley. 'I've been thinking ...'

And she explained – how she'd felt stuck here, in Kilcraven, like she was waiting for something to happen or to die. Like the guards hadn't just taken her job when they fired her – they'd taken her dignity, her purpose. Her future.

And when she'd been working on the investigation, she explained, it was like she'd come alive again. 'Suddenly, I could picture a life – somewhere else. Maybe in America, maybe in Australia. Just somewhere – starting over.'

'But then I met your Uncle Colm.' She shook her head. 'And I saw what it would look like – to run away. To carry the mountain around with you, instead of just climbing the damn thing.' She looked at him. 'I think ... ' She hesitated. 'I think that staying here – if it's me choosing to stay here, I think that's starting over in its own way, isn't it?' Emma looked at Charley. 'I'm proud of the library and my life here. And I know it's not as glamorous or exciting as becoming the first female Garda Commissioner or even being an inspector, but it's important to me.' She smiled. 'And I think that's what moving on looks like to me – staying here.'

*

In a few more years, Kilcraven might be gone forever – buried underneath housing estates and low-rise condos. They might be anywhere – but for the rest of their lives, they would be right here. In this moment. In Kilcraven.

Because Kilcraven wasn't the country lanes or the low fields – it was the hiding places they found in them. It was the call of a shearwater; the ballet of a jackdaw; the sound of rain outside a dark window and the warm stretch of the stove inside.

It was a poem the drunk forgot to write down and, in the morning, couldn't remember. It was both an accent and a habit. It was just a trick of light.

Kilcraven was what made them, broke them, found them and by morning, forgave them, every day of their lives. And when it finally found them, frightened at the station – it called them home.

Chapter 57

Long, long ago Kilcraven became briefly famous – when a villager died so spectacularly that people travelled from all over the country to watch it happen: from Antrim, Galway, Dublin, Clare, anywhere they got a newspaper.

Before the Great War, before the Famine even, a man named Thomas lived in a small cottage next to what was now the causeway, but back then was just the open coastline. He was poor. The wind, cold and wet, whipped off the ocean and passed through the slated walls of his cottage like ghosts in a hurry. Consumption dripped down off the ceiling of the miserable cottage. And eventually, Thomas began to die.

It took a long time for Thomas to die, however, and it was not an easy death. From the day the disease first racked his lungs, to the day he died six years later and every day in between, he was on death's door. But, for six years, the door remained shut.

This, of course, didn't make Thomas famous – there were thousands of people dying of consumption at the time, and his performance was fairly uninspired. But then, something strange started happening.

The first people to see the lights thought they'd gone mad: it looked like blue stars were floating all around the inside of the cottage. They rushed in and found Thomas in his usual state, dying in the corner. But there were bright lights, brilliant stars of red and yellow and purple, hovering above his body. And then, they disappeared.

The next night, more villagers came to witness the lights and weren't disappointed. This time they fell from the ceiling like purple meteors, crashing into Thomas's chest and disappearing somewhere deep inside his body.

Over the next few months, as the news spread across the country, the village was overrun with visitors, all coming to see the miracle. And, as miracles go, it was reliable. Every night, like clockwork, the visitors crowded into Thomas's cottage, the lights appeared, and Thomas ... well, the stories never said what Thomas did. The stories never seemed to notice Thomas much at all.

And then one day, Thomas died. And the lights stopped.

And then slowly, bit by bit, then all at once, people forgot. They forgot about Thomas. They forgot about the lights; and the lights, whatever they were, never appeared again. The currents in Kilcraven harbour shifted, and the cottage slipped under the waves and disappeared. By the time the currents returned and the foundations were visible again, nobody remembered who had lived there or what had happened. Generations walked by, without stopping.

*

The same thing happened to Kilcraven in the winter of 1988.

There were a few headlines in the papers – the murder in the Big House and the brilliant librarian. But then the Troubles rumbled again, and the economy continued to fall and Kilcraven slipped back under the waves.

But a few days after Ian's sentencing (thirty years, with no chance of parole), the whole village of Kilcraven came together at the library.

The revelations about what Ian had been doing in the village shocked everyone (everyone except for the ones he had blackmailed, of course). There were whispers in the village at first, about what the victims had been caught doing – affairs, tax evasion, et cetera – but when it turned out that almost everyone in the village had either fallen victim or was related to a victim, the rumours quickly died out.

And in the end, the homeowners had all been assured that the deeds of sale, as part of a criminal enterprise, would be voided. Life in Kilcraven could get back to normal. But first, they had to celebrate.

There was a festival-like spirit in the air. Fintan had thrown open the doors of Nolan's, and people were spilling out onto the road, back and forth between the library and the pub, pints in hand. In the library, they were pushed in close together, happily elbowing for space, to congratulate and thank Emma. As the evening drew on, the congratulations were repeated and the thank-yous became heartfelt to the point of cardiac arrest. Emma's hand was tired from handshakes – the front of her blouse was soaked with the spills of a hundred pints.

But she was happy. Everyone was. A catastrophe had been avoided and order restored to the village. Although, some people weren't so sure.

'Would it really have been that bad?' Connie asked his wife quietly. 'I get that stealing people's houses was bad. Poor form and all that. But would a big luxury development not give the place a boost? Maybe we'd have even got a McDonald's,' he added hopefully.

Nuala looked at him in disgust. (Which, to be fair, was how she often looked at Connie.)

'And turn into Ballyrae? The fishermen can't afford to live there anymore. Nobody can.' She snorted. 'There'd be no place for the likes of us, any of us – whether they stole our houses or not, they'd drive us out of here one way or another.'

'Or they'd make us into servants again,' Maeve cut in cheerfully, handing them both a pint from across the road. 'The English way.'

Connie grunted, reluctantly ceding the point. He was about to change the subject when there was the chime of a spoon on glass. The crowd quieted down.

Emma stood on a small, upturned box. 'I'm not really one for speeches,' she began, then hesitated. 'It's just ... as much as you all have been thanking me, I just wanted to say thank you in return.' She smiled at Sam, at Charley, at Frances and Jimmy and Maeve. Then at the rest of the village, who all smiled back at her. 'The library is a special place. It's been a second home for me, these past couple of years. But it's only special – it's only home – because it's filled with ye.' Her face turned red. 'Anyway, sláinte.'

And when she raised her glass to the village, the village raised theirs back.

As the church bells rang out on the Angelus, all the old clocks rang out across West Cork. Spring was here.

Acknowledgements

I wrote this book to make myself laugh, to give myself some comfort and joy when I needed it most. It did that and more – and I hope it did the same for you.

But there are plenty of people in real life who also brought me comfort and joy and without whom this book would not exist.

In particular, thank you to Mom and Dad, who have always believed in me, even when this was perhaps wishful thinking on their part. You're an inspiration in many ways – and look, no hedgehogs!

And my entire family – Kathleen, Tom, Caroline, Walt, Kelly and Mary Claire; my nieces and nephews Annie, Walt, Pat, Hailey and Henry; my cousins, aunts and uncles and more – of whom there are far too many to name here. But thank you all.

And to the friends along the way – thank you.

I am indebted to Katy Loftus for all of her wisdom and encouragement. Thank you to Aoife K. Walsh, Djinn von Noorden and everyone at New Island Books for taking a chance and making this journey so wonderful.

And thank you to my agent Charlotte Seymour for believing in me and for all of the support and care you took to make this book a reality. Here's to many more!

Thank you to Trish and Liam, for everything.

And, of course, thank you to Lisa.

But above all, thank you to Josh and Lauren. You made it all come true.

Reader Guide

1. The novel begins with Emma Daly having returned to her home village, Kilcraven, after a career setback. How does her past ambition — and the scandal associated with it — shape her identity, her relationships and the way she approaches the murder she witnesses?
2. Kilcraven feels like a character in the story. What role does place, community and local memory play in the novel? Would the story be very different if it were set elsewhere?
3. What do you think motivates Emma to investigate — guilt, redemption, curiosity, loyalty or something else? Does it change as the novel progresses?
4. Several characters carry secrets from the past. How do these past secrets drive the present narrative? Can you identify a moment where the past intrudes most strongly into the present investigation?
5. Female characters in the novel, such as Emma and Mary, navigate roles and expectations in a small rural Irish setting in 1988.

How do issues of gender, class and local reputation show up in their choices and constraints?

6. There are characters in the novel who are pushing to learn the truth, while others 'don't want to know'. Why do you think people choose silence?
7. Emma left the village years ago and returned as both an insider and an outsider. How does that dual position shape the way she sees the village — and how the village sees her?
8. The novel contrasts official power (police, church, wealth) with individual conscience. After finishing the book, do you come away more cynical or more hopeful about justice?
9. What moments in the plot or aspects of character resonate the strongest with today? Are there parallels in our time with how communities deal with change, the legacy of the past or truth-seeking?
10. And finally, what do you think the title of the novel, 'All the Old Clocks', refers to? Does it just apply to the natural world, or is there more to it?